I0645189

Praise for *Gentleman of Misfortune*

"Quality fiction and real history make a great match, and Sarah Angleton's *Gentleman of Misfortune* offers the best of both. This is an engaging story with surprises on every page".

—Jeff Guinn, *New York Times* bestselling author of *The Last Gunfight* and *Manson*

"Against a thorough and expertly researched historical setting, charismatic miscreant Lyman Moreau cloaks his tooth-and-claw survival instinct in the appearance and manner of a gentleman. As he moves constantly to stay ahead of the law, he leads the reader into encounters with mischief, mummies, murder, and Mormons. An intriguing and entertaining reading adventure."

—J. J. Zerr, author of *Sundown Town Duty Station* and *The Happy Life of Preston Katt*

"*Gentleman of Misfortune* is an intricately constructed historical novel inspired by a lesser-known part of Mormon scripture ("The Book of Abraham"). Mormon prophet and founder Joseph Smith appears as a black market buyer of Egyptian goods in this suspenseful, ominous, and captivating saga."

—Midwest Book Review

"*Gentleman of Misfortune* by Sarah Angleton is a fascinating story built around tantalizing facts . . . well-researched and delightful to read."

—M. M. Holaday, author of *The Open Road*

Also by Sarah Angleton:

Launching Sheep & Other Stories from the Intersection of History and Nonsense

Gentleman of Misfortune

Smoke Rose to Heaven

to

Heaven

A Novel

Published by Bright Button Press

Cover Design by Steven Varble
Author Photo by Karen Anderson Designs, Inc.

For more information contact:

Bright Button Press, LLC
P.O. Box 203
Foristell, MO 63348

Publisher's Cataloging-in-Publication Data
provided by Five Rainbows Cataloging Services
Names: Angleton, Sarah, author.
Title: Smoke rose to heaven / Sarah Angleton.
Description: Wentzville, MO : Bright Button Press, 2020.
Identifiers: ISBN 978-0-9987853-6-3 (paperback) | ISBN: 978-0-9987853-5-6 (ebook)
Subjects: LCSH: Mormons--Fiction. | Assassins--Fiction. | Conspiracies--Fiction. | New York (State)--Fiction. | Historical fiction. | Suspense fiction. | Bildungsromans. | BISAC: FICTION / Thrillers / Historical. | FICTION / Thrillers / Suspense. | FICTION / Historical / General. | GSAFD: Historical fiction. | Suspense fiction. | Bildungsromans.
Classification: LCC PS3601.N55441 S66 2020 (print) | LCC PS3601.N55441 (ebook) | DDC 813/.6--dc23.

For Paul

Smoke Rose to Heaven

to

Heaven

A Novel

SARAH ANGLETON

Bright Button Press • St. Louis, Missouri

1

1872

The fortuneteller had forgotten about him by the time the man worked up the nerve to knock on her door. Ever a keen observer, she had spied him earlier in the evening. For hours he stood just across the street, rebuffing the advances of prostitutes and evading the notice of the roaming packs of drunken sailors looking for trouble. The man appeared respectable enough, tall and slender in a dull brown sack suit. Respectability was rare on Water Street, and she assumed he must be a missionary.

Her evening had been busy with customers dropping in one after another. Several of the men she saw were newly arrived immigrants bound for work on the construction project for that ridiculous bridge to Brooklyn. Soon they would descend into the caisson that was described as the pit of hell and from which few men arose again unscathed. The workers came to her for hope, something she could not offer them. Even without the gift of supernatural sight, she could see their fates far too clearly.

Bidding farewell to her last customer, she watched him stumble into the night before locking the door. Exhausted, she dropped into the seekers' chair to catch her breath and reflect on how even simple tasks had grown difficult. Then came the quiet yet insistent knocking at the door and she remembered the lurking, respectable man she'd seen outside earlier.

The fortuneteller opened the door and sensed immediately that the man was in danger just as certainly as she sensed the name by which he identified himself was not his own. What she failed to anticipate was that he would know her name.

"Pardon me, Madam, my name is Silas Allen. I'm looking for a woman by the name of Ada Powell." He paused, perhaps trying to read her expression, though the fortuneteller would reveal nothing. Undaunted by her stoicism, Mr. Allen continued, "Are you Ada Powell?"

His tentative speech failed to mask that his words were more statement than question. She drew a labored breath, cleared her throat, and motioned for him to take a seat at her table. Ada Powell was indeed the nearest she had to a true name, but she had not heard it in years.

Ada took her own seat across the table from her visitor and examined him more closely before deciding how to respond. He was of middle age with coarse features, wild brown hair, and dark, tired eyes. His broad shoulders and calloused hands suggested that he was no stranger to manual labor. He wore a frayed coat that was clean, and a white shirt, crisp and fresh. He slumped slightly in the chair, a weary soul and, Ada decided, one who meant her no harm.

"Mr. Allen," Ada began, careful not to betray her apprehension. "I have been called Ada Powell, though by few, and not for some time. May I ask how you have come to know this name?"

He made no attempt to answer her question, his expression breaking into a wide, crooked smile that made him appear several years younger. "Miss Powell," he said, leaning forward to rest his arms on the table between them. "I'm glad to make your acquaintance at last. I am hoping you might help me solve a very old mystery."

Relieved by his response, Ada returned his smile. For many years she had been in the business of solving very old mysteries, and for a moment, she allowed herself to consider that Mr. Allen's arrival at her door did not portend some terrible danger.

"You certainly have my attention, Mr. Allen. How is it you think I may be able to help?"

He sat back in his chair, plunging his right hand into the pocket of his coat and drawing out a tattered book. "I wonder if you've ever read this." He slid it across the table.

Ada coughed into the back of her hand before reaching for the well-worn book. She ran her thumb over the gold letters on the cover—*The Book of Mormon: An Account Written by the Hand of Mormon Upon Plates Taken from the Plates of Nephi*. Missionaries were a common nuisance around the Seaport, but none had ever dared intrude upon Ada's business. A wave of anger washed over her. She pushed the book toward him. "I'm not interested, Mr. Allen."

"Oh, no, no. I gave you the wrong impression, but I'm glad to know you are familiar with the work. I wonder also if you have read this one." From his left pocket he took a second slim book and handed it to her.

"*Mormonism Unveiled* by Eber D. Howe." While Ada read, a shiver traveled down her spine. She knew the book well, but that someone might connect her with it was an uncomfortable notion. "So, you are not a missionary, then?"

Mr. Allen sighed, sitting straighter in his seat. "Once. Now I am an apostate."

"Lucky for me, but I don't understand. What exactly is this mystery of yours?"

"No doubt you have heard of the many legal entanglements and alleged violence of the Mormon sect in the Utah Territory over the last many years."

Ada nodded. She had read the accounts of the tragedy at Mountain Meadows where a large wagon party made up of Arkansas farmers and their families fell under attack on its way through the Utah Territory. Initially blamed on unfriendly Indians, violent details soon emerged that placed the blame squarely on the shoulders of the Mormons. There were other rumors as well— stories of apostates murdered as atonement for their sin of attempting to leave the church, of a greedy prophet who forced young girls into illegal marriages, and of a territorial government run on corruption.

"I was a devoted member of the Latter-day Saints as established by the prophet Joseph Smith, but I found I could no longer support a faith built on deceit and brutality. I guess you could say I've been on something of a quest."

"And your quest brought you here? I think you've been misled, Mr. Allen. I know little of Brigham Young's church. Only what is reported in the papers."

"Perhaps not, but I've heard you have a gift for finding things that remain hidden from others." Mr. Allen tapped a finger on the cover of Howe's book that now lay closed in front of Ada. "You see, this book describes evidence that might finally cause this whole false religion to crumble. The evidence has been lost for years, though there are those who have attempted to find it."

"And what exactly is this evidence?" Ada wanted to trust this man. He seemed at once so vulnerable and yet self-assured, much like Ada herself. She was drawn to him in that way she always felt drawn to those who sought truth within faith.

"There is a novel, written many years ago, by a preacher named Solomon Spalding. The book was not published in his lifetime, but was known to many of his acquaintances, as it was his habit to read aloud long passages from it."

"*Manuscript Found*," Ada whispered before deciding she shouldn't.

Mr. Allen's troubled eyes widened with enthusiasm. "Yes, yes!" he cried, beginning to stand. Seeing that Ada maintained her calm demeanor, Mr. Allen regained his composure and lowered himself once again into his chair. "There are many who have said that it is the true source of *The Book of Mormon*, that the prophet plagiarized the work and claimed it as Divine revelation. I've been looking for it."

"And you believe I can help?"

Mr. Allen shifted in his seat. Ada feared he would stand again and begin pounding on the table as a fiery end-of-days preacher might strike a pulpit. He restrained himself, but it was with new vigor he brought several loose papers from his coat pocket. Mr. Allen shuffled the pages, crumpled and covered in scrawled notes, clearly familiar enough with their contents and organization to know where to find what he needed.

"Ah, my dear Miss Powell, I fear you may be the only one who can help. According to Mr. Howe's book, the many works of Solomon Spalding were stored in a trunk by his widow Mrs. Matilda Davis, but when she allowed Mr. Howe access to them, he found the trunk which should have contained multiple stories contained only one."

"So you believe *Manuscript Found* was removed from the trunk before that time?"

"I do."

"By the widow?"

Mr. Allen shook his head. "I should think she'd stand to gain more from the fame that would accompany revealing the treachery of Joseph Smith than she would from hiding his dirty secret for him. No, I think someone else removed the manuscript, someone who would have had access but would have attracted little notice."

"And you have some idea of who that might have been?"

"I was hoping that's what you could tell me, Miss Powell."

Cold sweat prickled at Ada's forehead. This man probed a part of her life she kept locked away. Painful memories flooded her thoughts, and she wished more than anything to expel this man from the house, this intruder of the most sacred and secret parts of her inner self.

As her anxiety rose, the coughing began, and she was helpless to stop the forceful waves crashing through her abdominal muscles and up through her raw throat. She gasped for air, grateful to clasp the handkerchief Mr. Allen offered.

He shifted his attention to the cluttered bookshelf along the wall to his left until she regained her composure. When at last the attack subsided, Mr. Allen turned to her, his expression full of concern, but Ada cut him off before he could inquire after her health.

"Pardon me, but I don't understand what you think I could do for you, Mr. Allen. I'm afraid I wouldn't even know where to begin."

He offered a cautious smile. "Perhaps you could begin with your childhood memories from the brief time you lived with your mother and father in a boarding house in Hartwick, New York. Do you remember that?"

Ada felt the blood drain from her cheeks as she fought to maintain her composure.

Mr. Allen continued. "Zeviah Clark of Hartwick is a niece to Mr. Spalding's widow, and it is in her home that Mrs. Davison kept the trunk containing her first husband's writings. Do you know anything about the trunk, Miss Powell?"

Ada remained silent for several seconds, fixed in the expectant gaze of Mr. Allen's dark eyes. She instinctively understood him to be a kind man, seeking only guidance and not at all confident he would receive it. As she looked at him, his eyes softened, his shoulders slumped. If he suspected she had anything to hide, he was not demanding it from her.

"I lived many places when I was young," she began. "I was in Hartwick for a brief time and I believe we lived in a boarding house. Maybe it was with the Clarks. I was very young and I'm afraid my memories are not crisp. I'm sorry I can't be of more help."

Mr. Allen's face fell, the hopeful gleam disappearing from his eyes. "I see. Can you tell me anything at all? Were there other boarders, perhaps the whisper of a name you might recall? If you can't tell me anything, I fear the trail will go cold. The smallest detail, if you can provide it, might prove useful."

Ada stood, signaling that Mr. Allen should also rise, which he obediently did. "It's growing late, Mr. Allen, and I am tired. I'm sorry I could not offer you what you were hoping for, but I will try to comb through my memories and see if I might discover something to aid you in your quest. Can you come back tomorrow evening?"

He nodded and offered a cautious smile, thanking Ada for her time as he donned his hat and pushed his way through the door into the cold night. Ada watched after him, emotions she rarely allowed herself to dwell upon churning inside her. The breeze off the water was cold, the night overcast and dark. Ada shivered as Silas Allen made his way slowly along the now empty street.

When he faded from her sight she closed the door, enveloped once more by the warmth of the house. A fire burned low in the hearth, a pulsating glow of hot coals adding little light to that which spilled from the lamp on the table.

Ada breathed slowly, absorbing the rich colors of the room, feeling at once both comforted by the familiar space and burdened by the world she had constructed around herself. Her gaze paused on the bookshelf that had captured Mr. Allen's polite attention and she laughed.

Pushing aside books on herbal remedies and incantations, each more decorative than useful, Ada slid from among them a slim package identified only by two lines of faded script. She placed it on the table, considering the opportunity she had received.

Through the years countless strangers had passed through Ada's door to sit at her table and search not for her, but for what they hoped she could give them, a magical way to better understand the predicaments of their own lives.

But Silas Allen hadn't come to find himself. He had come to find Ada. And he had come to find the manuscript resting upon her table.

2

Ada dabbed at the bead of perspiration rolling down her left temple, the moisture soaking through her delicate glove. Though still early spring and not particularly warm, brilliant sunlight illuminated a world emerging from the depths of the cold winter and gave Ada the impression that she stood under a bank of gas theater lights. Unaccustomed as she was to self-exposure, the light served only to increase her anxiety at the task before her.

This sense of personal danger that now plagued her was not altogether unfamiliar to Ada, but it had been some time since she had known its full weight. Life had, at long last, settled into a comfortable routine of sorts for which she had been especially grateful in her weakened state of health. The ill-fated visit from Mr. Allen spurred Ada to action. The time had come to address the secrets in her past she had long been content to lay aside.

She glanced over her shoulders, both right and left, as though expecting at any moment to receive another gruesome surprise like that delivered anonymously to her doorstep the previous morning. Her diligence would do little to protect her, she knew, but still she scanned the quiet street. Ada was at least somewhat confident her pursuers would not approach her here in Friendship but would wait to see her next move, and she was anxious to get on with the business at hand.

Ada searched the neat row of homes lining Depot Street and drew a deep breath through trembling lips. Her eyes gravitated to the modest frame house she knew to be the one she sought. For Ada, locating the source of secrets had become nearly as natural as breathing. Glancing down at her skirt and jacket to see that all was in neat order, she tightened her grip on the handle of her bag and hastened toward the beckoning house before she could lose her nerve.

She knocked just twice against the faded wooden door before it opened. In the doorway stood a small elderly woman, her appearance both neat and tired much like the home she occupied. She smiled a vague smile, as if she were searching for Ada's face in her memories.

"May I help you?" Her voice was kind, her tone curious.

Ada said nothing. She had planned and practiced what she would say when she arrived at the door, vacillating between complete honesty and, as was her preferred mode of communication, well-disguised, misleading half-truths. When finally face-to-face with the woman she could only assume must be the prophet's wife, words failed her.

She thought of how she must appear, a stranger arriving at the door unannounced, her skin waxen, her cheeks hollowed by disease. Hoping to minimize the effect, she had chosen a modest dress with a high-buttoned collar and trim jacket that cascaded over a small bustle. Her curls, more silver now than she cared admit, had been pulled into a loose knot and pinned beneath a simple hat trimmed in a shade of blue that drew out the color of her eyes. However respectably dressed she may be, Ada was a tall, angular woman whose physical appearance often startled. Her heart pounded in her chest and her mouth went dry as the old woman scrutinized her.

At last she said, "Mrs. Rigdon, please forgive me for visiting your home without a proper introduction. My name is Ada Moses and I must speak to your husband."

"I'm afraid Brother Rigdon takes few visitors anymore." The woman still smiled, but her eyes, Ada noticed, had gone cold with the confidence of a diligent gatekeeper. "He is unwell, you see."

"I do understand, Mrs. Rigdon, but this is of some importance."

Despite feigning unfamiliarity when first approached by Mr. Allen, Ada had spent years studying the legend of the manuscript, examining the claims that had been made about it by both enemies and friends of the murdered prophet. She had long ago traced the trail to Sidney Rigdon, former advisor to Joseph Smith himself.

Tracking the reclusive old gentleman to Friendship had been simple. Public appearances were rare for him now, but he had been a notable lecturer for many years and was known through much of

Western New York certainly by reputation, if not often by personal acquaintance. Once she arrived in the little town, Ada needed only to follow her instinct.

"I would be happy to deliver your message to Brother Rigdon." Mrs. Rigdon, intimidating despite her diminutive stature, stepped through the door frame, placing herself in position to guard the entrance of her home from this unexpected visitor. "He is fond of correspondence. I know he would be delighted to advise you if that is what you require."

The old woman pulled the door nearly closed and crossed her arms, her now chilly gaze daring Ada to challenge the less than subtle suggestion that she leave. Ada did not yield her position but, gripping her bag more tightly, locked eyes with Mrs. Rigdon and began to cry.

Ada had never intended to appear vulnerable on this visit, but she recognized a hardened and stubborn woman when she saw one. She also recognized in Mrs. Rigdon the capacity for compassion. Ada allowed the tears to roll down her pale cheeks. As she did so her head pounded, her chest tightened, and the coughing began, as she knew it would. She surrendered herself to it, dropping slowly to her knees on the hard-packed ground.

Mrs. Rigdon reached for her, placing a gentle hand against Ada's back. "My dear, are you unwell?"

Ada could not get her breath to answer, but Mrs. Rigdon seemed not to require a response. Her right hand still upon Ada's back, Mrs. Rigon clasped the woman's left hand with her right, helped her visitor to regain her feet, and guided her into the house.

Mrs. Rigdon showed Ada to a chair and soon placed a steaming cup of tea in front of her, which she sipped as the fit subsided. Mrs. Rigdon studied her with the same eyes, so recently cold, but now softened and filled with concern. The old woman shook her head, her expression softened by compassion.

"Better now? Where have you come from, Miss Moses, seeking an audience with the prophet?"

Ada sighed. "New York City."

"Ah," Mrs. Rigdon nearly whispered. "Well, that can be a hard journey for a lady who should clearly be abed. Is it really so urgent that you speak with my husband?"

"It is. I should have come long ago, I fear."

"Surely it's never too late for God's mercy."

"I do not presume to know."

Mrs. Rigdon smiled and rose from her seat. "I will speak to him, Miss Moses. I am sure he will wish to see you, if it is truly as urgent as you say. Brother Rigdon will sort you out, my dear. No need to worry about that."

Ada watched the old woman disappear behind a rough wooden door to the side of the unlit fireplace. Silently she hoped, or perhaps she prayed and did not know, that the prophet would grant her an audience. She didn't wish to reveal to Mrs. Rigdon the true purpose of her visit. Sidney Rigdon was old and in poor health for much of his life, from what she understood, but the secret contained on the pages stowed in her bag belonged to him, if to anyone at all.

She was determined to return it to him. Mr. Allen's visit and his untimely end had been enough to convince her that this was not a secret that could die with her. Her time, after all, grew short as well, and so many of her own sins remained unresolved. If she did not succumb to the pain in her throat and lungs, the weakness of her limbs, this secret that was not truly hers to possess might bring about the conclusion of her story. Ada did not fear death, but she very much feared the consequences of things left unsaid.

The pages she carried were of little personal value to her, but that there were those who would kill to possess them, she had no doubt. Merely the unsuccessful search for them had been the cause of Silas Allen's gruesome death.

On the train, Ada had read the story in the newspaper. It described an unidentified man sliced from ear to ear, his blood drained onto the ground. What baffled the detectives, however, was that the man wore a clean shirt, unspoiled by even a drop of blood. The body was clearly redressed in a fresh shirt, a ritual Ada recognized, for she had been the recipient of the victim's bloody clothing, wrapped in brown paper upon her doorstep. No note accompanied it, but Ada need not know the names of the assassins to understand their purpose. She shivered as she remembered the discovery that had led her to board a train only twelve hours later and run to Sidney Rigdon to return his burden to him.

Mrs. Rigdon had not yet returned. It seemed her husband would not be easily persuaded to see his visitor. Ada struggled to interpret the muffled sounds drifting from the other room, for she always found it most useful to listen when it was assumed she could not hear. She detected the whisper of her own name, the scrape of a chair, and the pained breathing of an aged man. Phoebe Rigdon would not fail her, she felt certain. Ada was a dying woman, arrived on the doorstep with a need for absolution and no time to spare. If that was the part she must play, she would play it.

She finished her tea and waited. At last Mrs. Rigdon returned and showed Ada through the doorway.

"The prophet." Mrs. Rigdon's voice swelled with pride, her hands indicating a figure sitting in a chair next to the lone window. "Dear," she added to the old man, "this is Miss Ada Moses. She has something of great importance, I believe, to discuss with you."

The old man leaned forward as Ada squinted in an attempt to see him properly. Sunlight filtered through a single dusty window, casting wispy shadows across the room. A chair stood empty beside the door, facing the corner where the old man sat. Ada remained standing so as not to be thought presumptuous. Her manners as always were imprecise, her training in such matters as awkward and faltering as she often felt herself to be. As her eyes adjusted to the low light, Ada studied the image of the man she'd been seeking: Sidney Rigdon, a trusted advisor to a murdered prophet, fallen from a place of esteem.

An impressive figure, large and confident even in his frailty, he sat dignified and well-dressed with a worn quilt across his lap to shield him from the morning chill. Ada noted the dark, troubled shadows beneath his eyes. A well-trimmed and snowy beard gave the old man an air of authority and power. Still, Ada wondered just what she saw. The prophet's face carried on it the ravages of old age and poor health that one might expect, and his withered form suggested a need for a few good strengthening meals of the type surely enjoyed in younger days. But something more significant, more difficult to pinpoint, plagued this man's thoughts, she sensed.

His expression was one she often wore herself, derived from that nagging suspicion she was unworthy of the angelic mask she presented, that she may have lived a life that was nothing more than a deception. In her darker moments Ada admitted to herself she committed her crimes in the most terrible of circumstances, perpetrated upon the most vulnerable, the heartbroken, and the desperate. No matter the justification, Ada lived in increasing fear that she partnered with demons, a nagging dread that had plagued her since childhood.

She wondered if Mr. Rigdon bore such thoughts, and if he perhaps held the secret to the justification of deception for a noble purpose. Did he consider, as Ada did, whether or not his purpose had ever been noble, whether his deceptions were well-constructed enough to convince God Himself?

A bold, deep voice interrupted Ada's ponderings. "Miss Moses, is it? That's a rather curious name." The old man raised his head up and to the left as he spoke, giving him the appearance of one in deep thought.

"An invention," she replied, and noted his careful nod as he dropped his head back down to study his own wiggling fingers on the quilt. She had confirmed his suspicion and now Ada wanted more than anything to explain herself to this man, to make an impression on the one person who might ease her own feelings of guilt, remorse, grief.

"What is it you wish to discuss with me, Miss Moses?"

Ada did not know quite where to begin. She opened her bag and pulled out the bundled foolscap wrapped in brown paper. "I have something here that may interest you."

"Oh?" The old man leaned forward a few inches, as far as he was able, Ada suspected. "And what is that?"

"*Manuscript Found* by Mr. Solomon Spalding."

To Ada's surprise the old man laughed. "Miss Moses, I believe I have answered all the questions I can about that little piece of imaginary literature. Is that really why you have come to disturb my rest today? You wish to throw accusations at me?"

"No, sir. I don't wish to accuse you of anything, but I do have in my possession the lost romantic history written by Solomon Spalding."

His jovial smile faltered and he raised his head, once again assuming a thoughtful posture. It occurred to Ada that he could not see her well from certain angles, but rather had to adjust his view to bring her into focus. She held the papers closer to him in what she hoped might be his line of sight.

"And may I ask, Miss Moses, how you came to possess that manuscript?" He no longer smiled.

"You know what it is, then?" She lowered herself into the empty chair, resting the manuscript on her lap.

"Oh, I know what it is. I have always known what it is." He paused, raising his gaze to the ceiling. "And what it is not."

"What it is not, Mr. Rigdon, is not for me to judge."

The old man exhaled, and a low rattle resounded in his chest. He allowed his head to drop once again, his eyes focusing on his dancing fingers.

Ada continued, "I do, however, wish to explain to you how it came to me, if you'll indulge me. You see, it's a difficult tale filled with the details of a complicated life. My hope is that we might be able to help one another."

The old man's head snapped upward. "You mean to make a confession?"

"Of a type, perhaps. I do not seek forgiveness. I'm not sure I believe in it anymore than I believe in the one who offers it."

"I see," said the old man, the flush of excitement and purpose spreading across his wrinkled cheeks.

"Sir, please don't misunderstand me. I am not here seeking conversion. I abandoned any hope of that long ago."

"But do you believe God has abandoned you? You are here. Something, perhaps revelation from God Almighty, has brought you here, to me."

"I'll leave the revelations to you, Mr. Rigdon. I'm here because I am alone in the world and my time grows short. I want to tell my story to someone who will hear it for whatever it may be. I know you want this book." She indicated the bundled pages resting in her lap.

"It must have been in your possession for a long time. I assumed it had been destroyed."

"Not destroyed—merely forgotten."

In fact, nearly forty years had passed since the bundle first appeared in Ada's life. It was some time before she understood its secrets and its potential value, but though she rarely shied away from the promise of a profit, she had found herself unwilling to unleash such damaging power. Hesitant, even, when a seeker had at last knocked on her door.

Perhaps she had been wrong to possess it for so long. Were it to fall into the wrong hands, even if Ada felt unsuited to determine whose hands those would be, the secret carried within these ostensibly innocuous pages would alter the lives of thousands and forever taint a beautiful, if troubled, history.

Ada watched the prophet's lips move in silent prayer and then stop, a faint smirk replacing the piety she had just observed.

"I should like to examine your document, of course."

"You'll likely have your chance, but first I must ask you to listen to how it came into my possession. I cannot yet know for certain how this is going to end."

The old man shifted in his chair with great effort, drawing several deep breaths as he did. "It seems I have little choice, Miss Moses. Please take all the time you need."

3

Memory is a tricky thing to pinpoint, don't you find, Mr. Rigdon? But I think that the memories I have, imprecise as they may be and shaped over the years to new ideas and altered understandings of my maturing mind, make me who I am. That is, they led me to be the woman who sits, neither accusing nor judging, across from you on this glorious morning to give us an opportunity to consider one another.

The earliest of my memories of consequence is tinged in blood. Or rather, bathed in it. Of course I was only a child, seven years old, with cropped curls. This was 1831, around the time your Saints set eyes on establishing Zion in the backwoods of Missouri.

I was in the front room of our small but comfortable house. I don't know that we were wealthy, but I don't remember wanting for anything. My father was a newspaperman. He edited and printed the daily paper in our little New York town, and it enjoyed a successful circulation. He wasn't at home often during my hours of play, nor was he a nurturing father. I remember little interaction between the two of us. I do, however, recall his scent because later I would come to miss it.

He smelled of the printing press and his breath carried a hint of whiskey and tobacco smoke. Ink smudged his fingertips. It's his fingers, black from his late night work, that linger most freshly in my mind. When I close my eyes I can still see them dangling between his legs as he slumped on a wooden bench, elbows bent and resting on his thighs. His usually crisp white shirt was loosed and crumpled under his open wool waistcoat.

We sat in silence. He wasn't looking at me. Instead he stared down at his limp fingers. Short curls of his blond hair, the only feature I know for certain I share with him, fell forward over his ears and bounced as he shook his head side to side. At times this was an agonized, slow movement, but the pace waxed and waned with the tormented moans coming from the next room.

My childish mind did not comprehend what was happening, though of course I knew that the moment was serious. Children perceive the mood of the household even if they cannot fully understand or participate in it. Only when the sounds began to cease did I become frightened, in no small part because he looked up at me, directly into my eyes, and a connection of some shared panic passed between us in that instant. My father leapt from his bench and pushed through the door into the next room, leaving it open behind him.

I followed.

And that's when I caught my first sight of that terrible blood, the congealed mess of it pooled in unnatural clumps across the floor of the room. I only tore my eyes away from the crimson slime when I noticed the figure of my mother on the bed, pale and trembling.

No, trembling isn't quite the right word. She was shaking, rhythmically, from the tips of her toes to the flesh of her lips, as if in the throes of a religious trance. I could just see her fingertips bouncing out the beat at her side as she lay stretched on a bed—or perhaps it was a table.

The images are indistinct. I knew I wasn't supposed to be there, but I remained quiet, shrinking into a corner, and no one tried to chase me away. There was my mother with her faded complexion. At her side, opposite me, my father held her limp hand in his own healthy grasp, while her other hand lay helpless, dancing for me. She turned her gaze toward me, fixing me with puffy, stricken eyes, a blur of color against a ghostly face, but I couldn't keep my eyes locked on hers.

Another woman, perhaps a neighbor, delivered cloths, already stained pink with my mother's blood, to the doctor who stood at the feet of his patient and replaced the red-soaked rags that could not stop the deluge. The woman took the soiled cloths and shook her head, turning teary eyes to the floor, and hurried away to rinse out the blood and continue the futile cycle. I watched, transfixed, as the doctor reached his hairy arm up inside his patient, nearly to his elbow, withdrawing his hand again, to find it covered with clots of dark blood. His other hand massaged my mother's swollen belly, imploring her body to conform to his wishes.

I know I should have been sickened. I could see the others were frightened. Even now as an adult, it is difficult to express the emotions I experienced that day. The closest I can come is anger. More than anything, I was furious that no one could stop that terrible shaking. That no one, not even my mother, could control it.

But I was very young. I know now what I should have felt—intense sadness and grief, of course—if my mind could have fully comprehended it. She was dying in the most humiliating way I could imagine, lying there out of control while an audience, for all their efforts, did nothing more than watch. Together we held vigil as the quaking subsided and my mother slipped away from this world.

I have no recollection of a funeral. There must have been one. Probably the good townspeople who knew my parents came to offer condolences. I suspect that I didn't stay in our house during the weeks that followed, but rather was shuffled from one neighbor to another and melted into normal families for a time, playing with their children, behaving as though my life had not taken a tragic turn.

What I can recall is the day my father came to collect me from one such neighbor. I must have been there for several days, for I had a small trunk in my possession. In my mind I have a clear image of my father, dressed in his fine clothes, placing my trunk into a carriage, and then a very long trip across the countryside, ending at last in the village of Norwich in the Chenango River Valley.

Our carriage stopped at the end of a muddy road and as my father helped me down, he swore. I wore a lacy black dress of mourning and I remember that dirty water splashed from the road onto the delicate trim. In the end, my father picked me up and carried me down the lane, choosing to risk further ruin to his own clothes rather than spoil my appearance.

As we walked, we passed a row of frame houses, each with a rougher façade than our home though this roughness, I believe, pointed more to frugality than to poverty. The properties were all well tended. At the last house in the row we stopped, and my father placed me on the ground to knock on door.

He needn't have bothered because before his knuckles made contact with the rough wood, the door swung open to reveal an uncommonly tall woman wearing a simple brown dress and a comically wide grin.

"My dear brother!" the woman shrieked in what I can only assume was meant to be a joyful tone. The woman opened her arms and enveloped my father in an embrace that seemed to swallow him whole. The two were the same height and my father staggered under her exuberance.

When he broke from the embrace, he was smiling, too. "Harriet," he said with a chuckle, "it's good to see you." Then he looked down at me and squeezed my shoulder, guiding me toward the giantess. "May I present Ada Annette."

The woman bristled at the mention of my name, her mouth twisting in disapproval. "Annette? I hadn't realized. Whatever would have made you…"

"Her mother's idea," my father offered, shrugging and leaving me to wonder why my second name would cause such a reaction.

Not knowing exactly what was expected of me, I attempted a small curtsy the way I'm sure was shown me by my mother or one of the countless other women who had cared for me in recent weeks. As I did so, I stumbled, and had my father's firm touch not already been upon my shoulder, I would have fallen onto the path.

The giantess pursed her enormous lips, her cheeks shrinking into skeletal hollows. I shuddered, leaning against my father's leg. The woman crouched until her face was at my eye level, spreading her arms before me.

"I am pleased to meet you Ada. I am your father's sister. You must call me Aunt Harriet." Then she wrapped me in a tight squeeze with her arms like great lengths of thick rope against which I felt I must struggle, though I knew not to embarrass my father. Just as I was convinced I would suffocate, the giantess, now my aunt, released me and stood to show us into the house.

"I was so sorry to receive the news in your letter, Brother," Aunt Harriet said as she guided him into a simple wooden chair at the kitchen table. She sat in the only other chair in the room, across the table from him. I supposed I was meant to remain standing, for no one showed me what else to do. "I am sorry for your tragic loss."

"Ah, yes, well." My father sighed. "It has been difficult, obviously." He glanced toward me and then all at once I realized what he was about. I could count on one hand the number of times I had been alone with him in what must have been several weeks since my mother's death. He'd done nothing more than shuffle me from one place to another. Perhaps other adults had explained to me that he was a busy man and that he knew nothing of caring for a little girl, but I never suspected he wouldn't wish to raise me. As I looked from him to this mannish beast of an aunt, with her ensnaring arms and great abyss for a mouth, my throat began to tighten.

"Of course it has," the woman, my aunt, sighed and patted my father's arm with her absurdly large hand. "But you must remember that 'the Lord will not cast off forever, but though he cause grief, yet will he have compassion according to the multitudes of his mercies.'"

"Oh." My father looked into Aunt Harriet's eyes, his brow furrowed, his lips parted, as if he couldn't decide what to say. This had no doubt been an unexpected conversational turn, and I watched as he scrambled to determine its meaning.

In the end, he must have decided that she was in complete earnest because he replied, "Certainly I must bear that in mind. Yes, thank you. You always did possess the right words for the moment."

Aunt Harriet's lips spread once more into an enormous grin and she withdrew her hand from my father's arm.

"But how have you been, dear sister? I had some difficulty locating you. All is well, I trust?"

"Oh Albert, I've been managing, as always. I'm sorry for your troubles. John is a restless spirit, I'm afraid, and I do try to update our acquaintances, but we really have been all over the countryside it seems. We've only been here for a month, and with meetings and study, I'm afraid I have fallen behind. I pray that you can forgive me for not helping you bury Eliza and your little one. Did he have a name?"

My father started at the shift in conversation. He sat up straighter in the chair and cleared his throat, recovering from his momentary loss of composure. "Yes, he was Albert William. But, please don't concern yourself with all of that. We are fortunate to be surrounded by good neighbors. We've been well cared for."

The baby's name, or indeed that he had been a boy, was news to me. I had, of course, understood that my mother was to have a baby and that something had gone wrong. It had just never occurred to me that the baby must have died, too. That was why the silence had disturbed my father on that dreadful day. The cry of a healthy newborn gasping for its first breaths would have meant that all would be well. The absence of the noise signaled death.

I was angry with myself for not having thought of him, my baby brother, and I was angry with my father for not bringing my attention to him. He was more a part of me than any other living person, my very own brother. I would have loved to be a big sister, had in fact been looking forward to the responsibility of it. At seven years old, I was beginning to understand a bit about my little world and knew that I could have helped him, perhaps convinced him, at least, to live. I could have been the lady of the house, caring for the baby and holding us together as a family so that I wouldn't be standing in this bare, ugly kitchen while my father casually discussed the death of my whole reality with this supposed relative.

I hadn't even known he had a sister. She must have been older than he, I thought, as I looked at her drooping eyelids and wrinkled wrists. As she droned on, I only half listened, snatched bits here and there in an attempt to assess my situation whilst the grief and fatigue of the last few weeks welled up inside me.

"I am glad that you see reason in regards to the child," Harriet was saying.

Was I the child of whom she spoke? I tried to grasp at comments I'd heard, tried to piece them together, but could not. I'd been too preoccupied by my own jumbled thoughts.

"You can't possibly hope to raise her to Godly womanhood on your own."

"You're quite right, Harriet. I'm so relieved you understand."

"And I am certain that the Lord has blessed me with no children of my own so that I may welcome the girl into my home."

As Aunt Harriet spoke, a strange noise escaped my father's throat, a muffled sort of groan, and I saw that his eyes were moist with tears. I had never seen my father cry so freely, maybe not even at the death of my mother, and I felt sure that I was the reason, that I was so unwanted he cried at the thought of me.

After a quiet moment in which my aunt beamed in triumph at her younger, fragile brother, he spoke, his words strained and broken.

"I will, of course, send for her when I am better situated to care for her."

"You'll do no such thing. 'He maketh the barren woman to keep house and to be the joyful mother of children. Praise ye the Lord!'" Aunt Harriet lifted her eyes and her hands to the heavens, as my father watched, his eyebrows arched in what I interpreted to be disbelief. My aunt clasped her hands together above her head and brought them down to settle on the table once again.

Then she directed her gaze toward me, but her stare held a faraway look, giving me the distinct impression that she did not in fact care to see me at all. "We'll do very well together, won't we child?"

My expression must have betrayed my shock at being addressed so, after I'd been left safe in my own thoughts for such a long time. I knew Aunt Harriet expected a response, probably one of great joy and anticipation of the happy times we would have together as mother and daughter, but I couldn't muster it. Her focus snapped to me, searching. Her smile failed her and I caught the smallest cloud fall over her countenance, though my father did not notice, his attention fixed instead on the window.

"Of course we will," Aunt Harriet managed, hiding the rage I could see she felt.

And then I ran.

Out the front door and back through the muddy street, my feet kicking up flecks of muck onto my good dress. When I reached the end of the row of houses, I turned a sharp right, making my way uphill, toward a thick wood. I didn't stop until I reached it and then I sank breathless in the protection of thick branches. Not knowing how far the wood went, and fearing what else may be lurking amongst its shadows, I remained, tucked underneath a small shrub, further ruining my dress, looking out onto the weedy space between my refuge and the road.

I imagined they were right behind me, Aunt Harriet's long, lean legs propelling her through the street, her wide eyes scanning for evidence of me. Perhaps she had reached out her tentacular arms in an attempt to ensnare me as I rushed from the house, her strong fingers clamping down on the space I'd so recently occupied. My father I pictured as confused, slower to react to my outburst but just as angry at seeing his opportunity to abandon me with my relatives disappear through the mud.

I could only guess how long I remained in my hiding space. The afternoon had worn and given way to a chilly evening. In the failing light I couldn't see what approached me when I first detected heavy footsteps coming closer. My young mind could easily imagine at least a hundred ways that I might be in danger, the most likely being that I could simply die of fright. As the footsteps came closer, I heard a sound like a whip slashing across branches. I remained as still as I could, but the anticipation of what awaited me, were I to be captured, proved too much. When the slash came to my own dear bush, I screamed.

The next moment, two strong hands reached into the brush and pulled me from hiding.

4

He stood me up in front of him and knelt before me, a man quite unlike my father or any other I had known. His eyes met mine and in them I saw a curiosity that equaled my own. Even as he knelt, I could see that he wasn't particularly tall. Red whiskers, peppered with gray, adorned his thin face and his sleeves were rolled to reveal lean, sinewy forearms. Strong though he appeared, he could have done with a few good meals.

On his head he wore the low cap of a country laborer, askew. His left hand on my shoulder, he slid his right hand across the ground, prodding the grass, searching. Then finding what he sought, his fingers closed on a long, forked stick which he raised to eye level. As he did so, the skin around his eyes crinkled and his lips curved into a slow smile, revealing several gaps left by missing teeth.

"A useful little device." He rolled the stick between his fingers. "Though I believe this is the first time I've ever witched out the location of a runaway. I hope I didn't frighten you, Ada." His tone was kind, but I got the distinct impression that he'd rather hoped he had frightened me at least a bit. "You are Ada?"

I started to nod but thought better of it. Instead I kicked him, my foot hitting him square on the knee. The man fell back, catching himself with one arm, the stick he held breaking with a loud snap. I saw my chance to run, the blood pounding in my ears, but in the briefest moment as I turned to bolt into the woods, the stranger reached with his other hand and caught the hem of my dress.

It was enough to knock me off balance and send me to the ground where I scrambled to pull away from him, the rough grass tearing at my ruined lace.

The man winced as he jumped to his feet. Looming over me, he raised the broken stick above his head and with a loud growl of frustration, flung it into the woods.

He held out his hand to me then and, relieved as I was he didn't whip me with the stick, I let him help me to my feet.

"Well, now that you've got that out of the way, Ada, I think we'd better get you back to the house." He stood and turned to go, clearly expecting me to follow him which, despite my reservations, I did. He led me straight back over the path I had earlier traversed, up the stone walk, and into the little house where my father and aunt would be waiting, furious. He did not pause to knock, but walked through the door as a man who belonged to the place.

"John?" Aunt Harriet sat in the same chair she had occupied when I left. A single candle burned on the table and a leather-bound book lay open in front of her. She did not look up, but rather continued to bend low over the pages, squinting in the flickering candlelight. Her lips moved, shaping hints of words.

The man, who I deduced to be my uncle, grunted in response, but said nothing else. He kept a firm grip on my shoulder until at last Aunt Harriet ceased reading, wiping weariness from her eyes, and turned her attention to us.

"I found her, Harriet. Cold but not hurt, I think." The man patted my head, letting one of my curls slip through his rough fingers.

"That is a blessing for which she should be very thankful indeed." There was unmistakable anger in her voice. "Your supper." She motioned toward a tin plate upon which sat a small portion of bread and stew. My uncle claimed the seat across from Aunt Harriet and began to wolf down the meager meal.

My stomach grumbled in anticipation, as I had not eaten since breakfast and it had been a very long day. I stepped forward, clearing my throat, hoping this would signal my desire to be shown my own supper. As I did so, Aunt Harriet twisted her wide lips into an evil grin.

"Children who run away from home should not expect supper."

I knew then that my first impression of her had been correct. My aunt was not a tolerant woman. In her speech to my father she had expressed her intentions to raise me as her own, but her words contained neither love nor charity.

Attempting to display a brave face I asked, "Where is Father?" My voice quavered, betraying my true emotions. Even as someone so young, I understood I had lost some sort of a battle with the woman before me.

She seized upon the moment, eager, I realized, to emphasize her victory. Standing to her full height, her haughty chin lifted, she snarled, "Did you think he would follow you through the mud and beg you to come back home with him? You belong here now, child. You must learn your place. 'Foolishness is bound in the heart of a child, but the rod of correction shall drive it far from him.'"

Without another word, she walked out of the kitchen. With merely an angry flick of her wrist, she beckoned me to follow and, fearing her wrath were I to fail to heed her summons, I hurried behind her. What I found was a room, much smaller than the kitchen, with a low bed, my trunk placed at the foot. The room was bare of all other furniture but one wall contained shelves from floor to ceiling lined with rows of jars and bags of grains. A single candle sat flickering on the floor. I was to sleep in the pantry, a room with no windows.

"Undress and say your prayers. You do know how to pray?"

I dared not tell her I had never learned to pray and so I nodded.

"I expect you to go straight to bed." She turned to walk out, shutting the door hard behind her.

And so I went to bed without supper on my first night in Norwich, abandoned, frightened, heartsick, and hungry. I listened for a time at the door but heard no conversation between my aunt and uncle, only the occasional scrape of a chair. I climbed into bed, buried myself in the worn bedding, and cried until the tears would come no more.

My first morning in Norwich came early. I'd had precious little sleep and I felt as though I had only just closed my eyes when my aunt's insistent shaking roused me again. Aunt Harriet called me to rise with the sun, much earlier than I had been accustomed to doing at home, where my father's indifference had allowed me to keep any irregular schedule I saw fit. In my state of utter exhaustion I admitted this to my aunt.

"I'm sorry Aunt Harriet." I wished to sound humble, assuming that this is what she would want from me. I was at least an insightful child. "I am not accustomed to rising at this early hour and didn't rest well last night, so far from home."

Angry creases formed around her eyes. "This is your home, child, and in it you will rise with the sun for morning prayer."

Frightened, I breathed an apology.

Her expression softened. She wasn't happy exactly, but she no longer looked as though she might thrash me.

"Yes," she said. "You'll soon become adjusted. I can't imagine the life you've been allowed to live and what that must do to a child." She shook her head and handed me a pile of brown cloth that, upon examination, I found to be a simple child size dress otherwise identical to her own.

"Aunt Harriet," I said, "I have dresses in my trunk. May I wear one of those?"

"Certainly not. Silly lace frocks will not be the standard dress in this house. Clothing should be modest and practical and need be nothing more. You'll find no pampering here like you knew with that mother of yours."

I sucked in a sharp breath at her words, wishing I could scream and defend my mother, but already she was beginning to fade from my memory. Just the little things, like the smell of her skin and the timbre of her voice, slipped away, irretrievable, leaving me nothing to grasp and defend. My eyes filled with tears at the injustice of my helplessness as I wiggled into my ugly new dress.

One might assume that a young child crying over the recent death of her mother would elicit some sympathy, but if so, then one had clearly never met my aunt. Harriet saw no need for impractical emotions.

She dropped to her knees beside my bed and bid me do the same, watching to see that I obeyed her before bowing her head against folded hands.

Then she began to pray, not the murmured entreaties of a humble and penitent soul, but the self-assured ravings of a woman obsessed.

"Hearken unto the voice of my cry, my King, and my God, for unto thee I will pray." With the confidence of King David, Harriet approached the throne of her god.

Her abrupt attitude in prayer echoed that of her every action. After she said amen and prompted me to do the same, she led me to the kitchen table where a bowl of cold porridge awaited me. Ravenous, I attacked it as if it might be my last meal.

"Do you read, child?"

I swallowed my mouthful of porridge and answered, "A bit." My mother had been teaching me letters and I had been making some progress before she fell too ill to bother with the education of a daughter. I would not give Aunt Harriet the satisfaction of hearing me criticize the woman she so obviously despised, but at the thought of continuing my studies, a sense of thrill snaked through me, tingling in my limbs and settling in my barely satisfied belly.

"Have you read the Bible?" my aunt demanded in her brusque manner.

I started to shake my head. Then an image flashed into my mind of my father, in animated conversation with a man in the front hall of our home within days after my mother's death. The man held a thick black book. Periodically he would open it and glance down at its pages, reciting from memory antiquated words. As he spoke, the missionary attempted to put an arm around my father who deftly dodged him. I listened as my father's responses to the stranger became angry until at last he told him to leave and to take his damned Golden Bible with him.

It wasn't the vast knowledge for which my aunt was likely hoping, but it was all I had and I dare not tell her the truth. "Father reads it sometimes."

"Does he?" Clearly pleased at the information, my aunt's lips almost betrayed her with a smile. "Well, perhaps he would have made a fine father after all." Aunt Harriet took a moment to ponder this new information. "What do you know of it, then?"

"Oh, I find it interesting."

This was not the response she was looking for.

"Interesting how?" She drew out the question as she leaned over the table, stopping only when her face was mere inches from my own. Her posture frightened me, as I assume she intended, and I scrambled to find a response that would satisfy her.

"The language, I mean." It was the best reply I could I conjure. "The words sounded old and beautiful. I couldn't understand very well, but something about it made me want to hear more."

Aunt Harriet beamed at me then. I had answered well, something I learned to do consistently over the years or risk incurring her anger. She took away my empty bowl and laughed, so suddenly it may have surprised us both.

"Ada, my dear, there is hope for you yet." I wasn't sure whether to be pleased at her optimism or not. "We'll need to begin right away. There is little time, but if you work hard at your studies, I think we may succeed. Hallelujah! God is good."

My education began that very morning after we cleared breakfast away. Aunt Harriet chose for my first Scripture lesson the story of Noah and his legendary ark. There was logic to starting with Noah. It is one of the earliest stories in the Bible, starting in the sixth chapter of Genesis. Children are fascinated by stories and I was no exception.

I could envision the animals walking up the long plank, two-by-two, onto a large wooden boat where they would live peacefully together for weeks on end. It was a charming picture that ended with a rejuvenated earth and a beautiful rainbow splashed across the sky.

Aunt Harriet read me the story, asking me questions along the way to see that I understood the details. I was a quick study, my aunt was pleased to learn. She soon pulled out a small slate and told me to begin copying verses.

Her method for teaching reading and writing was simple. I copied a verse or two, and later long passages or even whole chapters at a time. She corrected my careless scrawl and then made me repeat the words I had written while pointing to each as I said it. This served two purposes: my reading improved rapidly, of course, but perhaps more important to my aunt, I memorized what we read together.

The first verses I committed to memory were Genesis 6: 5-7:

And God saw that the wickedness of man was great in the earth, and that every imagination of the thoughts of his heart was only evil continually. And it repented the Lord that He had made man on the earth, and it grieved him at his heart. And the Lord said I will destroy man who I have created from the face of the earth; both man, and beast and the creeping things, and the fowls of the air; for it repenteth me that I have made them.

"That is the power of God, Ada," my aunt said to me when I finished reading through the verses I had written. "It is only by His grace that we are allowed to live at all, and you can be sure He will wipe all human wickedness from the earth again."

"What about the rainbow promise he made to Noah?" I asked in my innocence.

"God promised never to flood the earth again, but he will not abide wickedness. Do not imagine for a moment that God will fail to unleash his vengeance on the earth. Every evil person will burn for his sins and the earth will cease to be."

At her words my eyes filled with tears. I did not wish to imagine that God preserved every living creature on the earth only to burn them up at a later date.

Seeing my tears, my aunt locked her cruel eyes on my innocent ones. "Are you wicked, child?"

I shook my head and wondered if I might be wicked.

Aunt Harriet stood and walked around the table, stopping directly behind me. She took my right shoulder in her firm grasp and leaned over me until her lips brushed my ear.

"Oh, but you are, Ada. You are wicked to the core and we will soon drive that from you."

We worked long hours, studying as we completed the household chores. My aunt never let a Scripture passage slip from my memory. If we had studied it, then she expected me to recall it at any moment. As we tended the vegetable garden, scrubbed the dishes, and swept the floors, she riddled me with relentless questions. We covered new passages each morning and reviewed in the afternoons.

I have whole chapters of Scripture memorized, and I have at times been grateful for them. My aunt would not be pleased, I'm sure, to know how I have used this skill. Sacred words, I have found over the years, can be powerful tools of manipulation.

I certainly did not appreciate my lessons at the time. My aunt was a tyrant in her teaching. Failure to memorize a day's lesson would result at best in an early bedtime without supper and at worst in a flogging with a stiff board.

Over time we became accustomed to one another and developed a routine. She learned, I believe, how far she could push me, and I learned how to avoid flares of her dangerous temper. I spent my days largely in fear, but my mind grew sharp, and when I succeeded, my aunt lavished love on me like none I could remember in my earliest years with my mother and father. So, in some small ways, I might even say that I was happy.

*****

"What a blessing your aunt must have been to you. The loss of both true parents is a large burden for a young girl to bear. I am sorry for your suffering." The prophet's eyes met Ada's. She knew that he could not see her clearly in this way, but his empty stare was nevertheless unsettling. Ada shifted in her chair, her throat as raw as her emotions after sharing these earliest of her memories. She took a long, slow breath.

"Your father committed a grave sin in so carelessly abandoning you in your time of greatest need. Rest assured that God will, by His power, bring all men to stand before him."

"That will do, Mr. Rigdon. I am unconcerned for the state of my father's soul."

"But we should be concerned for the souls of all men, Miss Moses, for all are beloved of God."

Ada shuddered inwardly at Mr. Rigdon's words, his voice once softened by sympathy now swelled with piety. Had it been concern for the state of Mr. Allen's soul that had ended his life, she wondered.

She recalled that evening in vivid detail. Ada had slept poorly, anxious for the return of her curious visitor, having at last decided to tell him her story, to give him the manuscript, and to wash her hands of the whole business. But Mr. Allen never arrived. Instead,

Ada opened her door to a sharp knock to find nothing but a brown package with the name Ada Powell written in a hand she did not know.

She glanced up and down the street. People milled about in early evening light. She saw men walking home from a long day of work, sailors just beginning to seek an evening of pleasure, and a few women of the type they would be seeking. No one seemed especially hurried or in any way concerned about her, the peculiar spiritualist standing in her doorway holding a paper-wrapped bundle.

Satisfied that she would not be able to identify the messenger, Ada closed her door and placed the package on her round table next to the manuscript that waited for Mr. Allen's arrival. She glanced at the clock as her fingers worked to loosen the package strings. When she pulled back the corner of the paper, she knew that Mr. Allen would never arrive.

In the package, folded neatly, was Silas Allen's white shirt and frayed coat, both soaked with blood that Ada assumed—no, that she knew—was his own. He would never hear her story, and so now Sidney Rigdon must.

Ada had imagined that she would be allowed to reveal her story uninterrupted. Perhaps she should have known that Mr. Rigdon, a self-proclaimed prophet of God, would have considerable skill at manipulating a conversation. She would not play into his diversions. At least not yet.

"God can sort out the souls of men. I very much doubt he needs my help." Ada allowed the trace of a smirk to cross her lips as she continued.

"It is true in some ways, Mr. Rigdon. My aunt was a blessing to me, but not in the way you imply. The harsh lessons she taught and her unreasonable expectations of me, though shaded in my memories by a constant fear, served to teach me much about myself, about who I wished—and did not wish—to become. And for one gift she gave me I will always be thankful because through her I met the one steadfast person in my life."

5

At this point I have said little of Aunt Harriet's husband, the peculiar imp of a man who pulled me from the underbrush. For the next year or two I saw very little of him. My uncle was more of a presence in the house than an actual body occupying it.

My aunt did not speak to me of his occupation, and I never dared ask. Instead I listened for clues and pieced together that he was a day laborer, hired as a farmhand during the seasons of harvest and planting. Often he would leave for weeks at a time following the whisper of work constructing railroads or dredging canals.

I dreaded these times not because I missed him, for there was nothing to miss outside of the uncomfortable sharing of awkward glances, but because my aunt grew tense and more dangerous during his absences. At first I assumed she longed for him to be near, but I suspect it was more that she mistrusted his intentions while away.

I soon began to understand why. When he was at home my uncle kept strange hours, waking before dawn, working through the day, and returning for his supper well after my aunt and I had eaten, only to disappear again soon after.

I knew he reappeared only during the darkest times of the night, slipping through the front door as silent as a shadow. Rarely did I perceive his return, the light shuffle of his feet or the deep sigh of fatigue. He never lit a lamp or stumbled into the table, cursing the dark night while nursing an injured toe. Like a vapor, he danced undetected through the darkened house.

Then one night I awakened to the insistent pounding of a fist upon our front door. My mind befuddled by sleep, I leapt onto the floor, shivering in the nighttime chill, and padded to my bedroom door, pushing it open only a crack.

Light spilled across the kitchen from the front doorway where a gangly stranger stood in the moonlight whispering, words edged with a panic that filled me with fear. The visitor pleaded with my bedraggled uncle. Uncle John's hair stuck out at odd angles and he stooped in his fatigue, but he straightened as the man spoke. I pulled back into the shadow of my own room, scarcely daring to breathe but also desperate to piece together the scraps of conversation.

"He's her only boy. It's bad, John. The doctor left about an hour ago, but Mrs. H. wants you to come."

My uncle rubbed his scraggly beard and shook his head. "Now, why would Mrs. Hodges want me? What's she think I can do?"

There was silence for a moment as the man seemed to consider how to respond. Apologetic, his voice wavering as though he were on the verge of tears, he finally spoke. "I told her you was good for this kind of thing sometimes."

"And what makes you think I am?" Anger coursed through my uncle's words, reaching a menacing crescendo that made my breath catch.

The man seemed also to shrink at the question. I could have sworn he was smaller than my uncle, though in truth he must have been taller by nearly a foot. "Look, John, don't deny you got some knowledge in this area. Mr. H.'s on the road, some big deal in the city. You know how mothers get. Just come see."

Uncle John grumbled, checking his volume. "I don't like doing business with women. There's always trouble."

The tall man leaned in close, his voice low and frantic. "She'll pay. I promise you that. She's in a state."

"There's more important considerations than just money. Hodges doesn't take any notice of me and that's the way I like it. He's not a man you want on your bad side is what I hear."

"So save his boy and you won't never have to worry about that."

This line of reasoning must have made good sense to my uncle because he asked, "How long's the boy been down?"

"Fever's lasted five days."

Uncle John let out a low hiss at the news. "Find me some good dark beer. Tell that woman of yours I'll be 'round as soon as I can."

The man dipped his head in a graceless bow, clasping his hands together in gratitude, and backed away from the doorway before turning to leave at a full sprint. My uncle watched him go and called after him, "And tell her not to go talking about this with that fool doctor or I won't come!"

He closed the door, plunging the kitchen into darkness. I heard no footsteps as he glided across the floor and wondered if he had even moved at all. Then I could sense him right next to me. The bedroom door slowly swung open, sending me scurrying backward into the black space of the room, the edge of a wooden shelf digging into my back. The faint outline of Uncle John peered through the widened crack, his face alarmingly close to my own. "Can't sleep, girlie?"

Foul breath washed over me and I would have screamed out had he not clapped a firm hand directly over my mouth, nudging me harder against the shelf, the splintered edge scraping across my back through the thin fabric of my nightgown.

"Now," he whispered, as he wrapped his other hand around the back of my head, silently daring me to struggle. "Since you're awake, I could use some help. So long as you understand you don't say a word to your aunt on the subject."

I nodded as much as his grip would allow and he let go. "We leave in five minutes whether you're ready or not. Dress warm," he added as he vanished into the darkness.

I pulled on my dress as quickly as I could and dug around in my trunk for a warm wrap to wear around my shoulders. Quietly, I let myself out the front door to find my uncle holding a lantern and mumbling to himself.

He still looked as disheveled as he had when he spoke with his late night visitor, but the lantern light reflecting off his bright eyes indicated that he was wide awake and focused, a bag slung over his shoulder.

"Come on, then."

My apprehension surged at his clipped words, though as he spoke he reached for me, pulling my wrap more securely up around my shoulders. His thoughtfulness lent me more comfort than did the wrap, and for the moment I was glad to come along on his adventure.

We set out into the night together. I had a difficult time keeping up. His legs could not be considered long, but his steps were quick and he set a demanding pace, making no effort to wait for me. As he had the only lantern, I was forced to run to keep up or risk being left behind.

He cut a path through the wood where he'd discovered me that first day we met. Since then I'd had some opportunity to explore it with Aunt Harriet as my stern guide to the wonders of God's creation, but I could never navigate it in the dark as my uncle did so effortlessly. He walked with a single-minded determination through the brambles, and as my breathing grew labored, his pace never slowed.

Finally, the wood began to thin and he stopped. Stooping, he snatched a plant by the roots. He turned to me and I saw between his gloved fingers several scraggly yellow flowers hanging limp from a cluster of green stems.

"A weed?" I asked, my question tinged with disappointment.

In the glow of the lantern his smile loomed, menacing, but by his tone I knew he was pleased. "Ragwort." He shifted the plant to pinch a single flower between his thumb and index fingers, inviting me to look more closely. "Can you recognize this plant if you see it again?"

I nodded. I had seen these plants many times in the woods, common enough they never demanded my notice before this strange night.

"Good. I need as many of them as you can carry in your fist." He handed me the lantern and continued to walk. How my uncle managed to press on so confidently without the aid of the light, I didn't know, but I scrambled after him, careful to keep him in my sight as I scanned the ground for more of the little yellow flowers.

We wound through a rough path that sloped sharply downward. He only slowed his pace to occasionally offer me a steady hand down a steep drop we happened upon. This was late spring and the night was chilly. My fingers stiffened with cold around my growing bundle of weeds. We hiked on for what felt like hours.

When he stopped at last, I could hear the babble of rushing water. We had come upon a small stream at the point where it trickled into the Chenango River, wide and dark in the moonlight.

My uncle turned to me then. "How about those flowers?"

Startled by the sharpness of his voice against the faint lapping of the water's edge, I lifted my fist, stuffed full of the plants. He took them from me and crammed them into his coat pocket, nodding his approval.

"Give me the lantern."

I did not question his command, though it filled me with dread. I hated to yield the light source so near the river. As clear as the night may have been, the river water was high at this time of year. My aunt, who seemed to relish my fear, enjoyed reminding me of the river's tendency to swell with the spring rains and claim unsuspecting victims from its banks, burying them in its depths.

My uncle spared no attention to my discomfort. He used the light to examine another plant. This one consisted of a cluster of slender stalks as tall as him. Small, narrow leaves with dusty undersides sprouted in pairs along the length of the brown stalks, dotted by drab, spiky flowers.

"This is it," he said as he handed me back the lantern and cut down the stalks with a knife he pulled from his bag.

"What is it?" I asked, breathless but grateful to have control of the lantern again.

"Meadow willow." He put his knife away and arranged the stalks in his hand as we began to climb up through the woods that led to town. "Willows like the damp soil along the river. There's some that say they can take away the ague."

"What's that?" My excitement grew. He may have terrified me, but I was also finding my uncle to be an endless source of knowledge. He was fascinating.

"It's fever," he responded, obviously as eager to teach as I was to learn. "Bad fever. The kind that gives you the shakes and like as not leaves you for dead."

"Is that what the boy's got? The one we're going to help?"

"Yes." His speech hesitated, but his pace through the woods never slowed. "Ada, since you're coming with me, I have to be clear. You can't come into the house."

I had just begun fancying myself his important assistant and his words felt like a slap. "Why?" My indignation sliced through the quiet of the woods.

"Because I won't have a little girl questioning my orders," he growled, then gentler said, "Healing is tricky work. I can't have you getting sick on me, but you can help with the mixing. Would you like that?"

"I suppose."

"Good. But stay out."

We stepped out of the woods and into a part of town with which I was unfamiliar. The world I occupied with Harriet was small, defined by little more than the woods between our small house and the river and the few blocks between home and church meeting.

Large houses, much finer than ours, lined the street. We veered off on a hard-packed drive leading onto a carefully gardened landscape of breathtaking beauty even in the darkness of night. A two-story house with a wide front porch rose proudly over a neatly trimmed yard.

I was about to ask who lived in such splendor when I saw a figure burst from the house, leap off the porch, and run straight for us.

The man hollered something indistinct as he ran and I recognized the voice as belonging to the man who had come to fetch my uncle for the sick boy's mother. His breaths came hard by the time he reached us. "Where you been?"

"Calm down, Ollie." My uncle spoke slowly and evenly, his tone somewhat soothing the frantic man. "Did you get the beer?"

"Yeah, yeah, I got the beer. Who's that?" He pointed to me as he panted. "I didn't know you was a papa."

"Harriet's niece," he replied, then more quietly as if his words were meant only to reach me, "My niece." He turned to follow Ollie to the house.

I went with them as far as the porch where he stopped me and pressed his fingers hard into my wrist. "Now remember what I said. You stay out here." He reached into his bag then and pulled out a heavy, smooth bowl of stone and a short tool of the same material shaped like a club that fit perfectly in his hand. Into the bowl he placed ten acorns from his pocket and began smashing them to pieces with the little club.

When they were crushed, he set the bowl down in front of me. "Remember what I said, girlie. You must not come inside. Now grind these little pieces into dust. Be real careful. Don't lose any of them."

He watched for a moment until satisfied that I had understood his instructions, then said, "Ollie, you bring the beer out to my girl. The two of you mix a drop in at a time just until you have a thick paste. No more than that."

He surprised me by looking straight at me as he spoke instead of Ollie, as if Uncle John thought me the more responsible of the two of us. The two men disappeared into the house, leaving me alone on the porch, pulverizing acorns in the middle of the night. Ollie reemerged from the house a few moments later carrying a large mug of beer.

His hands shook and some of the beer sloshed over the rim, splashing onto the porch. "Damn," he cursed and glanced up at me, startled, I think, to see me watching him. "Sorry," he stammered. He wasn't much to look at in a rough brown suit, his plain shirt hanging loose. I could tell he was the sort of man who takes orders a lot better than he gives them. The kind of man that a distraught mother sends away to find help because although he is more or less reliable for routine matters—he's no good in emergencies.

"Give me the beer." I held out my hand. He passed me the mug without question, crouching next to me on the porch. I splashed the tiniest amount into the bowl.

"Damn!" I whispered, a little concerned that I had already added too much. I think it was the first swear word I had ever uttered, and for me it was a glimpse into the power words might have to manipulate. Ollie gave me an uncertain smirk, let go a deep exhale, and stood. I mixed until the acorn dust formed a reasonable paste.

Ollie reached into his coat pocket and withdrew a small object that he held to his heart—a talisman. He proceeded to pace back and forth across the porch. "You work here?" I asked as I mixed, mostly because his constant movement bothered me.

He stopped and studied me, wondering, I can only assume, whether a little girl in a homespun dress was worth talking to. I sat up taller under his gaze in an attempt to appear older than I was.

"I've worked for Hodges for a lot of years. He's a lawyer, a big bug with influence, always off somewhere, leaving his pretty young wife and the boy at home because he has something more important to deal with. Mary's a sweetheart. Deserves better than that husband she's got."

I stopped mixing the paste and looked at him. Ollie knelt beside me, opening his hands to reveal the hidden object. It was a child's toy, a carved wooden horse of the kind my brother might have played with had he lived. Setting aside the acorn paste, I reached for the horse. Ollie let me take it.

Even with just the light of the moon, I could see the toy was inexpertly made. The proportions were wrong, the legs mismatched, but while fingering the unfortunate horse, I was filled with a deep sense of love and sorrow embedded within the unskilled craftsmanship. The horse carried a secret, one I could not know then, but still I felt the weight of it pull at me as I watched tears gather on Ollie's lashes.

I sighed and handed back the toy. "He's going to survive." I knew my words were true, even if I didn't know why. "My uncle is a gifted healer." I knew those words were true as well.

Ollie sniffed and nodded. Then he stood and tucked the toy back into his pocket. "I just take care of the place for Hodges—you know, the grounds and garden, and other things. There's no one else to watch out for them all when he's gone so much."

"I understand." Of course, it was only in retrospect that I understood fully, but I could see he loved this boy as his own.

Ollie reached out for the bowl of paste and I handed it to him. "I'll take this to John." He disappeared into the house, leaving me alone with my thoughts.

Pulling my wrap tight around me, I curled up on the porch swing and closed my eyes. I awoke to the sound of conversation, the sky still dark. I recognized my uncle's voice joined by another belonging to a woman. "Give him the paste once a day for seven days and the ragwort wrap across the belly every night, too. And see that those branches get burned out away from the house, and I mean right away."

"Of course." The woman nodded as she listened. "Thank you for coming. You have put the mistress's mind at ease. She's been worried so. She can't sleep and hasn't eaten in at least two days. She doesn't trust that doctor."

"See if you can get some food in her and get her to rest or she'll make herself sick, too. I'll fix her up something to help her sleep and send it along with Ollie."

He spoke to me next with a soft nudge on the shoulder. "Time to get up."

"Yes, Papa." The word slipped out before I thought. I looked him in the eyes, a knot of regret forming in my stomach. My uncle met my stare, exhaustion painting his weathered features. Embarrassed, I took the hand he offered me.

He pulled me to my feet and gently rearranged my wrap around my shoulders. Leaning forward, he whispered in my ear, "All right, Ada my girl, let's get you home."

That night my heart was full for the first time in years. Slipping through the quiet streets of Norwich, hand in hand with Papa, I believed that though I had lost so much of the life, I may yet have found a home that could suit me.

Though my aunt monopolized most of my time, I was eager to carve out moments I might spend with Papa. Still he was almost a phantom in the house, but his mysterious comings and goings now piqued my interest. We never spoke of the night I went with him to the Hodges house, and he was not encouraging when I asked him when I might help him again. Instead I got the impression that he avoided me whenever possible.

One Sunday as my aunt and I walked home from a painfully long worship service which, as usual, Papa had not attended, I mustered the courage to ask Aunt Harriet about him. She hummed the morning's hymns as we walked, as cheerful as she was ever likely to be.

"Aunt Harriet," I began, placing a hand in hers. If one did not know better, we could have made the perfect picture of a loving mother and daughter out for a Sunday stroll together. "Why does Uncle John not attend service?"

I was careful not to refer to my uncle as "Papa" in Aunt Harriet's presence. That name I reserved for him alone, though I wondered when I might have another occasion to use it. I also suspected that to use the endearing title in front of my aunt would bring swift punishment. She failed to be the mother I would have liked. Still she often displayed a sort of maternal jealousy for my affections.

Her humming stopped. Her pace slowed. I kept hold of her hand and looked up at her, encouraging her, I hoped, to share with me a morsel of personal information. There was much I longed to know of her and of Papa, even of myself, answers she might give me if only she would cease to speak in Scriptural riddles.

"Do not waste the effort on him, Ada." She placed her free hand on her stomach as if to hold back pain welling up inside of her. "'Unto the pure all things are pure: but unto them that are defiled and unbelieving is nothing pure; but even their mind and their conscience is defiled.' That's the book of Titus, Chapter 1, verse 15."

Whatever wave of emotion had passed over her, she had weathered it and now her previous pace resumed. Her humming did not. As that was all she had to say on the subject, I was left to imagine what sort of family this was into which fate had seen fit to thrust me. It was clear to me that my aunt and uncle lived quite separate lives and I could not be sure how I fit into either of them. I felt drawn to Papa, who seemed to want little to do with me, and repelled by my aunt, who always kept a watchful eye. And so I worked hard at my chores and studies and waited for my chance to cross over again into Papa's world.

6

Nearly two weeks passed before I found an opportunity to spend time with Papa. In those weeks, like always, he worked long hours—helping to construct a mill, I think it was. In the meantime, I resigned myself to long hours with my aunt, working diligently at my studies.

Aunt Harriet never insisted I call her anything but the title by which she first introduced herself to me, but she made it clear in other ways that she wished for me to think of her as a mother, far more suitable than my real mother had been.

In her care, my wardrobe of lacy frocks vanished to be replaced by more of the plain, rough dresses she herself wore. Nothing but their size indicated that they had been especially sewn for a child.

I grew thinner under her watch as well. No longer plumped up on sweet treats and extra helpings, I existed on careful portions of rough fare, usually a stew of garden vegetables and venison or rabbit. My uncle was a reasonably skilled hunter and we did not want for meat, but my aunt did not believe in excess. She rarely baked bread and when she did, it was a dense, chewy sort, very different than the lighter, more delicate bread I recalled my mother baking. I often refused it. In the first two years I lived with Aunt Harriet, I changed from a plump, giggling seven-year-old to a rapidly aging, slender, serious young woman of nearly ten.

My aunt held with the notion that within the heart of each child lay a smaller version of an adult. Under the influence of the proper rigors of study and toil, she believed this hidden maturity of mind could be coaxed to reveal itself in the outward appearance as well. She set about her work, eager to see me grow fearful of punishment and amenable to her will.

Fortunately among Aunt Harriet's staunch beliefs was a high regard for regular exercise, and she would not begrudge me that.

Often she accompanied me on an excursion through the woods, reciting Scripture along the way, continuing our lessons. She marveled over God's magnificent creation, but I could see she did not know it as Papa did. Her eyes slipped past the same plants he gathered and worked into powerful medicines.

She suffered for her lack of knowledge, and for her stubborn unwillingness to let him share his. During the changing of the seasons, frequent headaches trapped Harriet inside our dim house. Many days by the late afternoon, after hours of poring over the small print on the delicate pages of her Bible, she could not bear the exertion of exercise. And so she would send me on my own, with strict limitations on where I could go and when I was to return, generally by supper time when the sun began to set.

I relished those times when I could disappear into my imagination and, for a brief time, become the child I still was. I eagerly explored the woods, even down to the rushing river's edge, no longer afraid since hiking through so much of it with Papa. Along the way I collected wild flowers, closing my eyes to see if I might navigate as Papa had and discovering, as I stumbled over tree roots, that I could not.

I knew I was straying farther than strictly allowed, but the beautiful day called to me, and with Aunt Harriet safely incapacitated, my desire to thwart her influence overcame my fear of punishment. I kept going, lost in my meandering thoughts until something roused me from them.

First I heard him—or someone, because I didn't yet know it was him—but simply a funny sort of singing deep, soft, and lacking any melody I could place. My curiosity aroused, I moved toward the sound. I only had to walk for a few minutes before I found him, or rather them, because he wasn't alone. In a small clearing sat half a dozen men, including Papa, cross-legged on the ground circling a smoldering fire.

One of the men I recognized as Ollie who had called upon Papa to visit the sick Hodges boy. I did not recognize the other four men except that I thought they were the type of people I would cross the street to avoid. Each sat with his arms resting on his bent knees. Their eyes were closed and their heads bowed, relaxed, with chins resting on their chests. In contrast, Papa held his head high, his arms raised toward the sky, his eyes very much open. He did not pause in his song—a kind of chanting, I now understand—in a language I didn't know. As I approached, his eyes locked on mine and he nodded, a trace of a smile fluttering across his face.

I have often wondered that I wasn't frightened. Before tending to the Hodges boy, I certainly would have been. For two years the imagined mystery of my uncle had struck more terror in my heart than even the very real cruelty of my aunt.

But now he was Papa, the man who had welcomed my help, sharing his wisdom with me, pleased at my interest. It never occurred to me that I might be interrupting some important ritual where my presence would be unwelcome. After all, this was not something I was meant to see or it would have been performed in the open, rather than tucked back into the woods, away from prying eyes. Papa's expression contained more than surprise at seeing me. His gaze communicated a gentle welcome and I obeyed my urge to stay. I sat down, cross-legged just outside the circle, relaxed the muscles in my neck, and lowered my head.

I found it wasn't necessary to know the meanings of the chanted words. Whatever this magic was that caused my body to relax came from Papa's voice itself more than from the words he uttered. The incantation surrounded me, possessing my mind, enveloping me in a peaceful mist. I grew aware, while listening, that I was no longer still. My body responded in some new way to the lilting tones. But I didn't focus on my actions. Instead I let myself glide along, propelled by the rising of the tuneless song that grew in tempo and volume, wild and natural. My body followed the swell, dancing of its own accord.

Then, just as it reached a climax, the chanting stopped. I opened my eyes and issued a soft scream of surprise at what I saw. I stood inside the circle of men, all still seated, but with eyes open and trained on me. I dared not move. No one said a word for a moment, and then I heard my uncle speak from behind me.

"Gentlemen, we've received a special message tonight, one of great importance. Our treasure is surely near. The smoke rises in a thin wisp, a good omen if ever I saw one. And now we've had an angel dance among us."

The men began to talk amongst themselves, repeating expressions of awe and utter belief. Then one of them asked the obvious question: "Who is she?"

My uncle stood and draped his strong arm over my shoulder, hugging me tight to him. "Ada here is my young niece—a child, I hardly need to point out—too young to be wandering about this deep in the woods all alone."

The men nodded agreement around the circle and whispered theories to one another.

Next my uncle spoke directly to me, loudly enough the others might hear. "Why are you here, girlie?"

"I was in the woods," I began, focusing on Papa's face to see whether I was saying the words he wished to hear, the habit I had developed when speaking to my aunt. He smiled encouragement and so I continued. "I heard a low noise I thought was singing."

"And you were drawn to it?" He was not angry the way my aunt so often was, but I understood that he was leading me in a particular direction and I happily obliged.

"Oh yes." I spoke in a whisper so the men had to strain to hear me. "I couldn't help myself. I had to find it." They leaned their heads toward us to better hear what I had to say. Some began to stand and to inch closer to me. Papa held me more tightly. Grateful for his protection, I continued. "I don't know how far I stumbled through the trees before I came to the clearing. Time no longer mattered. I had to find the source of the sound, and when at last I did, I sat as you were sitting, just there." I looked around, catching the eye of each man as I did so, and indicated the place where I'd sat.

"And then what happened?" The question came not from Papa, but from one of the men who stared at me with wide eyes, captivated.

I relished the opportunity to exercise my imagination, to manipulate my audience. And so I kept going. "I can't explain it. I found myself getting lost in the sounds of the chant. I was only slightly aware that I was moving at all."

"You were dancing, my dear." Papa's voice was gentle. "You danced around the fire, in a trance."

"A trance?" I wanted Papa to elaborate, to explain what had just happened to me, but instead he spoke to the circle of men.

"The spirits are with us and tomorrow under the new moon, we dig!"

"Why wait 'til tomorrow?" one of the men cried out, accompanied by murmurs of agreement.

Papa spoke without hesitation. "We can all agree we beheld a wondrous sign tonight. The spirits that will guide us have chosen to work through young Ada. I doubt it would please them if we were to endanger her. I need to take her home. It's growing dark."

I realized he was right and that's when I became frightened. The sun was almost set entirely and stars broke through parts of the sky. "Aunt Harriet will be furious," I groaned.

My uncle said goodnight to the somewhat placated gathering and guided me into the cover of the woods. "Even your aunt can't be angry with you when she hears why you're so late."

"Papa, what happened back there?"

He grinned. "What happened is that I got very lucky. You bought me some time with some of my business associates."

"Those didn't look like good men to me."

"They're not, girlie." He chuckled and added, "But then, neither am I." I didn't know what to say to that, but Papa was eager to talk. "You were very good back there. You've got good instincts and you can tell a story."

"It was true." I shrugged in the darkness as we walked on. Once again I found myself wondering how Papa knew just where to go through the dense wood with little light remaining in the sky. He never hesitated, never stumbled. As long as I remained tight on his heels, neither did I. "At least it was sort of true. I said what I thought you wanted me to say."

"And that was the real beauty of it, Ada. You're a smart girl."

"You said I fell into a trance. What did you mean, exactly?"

"A trance, a true trance, is an altered state of reality when your mind goes somewhere on its own and your body does as it feels. Some people think it's a way to talk to God or to spirits."

"I did that?"

"If you believe you did, then I think you must have."

Papa always responded to questions of faith in this way, with elusive answers that encouraged exploration of truth rather than with rigid definitions of it. In that way he differed starkly from my aunt for whom truth was always absolute. I myself find that my perceptions of truth fall somewhat between the two, but of course it would be many years before I would come to fully understand and appreciate the depth of their respective wisdom. As a child, I had much more concrete worries.

"Papa, you said Aunt Harriet couldn't get angry at me about where I've been, but she's not going to like knowing I've been trance-dancing around a campfire in the woods with dangerous men. I should have been home hours ago." I could almost feel the lashes I would soon receive. Dread stole the warmth from my body as the trees became thinner near the edge of the woods.

Papa stopped just as we reached the open ground and knelt in front of me so his eyes were level with mine. The large moon cast a bluish light across his bearded face. "Ada, do you trust me?"

I nodded.

"And do you think you could do that again—tell a story like that, so convincing and heartfelt? Could you put on a show like you did tonight?"

"I think I could."

"Good." He looked down at the ground and released a slow breath. "This is going to be a beautiful partnership, this is. And we'll just tell Harriet that you sprained your ankle in the woods, called for help, and eventually I heard you and rescued you. She can't be mad at that."

"But, Papa," I began to protest, "she'll never believe…" I didn't finish because at that moment I felt his heavy boot kick at my leg and he stomped hard on my foot. Pain jabbed at me, the surprise of it nearly making me lose consciousness as I fell to the ground.

*****

"What can possess a man to do such a thing?" Rigdon shook his head, his clouded eyes narrowed in anger.

"Do not judge Papa too harshly, Mr. Rigdon. It was a fine line he walked between me and my aunt. I didn't truly appreciate that myself for many years."

"For some actions there is no justification, nor forgiveness."

"Yes, perhaps that is true when one is attempting to earn his way to heaven, and atone for his own sins, but Papa never seemed that interested in Heaven." Ada wondered, not for the first time, if Mr. Allen had still been interested in Heaven and if his sins had been adequately atoned for to see him safely there. She closed her eyes and the image of the blood-soaked shirt swam before her. Her breathing became shallow, her chest tightened, and she could feel herself swaying in the chair, momentarily disoriented.

Ada reopened her eyes, steadying herself. Sidney Rigdon, she noticed, moved his lips as though to speak, but then must have decided against it. Instead he raised his right hand just inches above the quilt on his lap, signaling for Ada to continue.

7

Papa dropped to his knees and cradled me in his strong arms. I pounded my fists against his chest, wriggling to break free of him. I could feel him flinch as each of my punches landed, but still he did not let me go, and my impotence filled me with rage. As justifiably angry as I was with Papa, I was more embarrassed that I had trusted him—thought even that I might love him or that he might love me.

He said nothing but held me closer to him as the strength of my attack faded, letting my indignant screams fade, before he spoke. Never releasing me, he whispered, "Ada, dear, how many times am I going to have to carry you out of these woods and back home to your aunt?"

And then a smile broadened across his drooping cheeks. For the first time, I wondered how old he was. He was not a young man—his weathered skin folding down his neck revealed that much—but despite a light peppering in his beard, there was no gray in the thick waves of hair on his head.

"You broke my ankle!" My fury bubbled out and fueled another attempt to escape his grasp.

"Ada!" His voice, so loud and so sudden, stopped my writhing at once. I looked into his eyes, gray and patient. He continued in a calm, low voice, "I can't carry you if you won't be still, and if I can't carry you then you'll have to walk, which I don't recommend in your condition."

He was right, of course, and serious in his threat. Whatever I felt about the cruelty he had just revealed to me, I was still at his mercy. I turned my face away from him without a word, but I stopped struggling against him. I wrapped my arms around his neck and leaned into his warmth, resentful that I still craved from him a father's love.

We walked toward home in silence. Then, steps away from the door, he said, "It's not broken, you know. I can break a little girl's ankle if I intend to." His breath was hot on my neck, but his words still sent a chill through me.

Aunt Harriet ran to meet us and snatched me from Papa's arms. "What happened to her?"

"This curious girl was climbing a tree, to get a better look at a bird's nest."

This was news to me, of course, but even if he had recently broken my trust in him, I was beginning to understand when I should stay quiet and let Papa tell his stories. I made no attempt to contradict him. Instead I lay my teary head on my aunt's shoulder, surprised as always to feel her brawny strength.

She sighed and clicked her tongue. "Fell out of a tree? Why would you behave so foolishly, child?" All I had strength enough to do was sniffle and await my unjust punishment.

"When I found her," came Papa's voice, "she was trying to hobble her way out of the woods. Almost made it, too."

"And what were you doing in the woods at such an hour?" Aunt Harriet directed her question to Papa, spitting venom with her clipped words.

"The girl is safe," he grumbled.

Aunt Harriet's body tensed against mine as though she was not at all impressed with that truth, but she refrained from further comment. Instead she turned to the house with me in her arms, leaving Papa to trail after us.

When she got me inside, Aunt Harriet placed me upon my bed and pulled the quilts around me. "You were extraordinarily foolish, child, and extraordinarily fortunate. You have much to be thankful for. You'll not be able to kneel tonight. Say your prayers in bed. I suppose you're hungry. I'll bring you some supper."

I watched her walk out of the room and did not hesitate to bow my head. I was thankful, surprised and thankful, that Papa had much cooler wits than I and that together we had outsmarted Aunt Harriet. There would be no punishment this time. I still didn't understand what I had been a part of in the woods that evening, but I knew well enough that my aunt would not have approved. My ankle throbbed, each pulse an outlet of the fury I still felt, but my breath was slowing, and I found that as the pain dulled to an ache, so did my raw anger settle into a reluctant acceptance.

The sound of his heavy boots on the wooden floor stirred me from my thoughts. "It's just me, girlie. Go ahead and finish your prayers." He stood next to my bed, strips of white cloth dangling from his hand.

"I don't pray. Not really." I don't know why I said it to him, but it seemed important that I do so.

"Prayer can be a powerful practice, girlie."

I was so surprised at his statement that I wasn't sure how to proceed. He offered no more words of explanation, but folded back the quilts to expose my injured leg. Gently he lifted my bruised ankle and laid the strip of fabric beneath it on the bed. The pain quieted as he applied a salve, then wrapped and knotted the fabric around my injury.

He spoke as he worked, quiet words that were not meant for me. My eyes grew heavy at the soothing sound of his voice, and I allowed my body to relax and my mind to drift. Before I fell off to sleep, I whispered a small "Thank you."

Papa leaned close, his whiskers tickling my cheek. "You're welcome, Ada."

I must admit that Aunt Harriet, for all her many faults, was a kind and diligent nurse, and it would not be dishonest of me to say that I enjoyed my first days of convalescence, for with it came some degree of immunity from her wrath. This was because she would not allow me to work alongside her, but instead instructed me to read aloud at the kitchen table or outside under the fruiting trees as she tended the garden and the few hens we kept.

Though I still stumbled through most new passages, my memory was strong and my reading vastly improved since I'd begun under Aunt Harriet's tutelage. Even she acknowledged my intelligence in her more gracious moments.

Sometimes when I'd reach a passage among the Psalms, she would begin to sing. I always stopped to listen because soon the words that so clumsily fell from my mouth would be transformed into something indescribably beautiful. Her enormous mouth, at other times quite frightening, would open wide with melody.

I suspect my father was also a singer—a deep, smooth tenor. I recollect it sometimes, just flashes of memories. In them he comes home late at night and in high spirits, bellowing jolly notes. He catches up my mother in his arms and dances her about the house as I watch, creeping from my bed where I should have been asleep for hours.

Of course now I realize he must have been exceedingly drunk at those times, perhaps more frequently than I know, for my mother, her features indistinct to me, is nevertheless undeniably cross in these images. When I was younger it seemed the most romantic thing in the world, and I wondered how anyone could ever be angry while dancing or while listening to the sweet sound of that voice.

Aunt Harriet's tune did not match his frivolity, but it was joyful in its own way and her voice easily as sweet. I thought there must have been music in their home when they were young. As she sang, locked in her own heavenly dreams, my imagination wandered to another distant childhood, directly connected to my own, in which a sister sang to her young brother until he copied her, matching her every tonal shift, and then gradually found new notes with which to form perfect harmonies. Perhaps their parents—my grandparents— had been great musicians, composers of fine concertos. I liked the idea that I descended from creative genius.

I never asked my aunt about her singing, partly because I didn't want the mirage of my history shattered, but also because the music felt sacred. When she sang, I saw past Aunt Harriet's rigid faith in the cold words of her beloved Bible. I could almost glimpse the intangible meaning of it all that, in her way, she tried to convey to me. She believed, with her whole heart, the words she forced into my mind held a promise for her and for me. Perhaps if she had ever concretely expressed that to me, our life together might have turned out differently.

On the third day of my recovery, the bruising turned a dark shade of yellow. I could walk with support and, I discovered, when pressed, I could also run. Aunt Harriet sent me to bed early, just after supper, as she had been tending to do since my accident. That was fine with me. Constantly needing to concentrate on my movements, stepping carefully and leaning on any support I could find, proved exhausting. Snuggled into my bed, I was nearly asleep when Papa burst through the front door of our house.

I was used to Papa coming in and out at all hours and so I would not have thought anything of it except that he normally moved with such care. This night was clearly different. I heard Aunt Harriet's quick footsteps running into the front room.

"What is it?" she demanded, her voice edged in fear.

"Pack," came papa's voice. He was not panicked, but his words were firm. I pulled myself up in bed and tried to decide what I should do when at once I heard my name.

"But what about Ada?" Aunt Harriet's voice quivered. "You promised me if we took her in, things would be different."

"So I did." Papa sighed and I heard him scoot a chair across the wood floor. Maybe he sat in order to give his words more emphasis in an otherwise hurried moment, or perhaps he had led my aunt to the chair to deliver unwelcome news.

"Harriet, I'm sorry. I know this was not what you wanted for the girl, but I was so close this time. Beman and Smith were onto something; the hacks were just in the wrong place. I know I'm right on it."

"You try to comfort me with your sorcery? I wouldn't care if you thought you'd found the lost treasure of Blackbeard! As the Proverbs say: 'A whip for the horse, a bridle for the ass, and a rod for the fool's back.' What I don't know, John, is if you are the fool or the ass."

"Spare me your sanctimony, Harriet. The golden streets of heaven never put any food on the table and you know it. But if we don't leave now, we may not be around to be worry about that anymore."

"Then go. Ada and I will manage."

I wanted to scream when I heard her say that. As much as I might distrust him, without Papa around I knew Aunt Harriet would soon suffocate me. I had come to regard him, if not as a parent, then maybe more like a guardian. He was someone who could be kind, someone whose cruelty at least had purpose. I could not bear the thought of losing him.

"You're in as much danger as I am. So is Ada, especially Ada."

"That's ridiculous." Aunt Harriet's voice grew louder. "She's a child. How could she be in danger?"

There was a pause in the conversation at this point, utter silence.

"John, why is Ada in danger?"

"The day she had her accident..." He paused. Dread seeped into every part of me. My ally was about to betray me. My ankle ached and I grew enraged at the injustice of it all, the pain I should not have suffered if it was all to be for nothing. I barely heard him over the indignant pounding in my ears, but he continued his confession. "She didn't fall from a tree. She stumbled on me earlier in a clearing in the woods, me and a group of men, reading the smoke. I've been running out of time for a while. I know I can find that gold, but patience is starting to wear thin. Ada helped me stall. I doubt she even knew what she was doing."

"Liar! 'Thou child of the devil, thou enemy of all righteousness, wilt thou not cease to pervert the right ways of the Lord?!'"

"Stop spitting your Scripture at me, woman!" I'd never heard fury in Papa's voice before, and I confess it scared me even more than did the wrath of Aunt Harriet, which I knew I would soon feel.

"Yes," her voice was much calmer now, cold and evil. "I imagine it burns in your ears."

I heard the scrape of the chair and then heavy footsteps moving toward the closed door of my bedroom.

"Stop!" Aunt Harriet screamed. "Don't you even think of touching her, you Devil!" A sudden thud against the door forced it open into my room and light poured in from the glowing fireplace in the front room, spilling across Papa's form, slumped on the floor. He shook his head slowly, catching his breath, and looked up at my aunt towering above him.

I opened my eyes only enough to just see them. I knew I couldn't impersonate a sleeper. They were clever enough to see through that ruse, and so I stretched and rubbed my eyes, pretending to adjust to a state of wakefulness.

"What happened?" I tried to project innocence, desperate for them to believe I hadn't heard a word they had uttered.

"Get up." My aunt commanded. Papa looked at me, his sorrowful eyes offering a sort of apology. He made no move to retaliate for the violence he received at Aunt Harriet's hand. Instead he pulled himself up and disappeared through the door. My aunt ignored him and continued to look at me. "Pack your things. We're leaving."

56

8

In less than an hour we'd packed up the necessities and Papa returned, this time with a horse and wagon. From whence they had come, I didn't know, but as I would grow to learn Papa was especially skilled at finding what he most needed.

The wagon was not large, the horse not young. But it wasn't the time to be particular. Without a word, Aunt Harriet helped Papa load our possessions and I was shocked to see how little we owned. For my own, I had only two everyday dresses, a nightgown, and a Sunday dress, not that different than the others really. All of these garments fit easily in my one small trunk. My aunt and Papa could not have had more themselves. We took almost nothing from the sparse house because, I suddenly realized, none of it had been ours anyway. The house must have come furnished. My aunt packed only her few cooking pots and utensils. The rest of our cargo was food—mainly grain, salted pork Aunt Harriet had obtained through trade with her vegetables, two hens, who were not at all happy to be situated in the wagon, and baskets of anything Aunt Harriet could quickly harvest from her garden.

I remember thinking we were fortunate not to have more because neither the horse nor the wagon looked like they were up to the task. Aunt Harriet must have thought the same thing. Though she'd said little during the process of packing to leave, other than the occasional command to me, she did not hide her concern when she first saw the rig.

"You can't be serious, John." She might even have been frightened, if I could believe it possible.

"He'll do." Papa nuzzled the horse's nose.

"And if he doesn't? Aren't we in a hurry?"

"We'll manage." His calm swept over me, as did the note of finality in his voice. My aunt said nothing more. The two worked together, in perfect synchronization, following what I could only assume was a well-rehearsed routine. I helped as much as I could. Mostly I remained out of the way, watching, aware that I had never seen my aunt and uncle work together on a single task before this moment.

All was perfectly silent, with the exceptions of the occasional clunking of some household item as it was set into the wagon and shifted into place and the nighttime noises of busy insects. Then I saw the lights and fear struck my heart. Papa and Aunt Harriet saw them, too. Far off in the distance, flickering torches approaching.

Aunt Harriet drew a sharp breath and ceased to move. Next to her, Papa dropped a crate and clasped her arm. At his touch she came back to herself and leapt surprisingly gracefully into the pod, nearly landing on top of the caged chickens, who squawked their surprise. Papa lifted me into the wagon where I sat on a barrel of grain. In a flash Papa was in the front of the wagon and we were off with a loud slap of the reins.

In the darkness I could hear Aunt Harriet crying, sniffling occasionally as she tried to soothe the hens that did seem to settle as she whispered to them. I lost the sound of her as the wagon jolted forward at Papa's urgings. The horse proved stronger than he looked and we flew out of town faster than I expected. What a sight we must have made—an old horse pulling an impossibly loaded pod filled with rattling cooking pots and squawking chickens, running for our lives from an angry mob.

We outpaced the lights. The men who carried them must have slowed at our house, an attempt at determining which way we had gone. Papa maintained his speed, the most the old horse could have mustered I'm sure, until he found a path in the woods that suited him and we pulled off the road. Much more slowly then we continued, the horse willingly following Papa's uncanny guidance through the trees.

The long, bumpy ride gave me time to think about recent events. Bolstered by the excitement, I had run from house to garden to wagon, on my aunt's instructions with almost no thought of my injured ankle, and now it throbbed in protest. Still I had more curious things to ponder.

My aunt, taller than Papa by several inches, had thrown a fit to be sure, but in the end had yielded to his instructions. The only possible reason for that was fear—fear of our pursuers, but who they were and for what purpose they came at us, I had no idea. Still, I thought it wise to be afraid and it chilled me. Whatever had happened had something to do with me and most likely with what I had seen in the woods with Papa and those men around the fire. Papa had said he thought he could find some sort of a treasure, but that he was out of time.

No matter how I tried, I couldn't quite fit the pieces together, but I also had other, more pressing concerns. I had seen my aunt throw Papa crashing through a closed door. Her anger would not remain at bay for long and I would face a terrible consequence for my lies. I feared the certainty of her rage more than the danger causing us to flee our home.

These thoughts swirled in my mind as the bumpy motion of the wagon eventually lulled me to sleep. When I awoke, the sun was high in the late morning sky and I lay on the ground, in a small clearing, surrounded by woods. I didn't know where Papa was, but I was wrapped in his coat, and my aunt sat on a stump about twenty feet from me, stoking a small campfire. Next to her, in two jumbled piles, were our meager possessions. I didn't see the wagon, nor did I see a road. Tied up to a slender tree, the horse stood happily munching the shoots of grass that poked through the litter of the forest floor.

I stood, gathering the coat closer around me, willing it to shield me from my aunt. My ankle still ached, but it could support my weight. I wished I had more of the salve Papa had spread over it that first night. Limping toward the fire where my aunt sat silent, I somehow found the courage to speak. "Where are we?"

Aunt Harriet looked up at me, her eyes ringed by dark circles from a sleepless night. She seemed smaller somehow. Her mouth, clenched in worry, no longer filled her entire face, which was drawn and pale.

She sighed. "We drove north, along the river. Your uncle thinks we're about a mile out of some village where he has an associate." She wrinkled her nose as she spoke the last word, as though the sound of it brought to her mind a foul odor.

I didn't think it wise to ask about the associate, so instead I asked, "Is that where we'll be going, then?"

My aunt's lips formed a tight line, indicating that she'd had about enough of my questions, but she answered me all the same. "Your uncle has just gone ahead to get some information if he can, and hopefully a better horse. The one he stole in Norwich is about half dead I think."

"He stole the horse?" My eyes grew wide at the thought. Somehow I had found myself as part of a gang of horse thieves, living off the land and running for our lives. Aunt Harriet was less delighted by our situation.

"I misspoke, of course, Ada. 'Thou shalt not steal.' We'll see that the horse is returned once we've found more suitable transportation."

I hoped she couldn't sense my disappointment. "Why did we have to leave like that?" The moment the question left my lips, I knew I shouldn't have asked it. Fury flashed in her eyes and energized her body. I thought of the way she pushed Papa down, as if he were a rag doll, and took a quick step back.

"Why did you lie to me, child?"

The question surprised me. She hadn't lunged at me, at least not yet. I chose my next words carefully.

"I didn't know what to do. I never meant to be gone so long. I was frightened by what I saw in the woods."

Her expression softened. She stood and reached for me, and so I went to her and accepted her embrace. After a moment, she loosened her hold, clasping my shoulders in her strong hands. I raised my chin and met her eyes with mine.

"John is a very persuasive man, but you must remember, 'The eyes of the Lord are upon the righteous, and his ears are open unto their cry. The face of the Lord is against them that do evil.' Your uncle would do well to remember that, too."

"Yes, Aunt Harriet."

She guided me toward the fire as she let go of my shoulders. "And, Ada," she continued, indicating that I should sit on the stump where she had been. "Let that psalm also remind you to 'keep thy tongue from evil and thy lips from speaking guile.'"

As she said this, her arm flew across her body, swinging back again to land a painful slap across my cheek. The blow shocked me. The force of it knocked me off the stump. With her shoe, Aunt

Harriet quickly swept a smoking coal from the edge of the fire and was on top of me in an instant, pinning me to the ground. Her fingers tangled in my hair and she pushed my face toward the charred wood, landing my lips directly on it. I wanted to scream out but could not. As the coal disintegrated, blistering the soft, pink flesh, my lungs screamed for air I could not deliver.

When nothing but ashes remained beneath me, my aunt's grasp tightened on my hair. My scalp screamed in agony as I gulped fresh air through charred lips. She pulled my face close to her own, her mouth widening so that for a brief moment I thought she might consume me.

"Perhaps next time you'll remember that I am not your enemy."

I remained in a heap, unmoving, next to the fire until I heard Papa return some time later. At the sound of his cheerful voice, I lifted my head, even more painful now that the wounds had set. When I tried to look up for him, I found that the right side of my face, where Aunt Harriet's blow had landed, was quite swollen and I could only manage a sliver of vision through that eye.

"I brought us a friend and got us some food." He held up for Aunt Harriet's inspection a handful of golden yellow berries and several dead squirrels.

Aunt Harriet nodded approval at the food, but scowled at the man who stood beside my uncle. "We needed a better horse. I don't suppose he's going to pull the wagon for us?" She jabbed a finger into the man's chest as he backed up a step.

"S'no way to treat someone who's tryin to help," the man said.

Aunt Harriet only snarled and walked away from the campsite, leaving me alone with Papa and the stranger. I wondered how Papa's mood would change when he saw my face—whether he would come to my defense.

He sat by the fire on that awful stump on which my aunt had attacked me and hummed to himself as he and the stranger gutted the squirrels with their long knives. I lifted my upper body and brought myself to a sitting position. Papa stared intently at his work. My aunt was gone, I assumed to find more wood scraps for the fire that would now cook us a hot meal. We needed it after the rush of our narrow escape.

When he had finished cleaning each little carcass, Papa skewered them in a long row on a freshly cut twig. "That should make a nice roasting stick when your aunt feeds up the fire." Then he looked directly at me for the first time since returning to the camp. Emotion flashed across his face so briefly I could have imagined it. I wondered if it was anger at the brutality of my aunt or pity for my despicable helplessness. Whatever it had been, it was gone as quickly as it had appeared, replaced by a stony expression that defied interpretation.

"My dear Ada," he said, somehow still in that cheerful tone. "Fell out of another tree, I see. You really should be more careful."

I didn't say a word in response. Never had I felt so betrayed—not when my mother died in her prime, leaving me to fend without her, nor when my father abandoned me to the nonsensical whims of his mad-cap sister. Righteous anger surged through me, filling every tiny crevice of my stiff and aching body. I was so physically and emotionally broken, I couldn't make myself speak. Instead, I stared, defeated, at Papa.

The strange man with my uncle at least gave some voice to the injustice of it all. "What the blazes happened to her face? Blame it all, girl, did that devil woman do this to you?"

Papa rose then, sighing, and nudged the stranger out of the way. He pulled a small bundle from his trouser pocket and crouched next to me. Then he took my uninjured cheek in one of his rough hands, still stained with squirrel innards, and began to speak in a soft, even voice:

"From the east came three angels. One brought fire and two brought frost. Come out, fire. Go in, frost. In the name of the Father, Son, and Holy Ghost."

As he spoke, his other hand applied some sort of a concoction from the little bundle to my seared lips and swollen face. Immediately I began to calm; the pain to subside.

"How did you do that?" I whispered through the cracked flesh of my mouth.

"I'll teach you." He leaned his bearded face close, touching his nose lovingly to mine. "But," he leaned back on his heels "I think for now we need to concentrate on keeping you out of the trees."

The stranger shook his head then, and let go a low whistle. "You always was a blame boat-licker when it came to that woman, but I never thought you was as cruel as her."

"Burnt lips heal better than burnt souls," Papa replied. He stood up and pointed to the stranger. "Ada, this is Mr. Seymour, an old business associate of mine."

The man smiled at me and I found myself wondering, certainly not for the first time, just what sort of business Papa was in. Though he wore a decent dark suit, Mr. Seymour's smile exposed a mouth full of crooked, half-rotting teeth, and he smelled as though it had been a long time since his last bath. He spoke roughly, but still, he was an adult and, in his own indelicate way, had defended my honor. I stood to offer a small, painful curtsy in greeting.

This seemed to please him. He lowered himself to sit cross-legged on the ground next to the fire and began to address Papa.

"What's happened to send you runnin'? Last I knew you was workin' it straight down there."

"You know me," Papa began. "I was working straight, sure enough. Harriet heard her brother lost his wife and she wanted Ada, and I promised her we'd have a home fit for her. We did, too, for near two years, 'til I caught wind of a legend."

Mr. Seymour nodded. "Injun gold in the Chenango. Yeah, I heard it. That old Joe Smith, the one that got himself a church, he dug there a few years back, he and Alva Beman."

"Yeah I know. I had a time, too, convincing folks it was worth looking after those burners worked it over. But I listened to the local talk and it all seemed likely down there around Norwich. I'd dowsed a couple of wells for some farmers in those parts and got myself a bit of a reputation. Pretty soon I had a little following. You know how it is."

"People clamoring for gold, yeah, yeah, I know it."

"So I got a little of the mystique going and started looking."

"Didn't find nothin;'?"

"Didn't get much chance. Might be I was close, but then the biggest toad in the puddle—a lawyer with dangerous friends— leaves town and his boy comes up with the ague and I get called on to heal him because the blame doctor's a quack."

"And the cussed boy died?"

I perked up a little at that. I'd never heard what had become of the Hodges boy after Papa treated him for his fever.

"No," Papa continued. "He lived, none the worse for it, but the housemaid never burned the blame willow branches I used and just piled them up at the side of the house, so the next person who wandered past them took up the sickness. The boy got better after about two weeks. His mother died in a matter of days."

"That's rotten luck if ever I heard it."

Papa nodded. "This man Ollie who was digging with me knew I was a healer and pulled me into this in the first place, comes and tells me that the big man is looking to kill me. So now I've got an impatient mob of diggers and a big bug sniffing after my blood."

"And you gotta pull foot." Mr. Seymour nodded like a man who knew what he was talking about. I began to get nervous, to question the wisdom of sitting still in this wood even long enough to eat our squirrels, but Papa was as calm as ever, rubbing his beard as he mulled over our situation.

"You got anything for me?" he finally asked Mr. Seymour.

"You know I would, John, but Norwich ain't that far, and now's not a good time to be a stranger around Sherburne. Our old pal Lyman blew through here a few months ago and left lots of folks mad and lookin' for someone to string up. I expect a man like you might do."

"Lyman was here? Last I heard he'd settled down to farm. Somewhere down near Pennsylvania, I think it was."

Mr. Seymour let out a low whistle. "I don't reckon a man like him could settle long for farming. Naw, he's in the patent medicine game. Made lots of money and plenty of enemies."

"I'm surprised I never heard he was here."

"He never stays around long enough for word to get very far. He's out of the state by now if he's smart."

Papa shook his head, amused but not smiling. "He's smart, but too cocksure to have made it out of the state. He's lurking nearby somewhere, gambling away all that new money, if I know him."

"Got himself a pretty little cherry to spend his money on, more like." Mr. Seymour slapped his knee and grinned.

Papa glanced at me and quickly redirected the conversation. "You gotta have something for me. I'd rather play straight, but either way, you're right. We're too close here. I don't have the means to travel very far right now, but I at least need to get out of the county and keep my head down until some tempers cool."

"Well." Mr. Seymour sat up tall and his face grew serious. "You might try Hartwick, east of here, the other side of the Unadilla River. It's growin' and I think a man with your skills would most like be welcome. Don't bring my name into it, though."

"You know I wouldn't do that." Papa clapped his associate on the back. "Thank you."

"You just take care of your girl here." He pointed at me and a blush spread across my cheeks. Then all at once he became stony faced. I turned to find Aunt Harriet stumbling back into our camp, her skirt partly lifted up to form a sling for a pile of thick twigs with which to feed the fire and more of the yellow berries Papa had brought earlier.

Mr. Seymour stood at her approach and said, "Good luck to you, John. Don't linger. Think I'll eat my dinner elsewhere." He moved his hand to his hat, awkwardly bowed his head in my direction, turned on his heel, and walked away through the woods without a word to Aunt Harriet.

9

As you might imagine, a well-loaded pod, pulled by a single tired, old horse didn't make rapid progress through the relatively untamed wilderness of western New York. Papa preferred still to remain off the roads during the daylight hours and we were four nights in reaching our final destination.

West of Cooperstown, Hartwick was a small farming community, hilly and pretty with well-kept houses lining the few shady roads that cross the town, a creek babbling right through the middle.

I'm sure the three of us were the picture of fatigue as we lumbered into the village in the early morning hours. Once again, Papa left me and Aunt Harriet with the horse and cart on the outskirts of town as he scouted ahead. It couldn't have been more than a few hours before he returned grinning.

"Well?" Aunt Harriet demanded, tired and sour from the long journey.

"I went to the general store and did some asking around. I found us a place." Papa's eyes danced as he delivered his happy news.

Aunt Harriet was still suspicious. "What kind of place?"

Papa nodded toward me and said, "You're going to love it! I met a man by the name of Walters who says he can line me up some farm work, and he says there's a big house on the east side of town that takes on boarders."

Harriet sighed. "A boarding house, John?" The righteous indignation in her speech had been replaced by exhaustion. In spite of everything, I felt sorry for her. I knew how difficult it was to be suddenly torn from the life you had known and to be forced into a new one, and I had gathered that this hadn't been an infrequent occurrence in her married life. I couldn't forgive her cruelty, but I could appreciate her grief.

"Oh, Harriet." Papa's voice softened. "You should see it. I met the owner, a Mrs. Clark. Her husband is away for a while and she's happy to have some help around. There's a cook stove and an ice box, and Ada can have her own room."

"Are there other boarders?" Though often charitable with her time, Aunt Harriet was, in fact, painfully private, attending only to the necessary conversations and service projects in the church but otherwise keeping to herself and her studies. I thought she might rather live in a crooked shack than in a boarding house where everyone knew her business.

"She said she's had a few drummers that come and go, all on the road right now, and so there's plenty of room."

Aunt Harriet looked unsure, but in the end, road weariness won her over and she consented to the arrangement.

Papa had perhaps exaggerated about the house. I wouldn't have called it large, but it was a sturdy white frame structure with a covered porch that wrapped from the front around one side. It consisted of only one story, with a sitting room that opened into the dining area. The kitchen was as modern as Papa had claimed and served to separate the front of the house, where Mrs. Clark resided, from the back where our bedrooms branched off along a narrow hallway.

I did have my own bedroom with what felt to me like a luxurious, feather-stuffed mattress. Faded pink wallpaper covered one wall against which stood a chamber-set like one might find in a hotel room. Next to that in the corner stood a sturdy wardrobe which wouldn't open when I tried the doors. A large window framed a clear view of an ample kitchen garden. I could not have been more delighted with my new home, however temporary it might prove to be.

"It's Ada, isn't it?" The gentle voice came from my bedroom doorway as I rearranged the meager possessions in my trunk, jumbled from travel. Startled, I looked up to see the pretty young landlady smiling at me. I stood and returned her greeting with a small curtsy.

"Yes," I said. "You have a beautiful garden, Mrs. Clark."

"Thank you, Ada." Then she cupped a hand around one side of her mouth and whispered, "You may call me Zeviah."

I liked her immediately.

"I thought to suggest to you and your mother that you might like to have a bath after your travels, but I think she drifted to sleep."

"It was a difficult journey. She's awfully tired." I didn't know why I excused her, but I was quick to add, "She's not my mother."

"Oh." Zeviah shrugged. "I'm sorry I assumed." Concern darkened her fresh complexion and I could see she was gazing at my bruised face. My burned lips had healed nicely with Papa's soothing balm, but a yellow shadow remained across my cheek. I didn't like to see her pity and decided then that I wouldn't allow this lovely woman to know my sad story.

"My mother and father are away." I tried to sound lighthearted, as if I truly had the unconditional love of two parents who would return for me soon. "My aunt and uncle have been very kind to take me in for a short while."

A twinkle returned to Zeviah's eyes, her expression once again easy. She said nothing about my discolored skin. "Well, we'll let your aunt rest, then. In the meantime, would you like a bath? I'm heating water and have a tub set up in the kitchen. I can even offer you a piece of cherry pie when you've finished if you like. I made it fresh this morning."

No one had made me such a fine offer in a long time, and I had to admit a bath would feel good. I couldn't remember the last time I'd felt clean. I followed Zeviah to the kitchen and the waiting bathtub.

As she helped me undress, Zeviah talked of Hartwick and of the people who boarded with her. Most, she claimed, were just the traveling drummers selling their wares and moving on, though, she admitted, she'd had a handful of unsavory types come through as well. Her husband had run off a few women of ill repute and was always after her to be more careful about whom she agreed to board.

"Is Mr. Clark away often?" I asked, lowering myself into the warm water and accepting a block of soap.

"Jerry travels with his work," Zeviah said with a sigh, "but he's home when he can be. I take in boarders for the extra money and because I get lonely without him. When we were first married my aunt and cousin lived with us, but they moved out a while ago when Aunt Matilda remarried."

Zeviah talked like this for a long stretch of time, telling me little bits about herself. I soaked up every detail, locking them away in my memory. This was so different than Aunt Harriet's lectures, full of forceful piety, never a word wasted. For all the time we had spent alone together, I knew little about my aunt, less in many ways than I learned about Zeviah the first day we met. I wanted to believe she reminded me of my mother with her easy manner and light-hearted chatter.

The bath water grew cool before I climbed out. I dried off and padded to my room to dress while Zeviah dished up two slices of cherry pie. As I passed the closed door to Aunt Harriet's room I could hear her muffled snores, and even though I was sure it was wrong, I wished she would never wake.

*****

"Do you have a question, Mr. Rigdon?" Ada gazed at the old man now leaning forward in his chair.

"No," he sputtered. "I mean, yes. Mrs. Clark, did you say?"

"Yes. Zeviah Clark is the niece of Mrs. Matilda Davison. You recognize her name?"

He nodded. "Where would I have heard that name before?"

"Why, Mr. Rigdon, I should think you'd know. Mrs. Matilda Davison was the widow of Solomon Spalding, the author of this book." Ada patted the bundled papers in her lap. "That name you know, I am quite sure."

The old man frowned, sinking against the back of his chair. "Yes, Miss Moses. That name I know. For a dead man, Solomon Spalding has caused me no small amount of grief."

"Ghosts can be troublesome companions, Mr. Rigdon."

*****

Papa returned to the house that evening sun-worn and laughing. I was in the sitting room when he walked through the front door and gave me a quick kiss. Aunt Harriet had risen somewhat refreshed from her nap and busied herself helping Zeviah in the kitchen. I listened to the largely one-sided conversation as Zeviah chatted pleasantly with my aunt, whose stiff manners appeared all the more awkward in comparison. Zeviah appeared not to notice, continuing to share, revealing that she expected the elusive Mr. Clark would be away for at least another three weeks.

"How was your day, girlie?" Papa chuckled as he spoke.

"I like it here," I replied. "What did you do today?"

Papa grinned. "I worked with Mr. Walters on his farm. He's digging a new well."

"And you helped him dig?"

"I will. I helped him figure the right place to dig."

"How'd you do that?" My uncle had many mysterious secrets, some of which I suspected I'd never fully discover, but a glint in his eye that night told me this was one he'd be willing to share. He opened his mouth to speak, but it was Aunt Harriet's voice I heard.

"Sorcery, Ada. And a hint of deceit. That's how he did it."

I looked at Papa for an explanation. He only shook his head and stood to face my aunt. "You look better rested."

"I am dead on my feet," she grumbled.

Zeviah peeked out through the kitchen doorway to offer a wave of greeting to Papa, but ducked back inside at Aunt Harriet's words.

"I think I can get some good work here," he continued. "Walters tells me there are lots of folks setting up and expanding their farms in the area."

"Oh, yes, that's true." Zeviah's cheerful voice floated from the kitchen.

Papa looked at Aunt Harriet, clasped her shoulders, and added in a low voice, "We can make this work."

She rolled her eyes and backed up a step, causing Papa's arms to drop to his sides.

"Uncle John," I said. "May I go with you tomorrow to see the well digging?"

My aunt sucked in her breath sharply at this and looked on the verge of spitting angry words at me and at Papa, but this time it was Zeviah who spoke, wiping her hands on her apron as she stepped into the room.

"Oh, that would be nice. I'd be happy to walk with her to the Walters place tomorrow so she could see what you're up to. I can bring her back or take her on a little walk through town when she gets restless."

Papa latched onto the opportunity. "That is very kind of you, Mrs. Clark. It would be a nice break for Harriet, too. I know she'll want to explore the town herself and get us settled."

Aunt Harriet must have been too stunned to speak and Papa, I could see, was determined not to let her.

Zeviah answered, "It's no trouble at all. Ada is such a delight."

Aunt Harriet squeezed my shoulder in a gesture that might have been tender had she not applied so much pressure. She dared not reveal her true nature in front of our new landlady and so she had lost, but I understood the look she gave me. I owed penance for my insolence.

10

I woke the next morning to the happy sound of Zeviah humming in the kitchen. Aunt Harriet had already gone out, she said, to seek a local minister. I had no doubt she was on her knees by now in fanatical prayer, determined to protect me from the evil clutches of my uncle and this vile woman.

Fresh and beautiful in a light summer dress, Zeviah placed a plate in front of me with two boiled eggs and a thick slice of warm bread spread with honey. She took a seat across the table from me with a plate of her own. "Your aunt is a very pious woman."

"Yes."

Zeviah seemed more to be musing for her own benefit than making conversation with me. "Not that there's anything wrong with piety." She took a bite of bread and chewed for a moment before continuing. "Of course, one can become so zealous as to lose sight of priorities, I think."

I pondered her words, wondering what she meant by them, but she did not elaborate. Instead, she changed the subject, filling me with tales from the Walters farm. It wasn't gossip, but rather the kind of information one should know about neighbors. She spoke of children and grandchildren, of kindnesses offered through the years. From her I glimpsed the joy of belonging to a community, one without secrets and hidden agendas. And I listened, eager to be a part of her world even as she stood to clear our empty plates off the table, setting them into a bucket of water on the cooktop and giving them a quick scrub.

When she finished with the dishes she said, "It's a beautiful morning. Shall we go to the farm to see what the men have gotten up to?"

I smiled and nodded. I couldn't wait to go to this farm I had just heard so much about and was eager to see what Papa was doing. Outside of his healing, which I had observed only a little, all I knew about his work was that Aunt Harriet rarely approved. That alone was enough to tease my curiosity.

The sun shone brightly, a gorgeous day developing. Zeviah hummed softly as we walked, soon leaving the road to follow a narrow winding lane carved with deep wheel ruts.

We found Papa and Mr. Walters quickly on the edge of the field nearest the farm house speaking too loudly. I looked at Zeviah for reassurance. She squeezed my hand, her eyes growing wide, but she did not hesitate to walk up to the quarreling men.

"It's not always an exact thing. We're close to this vein. The rod doesn't lie."

"Maybe not, but you sure do!"

"Just calm yourself down, Walters. Yelling at me isn't gonna help."

"No, of course, I wouldn't want to upset the spirits or anything."

"Don't joke about it." Papa lowered his voice, deadly serious as we approached. "I've seen them turn unfriendly."

"You're about to turn me unfriendly, John. I've a mind to shoot you. I doubt anyone would miss you."

Zeviah grabbed my hand and hummed a little louder, a clumsy attempt to block the conversation from my ears, but I'd already heard and my throat went dry with fear. Mr. Walters and Papa looked over, alerted to our presence by Zeviah's melody. Their argument quickly broke off as they turned to us. Mr. Walters gave us a grudging nod, but Papa's face lit with a large welcoming smile that reassured me. Even if Mr. Walters was serious about meaning to harm Papa, the man who lived under Aunt Harriet's thumb wouldn't be done in by an angry farmer.

"I wondered when you two lovely ladies might arrive," Papa said. "I was just explaining to Mr. Walters what I'm trying to do here. He's in need of a new well and I'm going to find a good place for him. Our first try hasn't been very successful so far."

Mr. Walters huffed. Zeviah shot him a stern look, squeezing my hand more tightly.

"Well," she said, her voice forcefully cheerful, "perhaps our being here will signal better fortunes."

Papa grinned and looked at Mr. Walters who appeared much less optimistic. He and Papa were both covered in dirt, and a number of shovels lay around a deep, narrow hole. It looked as if several men had been working on the digging, though where the others were, I didn't know.

Mr. Walters spoke to Zeviah rather than to Papa or to me. "I finally had to send the other men off. We dug fifty feet past where he said we'd find water and not so much as a little mud."

"I'm sure John knows what he's doing. He certainly comes highly recommended."

"Recommended by himself," Mr. Walters grumbled. "I don't know those names of references he's given. They could all be made up and him a no-account burner for all I know."

As they talked, I watched Papa. I still clung to Zeviah, who seemed to be the one person who didn't anger Mr. Walters, but I didn't take my eyes off Papa moving slowly over the land with his forked stick in hand. He almost glided across the ground so deliberate were his steps, moving in increasing circles outward from the unlucky dig site.

And then I saw it. As carefully as Papa moved, the stick, otherwise quite steady in his hand, gave an unexpected twitch toward the earth right above a large rock sticking up from the ground. Papa stopped and pivoted on one heel. As he did so, the end of the stick drew ever closer to the ground as if it wanted to leap from his hands. I gasped and Zeviah and Mr. Walters stopped talking, following my gaze with their own until we all three stared at Papa and his magic stick.

"Sakes alive. You ever see anything like that, Mrs. Clark?" Mr. Walters asked quietly.

"I've heard tell of it, but I admit I have never had the privilege to observe it before today."

Papa looked up, his face painted in victory. "What you have here, Walters, is a lot of clay in the soil. Throws the whole thing off the mark. I stand by what I said before. You keep digging in that first spot and you'll get to water, but seems to me this location would be better for your well."

Papa gave the branch a jerk and watched intently as the end bobbed up and down, his lips moving to a silent count. When at last it was still, he said, "Get those men back here. My reading is 120 feet, though if we hit a clay ribbon, might be it's a little more than that. Pull's a lot stronger here. With any luck we won't run into another problem."

"Can I feel it?" asked Mr. Walters, giddy now as he moved toward Papa, any sign of anger vanished. Papa handed him the branch and gestured for him to give it a try. No one could deny that Mr. Walters also felt something. His eyes grew wide and he laughed out loud. I couldn't see that the branch had moved for him as it had for Papa. Still, there was some kind of wonder afoot and I wanted to be a part of it.

"May I try, too, Papa?" I let go of Zeviah's hand and ran toward him.

He smiled tenderly as I reached him and whispered, "Not a word to your aunt."

My cheek, still lightly bruised from Aunt Harriet's blow, ached at the remembrance of his betrayal the last time we shared a secret, but my desire to experience the power of Papa's magic outweighed any apprehension. I nodded that I understood and reached to take the forked stick from Mr. Walters.

I held it with a light touch, as I had seen Papa do. As I inched my way over the area where I knew the branch had reacted, I didn't know what to expect. In some ways I found it easy to believe Papa was a confidence man of sorts and I might have loved him for that, for his undermining of all Harriet forced upon me. But I hoped he really did possess supernatural powers, that such powers existed at all, and that I might learn to harness them.

I crept, trembling with anticipation, and soon found myself overcome by a feeling of weightiness, like every part of me might be dragged right down into the ground. In front of me was the large rock. I would have stumbled into it except that, at the last moment, the end of the rod plunged. I stopped, tightening my grip on the branch as it pulled toward the earth, the strain of the stick toward the dirt so intense my hands grew sore and pieces of bark rubbed off onto my reddened skin.

Papa walked up behind me and placed a gentle hand on my shoulder. "Bounce it, Ada," he said, pushing down on my shoulder to demonstrate what he meant.

I gave the determined stick a downward shove, sure I would drop it. To my surprise it yielded, obediently bouncing up and down. Behind me, Papa counted, "One, two, three, four, five, six, seven, eight, nine, ten, eleven…" The branch stopped just as strangely as it had begun. It still pulled at me, tugging me toward the ground, but it became static.

Papa turned to Mr. Walters and said, "That's a good vein, that is. One hundred and twenty feet for sure. That's where you ought to dig your well."

"Wonderful!" Mr. Walters clapped his hands and laughed. "Your little girl's got a gift!"

"I think you're right." Papa's eyes twinkled as he locked my gaze. He leaned close and whispered to me, "You just found a gusher under a rock. Might be we ought to call you Moses."

I stayed to watch the men work most of the morning. After a time, Zeviah walked up to the farmhouse to visit with Mrs. Walters, but I would not be led away from the edge of the field. I wanted to see the water. Even having felt for myself the attraction between rod and earth, I still doubted, at least in some small part, that water would be discovered. A part of me needed to see it before I tried to understand the experience. I questioned Papa when he had finished a shift of digging and came to sit in the shade from which I watched.

"Papa," I said. "What happened to that stick?"

He leaned up against the tree trunk and closed his eyes, drawing in a long breath before he spoke. "Ada, do you remember when you admitted to me that you don't pray?"

I blinked, surprised at what I perceived to be a change in subject. "You said it was a shame I didn't."

"That's because the Great Something that's out there listens. For Harriet, the something is a remarkably cranky god. I don't know about that. What I do know is that when I ask the spirits, or what have you, sometimes they shine favor on my endeavors, and the rod is often how they do it. Does that make sense?"

"You want me to believe Aunt Harriet is right?" I didn't try to hide my disappointment. The only faith I held in Papa stemmed from what I assumed was our mutual disdain for my aunt. I was not prepared to comprehend that they shared a common understanding.

"Your aunt is right about many things, Ada." As he spoke he reached toward me and gently cupped my cheek in his dirty palm. "Not everything, mind you, but in her own way, she has things better figured than most folks, I'd say."

I shook my head at the suggestion. That made Papa laugh.

"Do you know the story of Moses and the Israelites?" he asked me.

"Yes."

"Do you know about when they were thirsty in the desert and Moses cried out to God? God told him to take his rod and find water under a rock."

"After Pharaoh let them go and gave them all those dreadful rules? I don't think we got to that story."

Papa smiled. "No, I guess you wouldn't, but maybe you'll read it someday."

I doubted very much I would read anything in the Bible that wasn't forced upon me. Reading some of the antiquated language was still difficult, and Aunt Harriet had me memorizing so many long passages from it that I had no love for God's supposed Word.

"Well." Papa rose from his rest against the tree. "I'd better get back to work."

I saw Zeviah walking back toward me from the house. Papa nodded to her and she waved back with one hand, the other grasping a bundle that as she got closer I could see was a piece of cornbread wrapped in cloth. She handed it to me as I watched Papa reclaim his shovel and relieve one of the men who had been digging.

"Thank you." I took a large bite.

"I thought you might need some nourishment before we walk back. You seem much too thin to me."

"Must we go? I want to see when they find the water."

Zeviah sighed and put an arm around me. "Yes, we must. I'm afraid I promised your aunt I would have you back in the afternoon for lessons. She was quite serious about it."

"Yes, she's very serious about lessons. About everything."

"A stern teacher is something you will be grateful for someday."

About that, Zeviah was correct. I possess no great feelings of love for Aunt Harriet, but it is as a result of her efforts that I can read and that I hold many of the sacred words of the Bible well in mind. For these gifts, I can be thankful, tainted though they are with malice and injustice. Zeviah never knew how polluted was my relationship with my aunt, but even so, her words eventually proved true.

11

Though we were there but a brief period, life in Hartwick settled into a calm routine for all of us soon enough, and even Harriet seemed grudgingly happy. Like farm animals that are suddenly thrown together and must determine how best to tolerate one another, Harriet and Zeviah had come to an understanding around the house and in regards to me.

Zeviah was not as devoted to piety as my aunt, but she did read from her family Bible daily, which pleased Harriet. When Zeviah claimed to be the niece of a Presbyterian minister, Aunt Harriet responded with a wistful gaze out the open kitchen window and a remark that it was indeed a blessing to have righteous men and women among one's family. After that, as long as our landlady didn't interfere with my long daily lessons, Aunt Harriet was pleased enough to allow me short outings with my new friend.

Zeviah never spoke to me of the Scriptures, and for that I was appreciative. Because she was often about the house during my lessons, she observed just how much study Aunt Harriet demanded of me. Had I been an unexceptional child of ten, I would not have been able to keep up with the strenuous pace. Zeviah was kind enough to comment on this as we went about our errands.

Most often we visited with neighbors or stepped into the shops along Hartwick's Main Street. Sometimes we simply strolled, hand-in-hand, alongside the creek and she spoke to me of her dreams and of her oft-absent husband, for whom she bore much love.

It was just such a morning when she surprised me with a question that contained within it an unexpected accusation. "Ada, do you think that now I have told you my deepest secrets, you might be honest with me about yours?"

"What do you mean?" I stopped walking and dropped her hand. I was not surprised at her accusation of my dishonesty, as I already felt guilty for misleading her. What bothered me more was that all of the inane details she had shared might really be the deepest secrets she possessed. I was both jealous of her contented life, one that was so ordinary, and also saddened by it.

"I don't mean to sound angry with you, my sweet. I just thought maybe you would be more comfortable talking with me by now and you might share some more about how you came to live with your aunt and uncle. How strange life must be with them."

"What's so strange?" I was evading her question. Though already the memories of life with my parents were beginning to fade, I saw other children, other families, in church service and at play. I did not doubt that life with my aunt and uncle was indeed strange, as she suggested. However, I did not want her to shatter the illusion of domestic tranquility I had conjured for myself these past weeks, an illusion made possible by her kindness to the characters that made up the nearest I had to a family.

Her eyes lit in relief that I was not angry with her and we continued our walk. "You know, I suppose I've never met a more oddly matched couple."

On that point we agreed, and I grinned to show her that we were of one mind. She giggled and I couldn't help but join her. The mood lifted. I attempted to shift the subject.

"Do you really not have any deep, dark secrets?"

Her giggle changed to a merry laugh and she studied my face for half a minute before recovering her composure and saying, "Dark secrets have a way of making us miserable. When we bring them to light, we are able to move on. So no, though my life has not always been trouble-free, I would say that I have no deep dark secrets. Just the good kind that really aren't secrets at all."

I could feel my face grow hot; tears threatened. I knew the truth of her words and was all the more miserable because I was not allowed to share my grief with Aunt Harriet. And Papa, though I thought I must love him, was not one to offer a great deal of comfort. The pain churned inside me until I felt I might be sick if I held onto it a second longer.

"My mother died," I whispered. I looked into Zeviah's kind eyes and felt the hot tears spill down my cheeks.

She wasn't laughing anymore, but stopped and knelt before me, her expression full of sorrow and tenderness. Before I could stop myself, I told her everything about the death of my mother and baby brother. I told her of arriving at Aunt Harriet's and of how my father had abandoned me there without a word. I stopped just short of telling her about the physical violence I had suffered at the hands of my aunt, and under the supposed protection of my uncle.

She listened intently to my whole story without saying a word. When I finished, she pulled me close to her. We sat holding one another for a long time, our tears washing away our grief on the sunny creek bank.

I felt safe and loved that day, though it lasted too little time. The morning had grown late and we hurried back to the boarding house only to find an elegant carriage parked in front and loud, angry voices coming from inside the house.

Zeviah ran faster than I would have thought was strictly ladylike, leaping onto the front porch and disappearing through the door. I followed, wary of whatever scene might accompany the shouting. I knew one of the voices to be Aunt Harriet's. The other was that of a man. I did not recognize his smooth baritone, but I couldn't help but notice the calm with which he spoke. Contrasted with Aunt Harriet's shrieking, it was easy to be sympathetic to him. His poise surely served to infuriate Harriet all the more. I stopped on the porch and tried to listen as Zeviah's voice joined the conversation.

"Goodness, Harriet, what is going on here? We heard you all the way down the street."

"What's going on is that this beast is not welcome here."

"Now, Harriet." The man's tone was both jovial and condescending. I peeked around the door frame to get a look at him. "Where are your manners? Madam, I assume you are the proprietor of this fine boarding house. Allow me to introduce myself."

The gentleman wore matching trousers and coat, both the color of black coal, a waistcoat of bright red silk, and he held a top hat of no small measure. Curls of thick, dark hair fell over his ears and his eyes sparkled.

He offered a graceful bow as he spoke. "My name is Dr. Lyman Durand and this is my dear friend and traveling companion Mrs. Mariana Laurent." With a flourish he indicated a woman standing silently behind him. "Forgive us for our intrusion into your peaceful home. I am an old associate of your tenants and upon hearing they were so nearby where I was traveling through, I stopped to pay my respects."

Zeviah gave an uncertain nod to the man and his traveling companion, who leaned upon his arm. The woman wore a silk dress with a tight bodice, cut lower in the front than common decency dictated, and full skirt made up of layer upon layer of gathered frills. It was a ridiculous costume for travel. She had a pretty face and shadow-rimmed dark eyes full of mystery, an effect accentuated by the turban sitting atop her head. It was sewn from the same bright red silk that perfectly matched both her dress and the gentleman's waistcoat.

"Sir," Zeviah began, staving off Aunt Harriet's fury with a subtle wave of her hand. "It seems suspicious to me that you should claim you wish to share your respects with this dear lady and yet you obviously cause her grief."

The gentleman's easy tone never broke, nor did his smile full of straight teeth. "It is true, I admit, that Harriet and I did not part on the best of terms when last we met. For that I can only apologize and appeal to her Christian mercy."

At this he turned to address Aunt Harriet directly. "I beg of you, kind lady, please allow me to repent of my former sins and win your favor, for your husband is a man I hold in high regard. I wish only that I may speak with him. Might I know where to find him?"

It was Zeviah who answered. "John is working on a neighboring farm. I could take you to him, but you must be weary from your travels." I thought I detected a slight tremor of either anger or revulsion as she glanced at the woman on his arm, who withered under her gaze. "May I offer you refreshment and perhaps you will dine with us this evening? Then you and John may visit in more comfort."

"I thank you, though we do not wish to intrude too much on your generous hospitality." He looked at his companion, her expression grown uneasy. "If you could perhaps direct us to a hotel, we will refresh ourselves there and return in time for a happy reunion supper."

All agreed, Aunt Harriet reluctantly so, and the visitors took their leave. I remained on the porch as they exited. When the gentleman passed through the door, he donned his top hat, but then spotted me and removed it again, tipping his head in my direction.

I found it difficult to focus on my lessons that afternoon, my imagination continually wandering to the new dandy who had appeared from Papa's past. He had referred to himself as Papa's associate, the same term Aunt Harriet used to describe the Mr. Seymour who sent us to Hartwick in the first place. I pondered over the meaning of the word, wondering if this Lyman were friend or foe. Over the years I would meet several of Papa's associates and often ask myself the same question.

Aunt Harriet pursed her lips at my distractibility but did not comment upon it. I suspected she felt much the same way. At last she ended our lesson, earlier than usual, claiming her head ached and she needed to lie down for a spell. Indeed she did look ill, which only added to my anticipation of the evening meal and the intrigue it promised.

My aunt was still abed when Papa returned to the house that evening. He kissed my cheek by way of greeting, as had become our delightful custom, but I could barely hold still even for this.

"What has you all riled up, girlie?" Papa asked with a light chuckle.

"We're to have guests for supper," I replied, eager to share everything I knew and hoping he would shed some light upon our sudden visitors.

"Oh? And who will that be?"

"Dr. Durand and Mrs. Laurent."

Papa looked at me, a trace of a mystified smile on his face. "Who?"

"Your associate," I explained, confused at his lack of understanding. "Lyman Durand."

Papa's face grew grim at the mention of the name. "You're sure? It was a Dr. Lyman Durand?"

"Yes, yes, and a lady Mrs. Laurent in a fancy red dress."

Papa scratched his chin before he patted my head with a dirty palm. "Guess I better put on a boiled shirt if we're to have company. Where's your aunt?"

"She's in bed. Her head aches again."

Papa nodded. "Yes, I suppose it would. Run along and help Mrs. Clark. I'll get myself ready for supper."

Dr. Durand arrived only twenty minutes later. Zeviah sent me to invite him in. He wore the same bright red waistcoat as before but had traded his trousers for breeches and his brogans for stylish pumps. I rarely spent time in the company of fashionable people, our own clothing being of rough homespun and made by Aunt Harriet's moderately skilled hands. Naturally, I thought he cut quite the figure, and I was all the more smitten.

"And who might you be?" he asked as he removed his hat and waltzed past me into the parlor.

"I'm Ada." I stood tall, doing my best to appear older. "Harriet is my aunt."

The gentleman settled himself on a sofa and patted the space next to him to indicate that I should sit as well. "But you're such a charming young lady. Are you certain you're related to Harriet?"

"I think so." I blushed at his compliment. Truthfully, I had harbored a secret and sincere hope that we were in fact no relation at all, that her claim over me was entirely imagined and one day I would escape her. "She's my father's sister."

"You're Albert's girl?"

I was astonished to hear this stranger speak my father's name. My breath caught. "You know my father?"

"More like knew him, I would say. We were boys together." The skin around his eyes crinkled as he spoke. A shallow dimple formed on his cleanshaven cheeks. "I spent many a day of my childhood with Albert, really with the whole family. Your grandmother treated me like a son. She was quite a woman."

The gentleman trailed off, enveloped by his own memories. Hoping to hear more about my father, I attempted to reclaim his attention. "Dr. Durand?"

The man said nothing but remained lost in his thoughts for several moments.

"Dr. Durand? Where is Mrs. Laurent?" I tried again.

"Hm?" he responded. "Oh, no, no, princess, you must call me Lyman, please."

He looked past me as he spoke and began to stand. I followed his gaze to see Papa, still filthy even in clean clothes.

"John, old friend." Lyman extended his hand, a genuine smile on his handsome face.

"Hello, Lyman." Papa shook Lyman's hand, though I was certain I detected hesitation. "What brings you here?"

"I heard a rumor about a man," he said as he looked at me with a mischievous grin, "and a little girl that could sniff water from rocks. But then I should be asking, what brings you here?" His jocular tone brimmed with enthusiasm, as if it had been Papa who had popped in on him instead of the other way around. "Last I'd heard you were way down south somewhere."

"And I'd heard you'd become a farmer."

Lyman laughed as if this was the funniest thing he'd ever heard. "I hardly think I'm cut out for such a reserved life. What about you?"

Papa crossed his arms and eased onto the arm of the chair. "A deal gone poorly, as it turns out."

"Good man." Lyman clapped Papa on the shoulder and settled himself back down on the sofa beside me. "Always one step ahead of the game, but mind you only one step. A dangerous way to live. And not too profitable, by the looks of it. You're a family man, now, John. You've got to think of your princess here."

"Well, look at this scoundrel. *Dr. Durand,* is it now? Telling me to go off the crook. It's not that I don't appreciate your concern, but we're doing all right here just now, aren't we, Ada?"

I nodded my agreement, focusing on Lyman's handsome face. I did like it there. I liked Zeviah and appreciated the layer of protection her presence provided me from Aunt Harriet's temper. That home, even if it was just a boarding house, felt far more real than the glorified shack we'd rented in Norwich.

Lyman's smile faded for a moment, though he was quick to recover it. I followed his gaze and saw that Aunt Harriet had walked into the room. "And here at last is the lovely Harriet! Haven't left this old scoundrel yet, then?" This had to have been the best performance I'd ever seen. I couldn't imagine that anyone would think Aunt Harriet lovely, but I found myself unable to doubt his sincerity.

My aunt glared at him and asked through clenched teeth, "Where's your companion, Lyman?"

Lyman grinned as though her question were a dull joke, though I failed to see what was so amusing. He looked from me to Aunt Harriet. "Too intimidated in the company of such brilliant beauties as you, I should think."

"'A whore is a deep ditch; and a strange woman is a narrow pit.'"

"Phew! Is that from the Bible, Harriet?" Lyman's voice was light and joking, but his expression had hardened. "I'll have to remember that one the next time a strange woman comes my way."

Aunt Harriet stood speechless and beckoned me to her side. I quickly obeyed and felt her firm hand clutch my shoulder.

Lyman appeared unconcerned about the offense he clearly gave my aunt but went on to explain himself. "Mariana is a friend who was in need of a change of scenery. We were traveling the same direction. I couldn't very well allow her to traipse around the countryside all alone now, could I? What's a gentleman to do?"

"Are you what passes for a gentleman these days?" Aunt Harriet snarled.

"Clever Harriet," Lyman mused. My uncle wisely stayed out of the conversation, but Lyman turned to him next and said, "'A contentious wife is like a continual drip.' I think that's in the Bible somewhere, too."

"You're a foul, loathsome man, Lyman. Come, Ada." My aunt's grip tightened on my shoulder so much that I had to bite my lip to keep from crying out. I had no choice but to go with her. I wanted to stay and hear more from this Lyman, my champion, as far as I was concerned, in my war with Aunt Harriet.

12

Dinner was an awkward affair that night, full of snide remarks
that only amused Lyman and, perhaps inwardly, me as well. He was
certainly a smooth talker, and though much of the strained
conversation was filled with innuendo not meant for my
understanding, I grew to like this stranger more and more with
every verbal jab at Aunt Harriet.

For her part, my aunt offered only curt responses when it was
required of her. She rubbed her temples throughout dinner and
bore the brunt of Lyman's mean-spirited witticisms with something
akin to grace. Her lips clenched tight and colorless, her every facial
muscle tensed, and at times I got the impression that had she felt
better, the two of them might have come to blows.

Papa engaged all of us as well as he could in small talk about
the more inane details of the farm work in which he had been
engaging and prospects for additional work that could keep us
comfortable in Hartwick for some time. What was notably absent
from this conversation was any reference to how Lyman and Papa
had come to know one another in the first place. Neither man
seemed keen to delve into the past, and Harriet, gently massaging
her closed eyes with her fingertips, her elbows bent and resting on
the table, was a closed book.

When Papa could come up with no more to say and Lyman
ran out of ammunition, an unnatural hush filled the dining room.
Zeviah came to a graceful rescue.

"So Dr. Durand, what business are you in exactly?"

"Well," Lyman began, his countenance brightening. He turned
his long and thoughtful gaze on our pretty landlady. "I like to say
that I am a doctor of philosophical medicine, an inventor of
miraculous patent medicines."

"You're a snake oil salesman?"

"Oh, now, when you say it like that, it sounds like I'm some sort of fast-talking criminal."

"Are you?" Zeviah asked as Aunt Harriet opened her eyes and nodded her approval.

"Nothing of the sort. I take my responsibilities seriously. I travel not for the purpose of self-promotion surely, but so that I may seek out those with previously undiscovered wisdom of wellness. I'm no miracle man myself, but I have met those who claim to be. I've tried and tested their remedies so that I may collect them together and offer the common country folk a genuine path to good health."

He smiled again as he finished this clearly well-rehearsed speech and looked Zeviah straight in the eyes. I could see that though she did not yet trust him, she had been moved by his claims.

He continued. "That is, in fact, how I happened to come to know our good man John, here."

"I don't understand, Dr. Durand. How is that?" Zeviah asked.

"Has he not told you?" He nudged Papa's shoulder. "John is a gifted herbal healer."

"Truly?" Now Zeviah turned her gaze to Papa who blushed beneath his beard.

"It's true," I blurted without thinking, excited to be able to add to the adult conversation. For my efforts I received a swift kick under the table from Aunt Harriet. I resolved to say no more.

"Well, you are a man of many talents." Zeviah smiled kindly at Papa.

Aunt Harriet would tolerate no more. She stood from the table, sliding her chair back with a loud scrape across the floor. "Time for bed, Ada."

I had not finished my supper yet, but I knew better than to argue with my aunt. I stood to follow her.

"Thank you for supper, Mrs. Clark." Aunt Harriet spoke with clipped words, indicating that though she might observe the niceties of civil conversation, she would not enjoy it. "Lyman, do have a pleasant journey. You will be leaving in the morning?"

"Yes, my dear Harriet." He stood as he spoke, guiding his own chair backward and offering us a genteel bow. "I'm afraid the road calls to me, but it is always a delight to see you. Good night, ladies."

I gave a small curtsy. Harriet merely grabbed my hand and pulled me from the room as I struggled to keep up.

We had only just entered the hallway off which our rooms were located when she said, "Undress and say your prayers. Be quick about it."

"Yes, Aunt Harriet," I replied, and then, "Are you still feeling ill?"

"The presence of Lyman Moreau should make every Christian ill." She nearly spat as she spoke his name.

I prepared for bed quickly, just as my aunt had instructed, but even as the silence filled with Harriet's soft snores from the other room, sleep would not come to me. I kept mulling over the things my aunt had said, not the least of which was Lyman's name. She had identified him not as Durand, but as Moreau. I wondered if that was even his true name. I somehow doubted it, just as I doubted he was a true doctor traveling benevolently through the countryside collecting knowledge of folk remedies. It would be dishonest to suggest that I minded being fed a story. In fact, I never really considered that Lyman had misled me as well as Zeviah. I felt more like an accomplice, and his lies only excited my curiosity.

I lay awake listening until I no longer heard noise coming from the kitchen, assuming Zeviah had cleaned up from supper and probably gone to bed herself. Then I rose, crept down the hallway and across the dark kitchen to crouch next to the doorframe that led into the sitting room where I could see flickering lights and hear voices belonging to Papa and Lyman.

"Got a nice setup for yourself here, John?" Lyman's tone carried a gentle mocking.

"It's comfortable enough for now. I'm off the crook here—no more than a day-laborer—but I can't keep dragging us all over the countryside. This place is good for Ada."

"That's exactly why you should consider my offer. New Barker is a good place for a little girl. Wholesome."

"You're not going to convince my wife any place is wholesome if you're in it."

"That's one thing she's right about." Lyman laughed. "But as I explained to Harriet, the road calls to me. I have some business to see to west of here and then, with your help, I plan to make another run at the patent medicine game. New Barker is too sleepy for me anyway. You could do well there, John."

"And what do you get out of that deal?"

"A business partner, for one. And a caretaker that I trust. A gentleman's got to have his country estate, right?"

This time Papa laughed.

"Look, I'm good at what I do—hoodwink the old ladies, charm the pretty young mothers, embolden the young men, and stroke the egos of the old timers. Showmanship I got plenty of, but real miracles are in short supply around here. You've got a gift. I need you."

"You know as well as I do that if I could bottle miracles, I'd have been a settled happy man by now."

"Who said anything about real miracles? You're the best there is, John. There's no good reason you shouldn't have your own town by now complete with a temple and a string of pretty little mistresses like that Smith fella got himself. I'm not asking you for bottled miracles. I'm looking for the best illusions you can pull off. You're the goddamned mystic, remember? At least you were until you saddled yourself with that wife of yours."

"That's a hell of a way to talk. I won't have that conversation with you again." Papa growled, and Lyman must have sensed danger, because he changed the direction of conversation.

"So, what about this girl? You're a father now?"

"Ah, Ada." The joy in his voice warmed me. "Smart as a whip. Harriet's had her reading Leviticus, the poor girl. She's been through something, though. First thing she did when she got to us was run away. Not bad for a tiny little thing. Had to witch out her hiding spot."

"How old is she?"

"About ten, I'd guess."

"Good age. Old enough for deceit but still young enough to feign innocence. You know, she could be very useful to you if you had a mind to try your hand at something new."

"What do you mean?" Papa spoke slowly, drawing out his words.

"There's seers and mystics all over these days. People clamour for more. I see it everywhere I go. And if the mystic was a little girl, young and innocent, just imagine the possibilities."

"That doesn't sound like something for Ada. She's got a real gift."

"Exactly. And she'll never know what to do with it if you don't teach her. You arm her with the right skills and that girl can go places. And take you with her."

"Only reason I'd go to New Barker is to give Ada some kind of a good life, not to make her into a criminal."

"I know that, John. Annette's granddaughter deserves a good life and she'll have it. I can see it in her eyes. Potential, she's got. And plenty of curiosity, too. Probably likes to eavesdrop, the little sneak."

I still can't understand how he got to the door frame without giving me the slightest indication he was even moving at all. He peeked around the wall that hid me, his delicate, musky scent awakening in me new sensations that made me blush. "Hello there. No need to lurk in the shadows. Your uncle and I have no secrets from a dear one like yourself."

He held out his hand as a gentleman to a lady and helped me off the floor. He still carried his top hat, and when I took his hand I felt like a princess at a ball, escorted across the parlor floor by a prince. Lyman always had an uncanny way of making a girl feel as if she were the most important person in the world, and I loved him for that.

I allowed him to lead me to the sofa where I settled in next to Papa, who put his arm around me. He smelled faintly of earth and I smiled, remembering the tug of the witching rod in my hands. Lyman remained standing over us, thoughtful. After a moment he spoke.

"That's a fine picture. A father and daughter, like it was meant to be."

Papa, tensing only slightly, said in warning, "Lyman, I'm not so easily manipulated as some."

"Oh don't get upset with me. I'm just saying if I suddenly found myself with a little girl, I'd want to take care of her. Give her some stability."

Papa gave me a gentle squeeze. "I think it's time to get you to bed, girlie. Lyman and I have some talking to do."

"I want to stay with you." I yawned.

He brushed a wayward curl from my forehead and whispered, "I'll tell you all about it tomorrow."

13

I woke the next morning early, having had a restful sleep full of
dreams of my handsome savior Lyman coming to whisk me away
from my brutish aunt. I lingered for a moment, remembering too
the gentleness with which Papa had tucked me into bed. Moments
like that stand out in my memory, testaments to the truth that,
despite his faults, my uncle was more a parent to me than ever my
real father was, whose image by then had become difficult for me to
recall.

The sun had barely risen in the sky and already I could hear
stirring in the house. Aunt Harriet would be awake and at the
Scriptures already or in the kitchen preparing the rough sort of
breakfast she was known for. I much preferred Zeviah's cooking,
but Aunt Harriet found it too rich and seized every opportunity she
could to prepare meals.

Pulling myself from my sleepy comfort, I padded across the
cool floor to the wall where the chamber set and wardrobe stood
side by side. Somehow this small routine was one of my favorite
parts of every day, though I would have had a difficult time
explaining why. The best I can do, even now, is to say that my
whole body tingled with anticipation as I splashed water from the
white basin onto my face. I thought perhaps this was because I felt
so grown up—having such luxuries in my very own bedroom, all to
myself, but as I would soon discover, it was much more than that.

I had no sooner finished cleaning my teeth than I heard a great
deal of excitement rise in the house. It was Zeviah's voice which
rang out in nothing short of wild glee. I pulled on my plain dress
and ran quickly from the room to see what had caused this
unexpected ruckus. What I found made my sentimental heart pound
with pleasure.

There in the parlor stood Zeviah, locked in the arms of a man
I did not recognize but immediately understood to be the long-

absent Jerry of whom she had so sweetly spoken. I watched the two embrace as only a couple truly in love, and recently reunited, will do. I remember reflecting that it would be a strange sight to see Aunt Harriet and Papa hold one another in this way, but for Zeviah and her Jerry, the moment was beautifully natural.

It had just occurred to me that perhaps I should not be observing such a private moment when I felt Aunt Harriet's tight grasp on my arm. "Leave them be," she hissed.

However, Zeviah turned toward Aunt Harriet's embarrassed whispers, then beckoned us both further into the parlor with a wave of her hand. "Mr. Clark," she said happily, "may I present our boarders. This is Mrs. Harriet Powell and her niece, dear Ada. Has John left for the day already?"

"I believe so," Aunt Harriet responded, rather graciously I thought. "He must have gone long before sunup. It is a pleasure to meet you, Mr. Clark."

"And you as well. Mrs. Clark has written such kind words about all of you. And," he beamed at me as he spoke, "I know she has grown very fond of you, Ada."

A warm blush spread across my cheeks and, not knowing what else to do, I looked to Aunt Harriet for guidance. She wore what appeared to be a forced smile as she said, "We'll take our leave of you for now. Ada, you may breakfast outside by the garden where we will review your lessons from yesterday."

"Yes, Aunt Harriet." I tried not to sound glum since this was a happy moment for Zeviah, but an inexplicable dread had begun to seep into my mind, and I feared this was not the start of a pleasant day.

Less than an hour later, I discovered how right my ominous feeling had been. Aunt Harriet and I busied ourselves weeding the vegetable garden and quoting scripture passages back and forth. Sometimes she paused to offer an explanation that I would be expected to remember and repeat back to her at a later time. Right in the middle of my recitation of the first chapter of Romans, just at the part where God becomes vengeful and turns all His people over to the ugliness of their sins, I was interrupted by the most awful shouting from inside the house.

I stopped speaking, looking to Aunt Harriet for explanation. She appeared as puzzled as I. Without a word to one another, we stopped our work in the garden to hasten toward the sound.

Dread filled my heart, my blood running cold through my limbs as the scene became clear. It was Mr. Clark's voice that raged.

"How dare you come into my home and spread your despicable lies! I'll have you thrown in jail!"

"Now, my good sir," Lyman said, "be reasonable. No matter what you may think of me, I am only in town to visit my dear friend here. A fine upstanding man. A family man. I had no intention of causing you grief. I will, of course, take my leave." Lyman spoke eloquently, though his contrite speech won him no favors with Mr. Clark. Next to Lyman stood Papa. With his hat in his hand and his head bowed respectfully, he was the very picture of repentance.

"This man," Mr. Clark roared in the direction of his wife now, "is a filthy burner and a whoremonger, and I will not have him nor his friends here a moment longer."

"You!" Mr. Clark pointed to Papa who met his eyes, but offered no other response. "You find yourself a different mark. I want you out of my house and out of Hartwick within the hour!"

The sound of a sharp breath reminded me of Aunt Harriet's presence standing beside me. I expected her to be as stunned as I, but to her this scene must have been familiar. I stood dumbstruck, staring at the three men and at Zeviah, who dared not object to her husband's accusations and who would not raise her gaze to meet mine. Aunt Harriet grabbed hold of my hand and rushed me through the kitchen. We were in the hallway just outside our rooms when I thought to protest.

"Wait! What's happening?"

"Lyman is happening," my aunt snapped. "And we are guilty by association. Pack your things."

"We haven't done anything wrong."

My aunt did not tolerate whining. I immediately regretted my tone. Fortunately she chose not to reprimand me, probably for lack of time. I knew from experience that a painful scolding may yet come my way. Still, in that moment, she knelt in front of me, clasping my shoulders in her strong hands.

"We are innocent, Ada, and the Lord above knows it to be true, which is all that matters. Lyman is a foul creature, and he is everything Mr. Clark said of him and more. Whatever he stands accused of now you can be sure he is guilty."

"Why must *we* leave?" I began to cry, thinking about another run across the countryside with no home in which to settle. "Zeviah can tell him. We're good people. He can't really just throw us out!"

"You and I are good people, Ada. Mrs. Clark may even believe that, but that doesn't change the fact that she will stand by her husband and his fury. We will not be allowed to remain here."

"She's my friend." I would not believe that Zeviah, in whom I confided my most painful secrets, would allow this to happen, but as my aunt's grip tightened on my shoulders, I knew she was right.

Aunt Harriet released me at last with a stern look and the command to quickly pack my trunk. Then she disappeared into the bedroom she shared with Papa, and I had no choice but to do as she instructed.

I had nearly finished packing my few possessions when Papa knocked on my open door, red-faced and ruffled as though he hadn't slept in days. In his right hand he carried one of the forked sticks he used to locate underground water veins. He sat down upon the corner of the bed and looked at me with sad eyes. "I'm sorry, girlie."

I had not thought to be angry with Papa and wondered whether I should be. However, my desire for explanation outweighed this consideration.

"What did Lyman do?"

Papa shook his head. "Lyman has at times been a good friend to me, but he's a swindler, no two ways about it. He's usually too good to get caught up like this, but Mr. Clark happened on him many months back, and evidently Lyman made a poor impression. He's crossed plenty of people who think he's nothing but a crook. And while I've known him to play the good man at times, he has always been one."

"Papa," I said, my cheeks wet with tears, "are you a crook?"

Papa hesitated for a brief moment before he answered. "I have a special set of skills and that sometimes brings me into associations with crooks."

I wanted more, but Papa left the explanation there. He stood and walked toward the door. Looking back over his shoulder, he said, "Best finish packing. Lyman's been taken to jail. We'll load his wagon and leave here as soon as we can."

Papa closed the door behind him, leaving me alone in the little bedroom that had been mine for the last several weeks. Even though I'd felt at home within its walls, now the room felt empty to me. My trunk was packed and I would have offered to help Aunt Harriet and Papa with the rest of the preparations for our departure if I hadn't been too lost in my own grief and bitterness.

Mostly, I resented Zeviah who had been my friend and confidante. She had seen and even respected Papa's particular set of skills. She could surely make her husband understand that Papa was no threat to their family and home, that none of us were. I kept picturing her standing meekly behind Mr. Clark as he shouted his scandalous accusations. She hadn't dared even a look at any of us.

Then I thought about our walks along the creek, our conversations, and her supposed secrets. I had been sure she possessed darkness I couldn't see, scars she kept locked away.

As a woman grown, I can reflect back upon the time I spent with Zeviah and understand that, more than anything, I was desperate to see something of myself in her. I don't know, Mr. Rigdon, if you can appreciate the struggle of a young girl trying to grow up without a proper mother. Most of what I had known of my real mother was obscured by the trauma of her death. And I could hardly look to Aunt Harriet as a model of what I wished to become.

In the short time I had known her, Zeviah filled the void in my heart only to then reject me at the bidding of her husband. It was a betrayal, one that left me vulnerable, like a little girl, once again watching her mother, the woman who was supposed to protect her from the world, shrink under a greater force. I wanted to hurt her.

Papa had left his witching rod behind him on the bed. Having no idea what I hoped to accomplish, I felt compelled to hold it, perhaps to gain some control over the whirling momentum of my unstable life.

I grasped the forked end in both hands, palms up as Papa had shown me. At once it pulled at me, its unnatural weight causing my muscles to tremble. I stepped slowly, following its urgings toward the source of intensity. Pausing briefly at the chamber set I recalled the tingling sensation that I had felt every morning and had taken to be merely anticipation of a new day in this relatively happy home. Now this magnified perception permeated every crevice of my body, threatening to drag me and the rod into whatever mystery lay hidden nearby.

The source of the weightiness, at once both terrible and thrilling, was not the chamber set at all. It had never been. Rather, it was the wardrobe that I'd all but ignored since discovering it was locked on the day we first arrived.

I stood before it, the unseen energy prickling at my skin. I no longer questioned the source of the attraction. My hands ached as the rod twisted against my grip. I let go, expecting the rod to fly against the wardrobe door. Instead, it dropped to the floor. Rubbing my raw palms together, I stared at the lifeless stick.

Then, without further thought, I slammed all of my weight into the doors. The lock gave way easily and I stared at the contents, searching, desperate for relief from the force that had drawn me so intensely. Several men's coats hung, neatly pressed, from the rod in the top of the wardrobe, and next to them one or two out-of-fashion ladies dresses. None of these were the treasure I sought. At last my eyes fell on a trunk, about the size of my own, resting on the floor of the wardrobe.

No lock barred my examination. I opened the lid, my forehead breaking out in sweat at the anticipation of what I might uncover. It appeared to be an ordinary stack of old papers, in two bundles— one thick, the other slim. The pages of each were written upon with the same careful script. The slim one bore the title of *Manuscript Story, Conneaut Creek*. I set that one aside, for it was the other bundle that caught my imagination. It was nothing more than a bundle of foolscap, identified only as *Manuscript Found*.

A curious title to find stashed away in the bottom of a trunk in a locked wardrobe, like some treasure awaiting discovery. I could not imagine what secret might be contained within its pages, but that it had been the source of the rod's pull, I had no doubt. What I did know was that someone—I assumed Zeviah—would not have wanted me to find it.

And so, without further consideration, I placed the slim bundle back in the chest and took *Manuscript Found.* I clasped the papers tightly in my hands, drawing several long, deep breaths. The room came back into focus as the tingling sensation subsided. I knew not what I held. Looking at the stack of pages covered in the author's cryptic scrawl, I doubted it would yield up its secrets that day. Quickly, I stuffed the manuscript into my own trunk, careful to conceal it under the small pile of homespun.

I closed the wardrobe door, checking that it latched so no one would notice the opened lock, and dragged my belongings into the hallway for Papa to convey to Lyman's carriage.

14

"Mr. Rigdon, are you unwell?" Ada shifted in her seat and wondered, not for the first time that day, whether she should be here, divulging so much information that she had long kept to herself. The aged prophet had, with no small effort, pulled himself into a straighter position, leaning just forward as if eager to speak.

"Why did you come here, Miss Moses?" The old man trembled as he spoke, though his voice remained strong and commanding.

She did not intimidate him, she realized. Even now that he was absolutely convinced she possessed the one treasure most important to him, he did not fear her. She envied his confidence. Perhaps that was the real reason she had decided to come to him—to satisfy her own curiosity. What must it look like to so fervently believe in the purpose of your created deceptions that you can rest easy, justifying the lies and schemes you helped to create?

It would have been simpler to disappear; her first instinct when she opened the package sent by Silas Allen's killers and stared at the bloody shirt. Her eyes had been drawn to the familiar frayed cuffs of the shirt Mr. Allen had worn when he followed the trail of *Manuscript Found* to her doorstep.

He had not been the first to seek the pages that might prove a prophet to be no more than a common confidence man, but Mr. Allen had been the first to find a connection to her. Ada suspected as he spoke that he may have had an extra sensory gift himself similar in some way to her own. She might have asked, had he returned to her Water Street home. Instead, she received only his soiled shirt, a dangerous threat. He had taken notes, notes which likely bore her name. The name alone was not a problem, for she had long since stopped using it, but he had been followed, and his murderers sent her an unmistakable message.

"I suppose I came because I was curious," she finally said. "Curious about how it might feel to reveal my nature to someone who can understand it."

"What makes you think I am that person?"

"I see your expressions as I speak. I watched the excitement flash through your cloudy eyes at my mention of my skill with the rod. Oh, yes, I am skilled. I can find deep water veins when called upon even when others cannot. As you might have guessed, however, my specialty was, and remains, secrets. I am particularly gifted at locating secret objects. If you've something you truly wish to hide, that is of great value to you, I am not a woman you want around.

"I didn't know for a long time why the manuscript drew me in. It was the first treasure I ever stole, but not the last, once I realized what I could do with my gift. Most of my discoveries have not brought me great wealth, though a few have provided some monetary compensation, in particular those that have passed from owner to owner by nefarious means.

"Perhaps I should have left the manuscript, tucked it back inside the trunk. Of course, as you already know, it was not Zeviah's secret I found that day. The trunk and its contents did not belong to her anymore than did the dresses that hung above them. She was merely an unwitting link in the chain of possession. The trunk belonged to her aunt, the papers held within to her aunt's deceased husband. And the secret, sought by both those who wish to expose it and by those who would kill to protect it, belongs to you.

"Had I left it, I wouldn't be here today discussing *Manuscript Found* with you. Instead it would have been discovered by someone with more malicious intentions. Imagine, with this one missing bit of information, what damage an enemy could have done to your religion."

"And so your intentions are not malicious?"

"There is more to my story, Mr. Rigdon. If you'll hear it, I think you'll see that I don't wish to be your enemy."

The old man relaxed at these words and he sagged once more in his chair, his shoulders slumping, giving him a more shriveled appearance. Ada preferred the straight-backed, commanding image of him, but she could appreciate that she had gained some small amount of his trust.

"So tell me about this gift with the rod." The old man's curiosity had gotten the best of him now and he asked the question eagerly.

"I know what you are thinking, Mr. Rigdon. My gift, as Papa always called it, captures your imagination just as it did Papa's and later Lyman's. Papa had been witching for water since he was a boy and he'd had more successes than not. How long he'd been attempting to witch for treasure, I was never sure, but all the effort ever brought him was disappointment. As his reputation with the rod grew, his opportunities expanded. Enthusiastic men looking for an easy path to wealth, as men will always do, discovered him, and he put his skills to good use.

"But despite the many tales, the eastern countryside has little treasure, at least not of the kind its famed treasure hunters seek.

"There is no lost Indian gold buried beneath its dry riverbeds. No smuggler's hidden stash forgotten and covered over by time. No golden Bibles tucked away in the hills.

"I've heard the stories of great wealth, too numerous to count. They're true, in a way. Where there is a whisper of undiscovered fortunes there is always a trail of fools who will spend their own riches to find it. All they need is a mysterious stranger who can locate it for them.

"And now I'll let you in on another secret as well. A man who can find treasure does not lead others to it. He finds it himself and becomes rich. A man who can make others believe he can find treasure leads them on a chase and then disappears with their money. If he's very good at what he does, he also becomes rich.

"Shall I continue?"

The old man nodded.

15

"Explain to me again why we must fetch the strumpet." Aunt Harriet was in about as sour mood as I had yet seen her. I was careful to hold my tongue, afraid that whatever I said might incur her wrath.

Papa seemed to feel the same way and had chosen to explain little to either one of us since loading the carriage. "Because Lyman asked me to care for her. And he's opening his home. He's behaving generously." He looked at Aunt Harriet with an expression I had rarely seen him use, but apparently it conveyed a subtle warning to my aunt, because she waved him away without another word on the subject.

Papa pulled the carriage up in front of the hotel where Lyman and his Mariana had been staying while in Hartwick. He disappeared inside and less than fifteen minutes later returned with the strumpet herself. Papa carried her loaded carryall and she leaned upon his arm, wan and weak. Papa handed her into the carriage. She pulled the bag onto her lap, settled next to me, and drew the carriage curtains.

Papa took his place in the driver's seat and soon the carriage began to rock. We were not transporting so many supplies this time as we had been when we left Norwich and the carriage was much more comfortable than the tiny wagon had been. Still, we were cramped. Lyman's horses, young and strong, moved at a good pace, leaving behind Hartwick and the enemies we had unwittingly made there.

Stifling silence filled the limited space within the carriage compartment. Mariana leaned her head back against the seat, her eyes closed and moist at the corners. Failing to grasp Harriet's explosive temper that only awaited detonation, she broke the silence. "Thank you for coming to collect me."

Stony faced, Aunt Harriet stared at the woman who still wore her scarlet turban and matching silk dress.

After a few moments of silence Mariana opened her eyes, a blush crossing her cheeks. "I know you may not think much of me, but before you judge me too harshly, you should know that I am not a common trollop as you assume. I am widowed. Lyman was an associate of my late husband. There is nothing more."

"An associate." Aunt Harriet repeated the word she never uttered without a scowl. "In that case, congratulations. You've chosen for your protector the most famous whoremonger in the New York prison system."

"And here I thought your husband was now my protector." Mariana leaned back again, taking from the top of her bag a handkerchief and dabbing at her eyes and brow on which a fine sheen of perspiration had begun to settle.

"Look who's so high and mighty," Mariana continued, her words barely a whisper that somehow felt more dangerous to me than a yell. "I know all about you, Harriet, a washed-up old maid who grabbed onto the first scoundrel that would have her. I see now Lyman was much too generous in his description of you. He's a good man who should demand your respect."

I admired her bravery in defending Lyman and in standing up to Aunt Harriet who, as far as I could tell, most people found nearly as intimidating as I did. But if she did not fear my aunt's wrath, I certainly did. I barely breathed, not knowing what to expect, yet convinced that it would be something terrible.

I withdrew into the corner of the bench seat I shared with Mariana, doing my best to fade into the carriage wall in case the two women came to blows.

The sinister smile that crept across Aunt Harriet's face was almost a worse reaction than I had imagined. She did not rail at Mariana. She laughed. "Whatever you think you have come to know about that man, I assure you, you've been misled. He's nothing but a shameless, no-account bastard." Aunt Harriet paused, glancing at me. I was careful to look out the window, pretending my attention had been captured by the passing scenery.

"As for me," Harriet continued. "Lyman and I were children together. I know him better than I'd ever care to. And since you have been so presumptuous as to comment upon my own marriage, even after John went out of his way to collect you, I'll tell you that my husband is a hard-working repentant sinner deserving of your respect. I see he'll receive none of it."

That was the first of only a very few times I heard Aunt Harriet say a kind word about Papa. She was more apt to remain quiet on the subject. I could not determine whether she was sincere in her loyalty or if she only meant to inflate her own righteousness in order to put Mariana in her place. Either way, her words moved me.

I knew nothing of this Mariana woman who slumped, weak, in our carriage and little of Lyman. The only people I had to cling to in my unstable world were Papa and Aunt Harriet. That was the first time I began to understand them as a couple. Their affections most often went undemonstrated but each, on some level, saw the best in the other.

I remember thinking that I lived in a cruel world and that if I were to survive, it was necessary to form connections wherever any sort of trust could be fostered. As often as I felt endangered by both Aunt Harriet and Papa, I thought that I had already seen their darker sides. Somehow there was a kind of comfort in knowing that I would never be further disappointed by their flaws. Maybe love really is about seeing the worst in someone and still being able to glimpse the good.

The conversation between Mariana and Aunt Harriet came to an abrupt end. The animosity between the two women did not. I felt sure Mariana was not the type to let someone else have the last word, but what little strength she possessed must have been exhausted because she fell silent, her breathing slowing as she drifted to sleep.

My aunt and I rode in silence for the remainder of the morning until Papa stopped so we could eat a roadside picnic.

My aunt took out the food Zeviah had thrust upon us, by way of apology I supposed, though it did little to assuage my anger at being so easily turned out. Papa helped Mariana from the carriage. She stumbled as her feet touched the ground. He helped her to sit and placed a hand on her forehead, letting out a low whistle.

"Fever," he muttered to no one in particular. Then "Ada, I need you to fetch me a plant with round, black berries. Don't wander too far. Can you do that?"

I nodded and was off before Aunt Harriet could stop me, rushing back into the tree line, careful not to lose sight of the road. It didn't take long to find a bush with berries like Papa described and I stripped several branches, my fingers stained purple as some of the soft orbs burst at my rough handling.

When I returned, Papa was busy applying a poultice to Mariana's forehead. She did not move and I thought at first she might be dead. I nearly gasped when her eyes fluttered at my approached.

Papa had removed her turban and with it, I was shocked to see, had come a clump of her long brown hair. I handed him the berries.

"Thank you, Ada." The voice was so hushed, barely competing with the low hum of insects coming from the grass, I almost missed it. Mariana's eyes, wide with sincerity, met mine and she reached for me, catching my wrist. An unpleasant prickling rushed through me at her touch and I felt heat rise in my cheeks, reddening as her complexion paled.

Her long, dark hair lay limp across her slender shoulders. Even in her weakened state she was undeniably pretty. I could not have explained why, but I knew I didn't like her.

Papa rolled a berry between his fingers, letting the juice fill the lines of his skin. "These will do nicely."

"What are they?" I asked, pulling my arm from Mariana's loose grip and turning toward him.

"Elderberries. You have to be sure they're ripe or they can be dangerous. And brewing a tea would be better, but I think it's best we keep moving. We need to get her somewhere she can rest."

We were in the middle of nowhere, as far as I could see, along the well-packed dirt road we had been traveling. "Where are we now?" I asked Papa.

"On the road," he mumbled, feeding the berries to Mariana whose lips puckered at the taste of them. When she had taken all of them, Papa turned to me, mussed my hair, and added, "We're headed south toward the Susquehanna River. Do you know where that is?"

I nodded despite the fact that the geography of the area was largely beyond my grasp. My lessons focused on a more heavenly landscape.

"We'll make our way there, then follow the river west to Lyman's farm."

"Lyman has a farm?" I tried to picture Lyman as a farmer, his coattails covered in dirt, his un-tucked shirt drenched in sweat.

Papa nodded. "His country estate, he calls it. Really it's just a little farmhouse with a few acres he inherited. He's offered to let us live there for a while."

"We're going to live with Lyman?" As intrigued as I was by the mysterious scoundrel that had been a friend to both my father and to Papa, I dreaded being run away from another home. I grudgingly found myself in agreement with Aunt Harriet. The man was bad news.

"Don't worry, girlie." Papa lifted my chin with a little nudge from his fist. "Lyman travels when he's not in jail. He says he's hardly there and needs someone to look after the place for him."

"He'll get out of jail soon, won't he? And you believe him? That he's not at his farm very often?"

"Oh, I wouldn't be surprised if he's out already. And, yes, I believe him. Lyman isn't one for staying still too long. It'll be safe enough for us to make a home there and we won't see Lyman for more than a few days at a time, I can promise you that."

It took more than a week to make the trip all the way to the sleepy little town of New Barker, tucked into a bend of the Susquehanna just north of the border with Pennsylvania. Autumn rains slowed us and made the way treacherous along the river so that we rarely traveled more than a few miles each day. Mariana's condition improved slightly under Papa's ministrations, but it was still clear travel was difficult for her. The one advantage to her weak state was that she spoke little, and once Aunt Harriet saw how ill our traveling companion really was, she picked no more fights.

For my part, I only tried to stay as far away from Mariana as I could, moving to sit beside my aunt, concerned that I might fall victim to whatever disease had taken hold of our unlikely fellow traveler. Papa told me not to worry, that Mariana suffered from the French pox and I couldn't catch it from her.

I couldn't explain to him that what scared me far more than her illness was that awful burning I felt at her touch, like she was stealing something from me, some kind of energy that would give her power over me.

When we finally arrived in town, Papa stopped to ask for directions to Lyman's farm. He spoke with a woman, clearly delighted to help, and their conversation lasted for several minutes before Papa returned to the carriage.

We found the house down a winding country lane, lined with shade trees, less than a mile from the proper town. As we pulled up in front, Lyman himself stepped out onto the sprawling front porch, dressed as always in a pressed suit, tall matching hat, and a magnanimous smile.

As if he hadn't a care in the world, he stretched out his arms as a showman and asked, "How do you like my country estate?"

Papa let out a low whistle. "Thought you said it was a little old farm house."

"Is that what I said?" Lyman smiled, but as he looked toward the carriage compartment, his unfettered joy evaporated. "You rescued dear Mariana, too. How is she?"

"She's better, but how long that will last, I couldn't say. I told you I can't work miracles."

I climbed out of the carriage and stretched, watching them. Lyman clasped Papa's shoulder. "If anyone could, it would be you. Thank you."

"Don't thank him yet" Harriet climbed out behind me, blinking against the sunlight.

"How'd you get here so fast, Ly?" Papa asked.

"Oh, you know how it is. I called in a favor or two. Just got here myself, really. I was surprised you didn't arrive before me."

"All this rain made for slow traveling along the river with a full carriage."

"And a half-dead woman," Harriet added with a scowl.

"Charming." Unfazed, Lyman approached the wagon and offered a hand to Mariana who, while disheveled from travel, did look like she felt a little better.

"Harriet, why don't you and Miss Ada go and look around while John and I unload the carriage?"

Aunt Harriet seized upon Lyman's suggestion and I followed her into the house, both of us leaving Mariana behind sitting on the porch steps to watch the men as they worked and chatted.

We found our way through the house, more spacious than it appeared from the outside. From the sitting room, a doorway led into a large dining room with a pass through to a modern kitchen with a brick oven on one side. A set of stairs led to a second story just off the main hallway at the front of the house, and we discovered a second stairway leading up from the kitchen.

We might not have noticed the second staircase upon our first look had it not been for the woman who descended it just then. She wore a dress of faded lavender with a corseted waist and a large bustle. She'd tied her auburn hair in a hasty knot on the back of her head and as we sized her up, several pieces fell to her shoulders.

"Oh, hello." The woman's expression registered surprise to find us in the house and she clutched her hand at her breast to showcase her astonishment.

"Hello," I replied. I would not have thought the encounter remarkable at all had it not been for my aunt's firm grasp on my arm.

"Well, aren't you a fine little lady?" The woman smiled at me and then locked eyes with Aunt Harriet who easily stood head and shoulders above her. Perhaps the woman expected a friendly greeting.

My aunt remained silent, returning the woman's stare. The tension grew for several moments until at last Papa and Lyman entered through the back door.

"Ah, I see you've met Grace." My aunt turned to stare at Lyman as he addressed the disheveled woman. "Gracie, it is time for you to be leaving lest your fortunes take a turn, I think. Out the back door would be best."

The woman curled her painted lip at my aunt before she turned on her heel and walked out the door.

Aunt Harriet finally found her voice. "We're leaving."

"I'm sorry, Harriet." Lyman spoke with mock contrition. "Did I offend you somehow?"

Harriet glared at Lyman, but it was Papa who spoke. "Be reasonable, Harriet. You know how Lyman is."

"Yes," Lyman interjected. "You know how I am. Just go pray for me or something. I'm sure that will help."

"And what about Mariana?" Aunt Harriet snarled.

"What about her? I told you, she is a friend in a bad way at the moment. I owe her nothing but my kindness which, thanks to John, I have been able to give her much of. Besides, she knows better than some what kind of man I am."

Just then we heard the bump of the front door closing and Mariana walked in. She moved slowly, but some color had returned to her cheeks and her eyes shined brighter. It pleased me to see both how Papa's medicines had helped her and how dreadfully travel-worn she looked.

Lyman rushed to her, offering his arm, which she took after a slight hesitation. "My dear, I told you I would return for you. I'm sorry to have made you wait." He gestured toward Aunt Harriet. "I was being scolded for all my sins, both real and imagined."

My aunt loosened her grip on me and sighed. I turned my face to study her and all at once I realized how weary she also looked. Large as she was, she carried with her an air of absolute certainty and authority that was difficult for most people to ignore, but the week of hard travel and tending to the needs of a sick woman, a headstrong husband, and a heartsick child had worn on her.

"Harriet," Papa said in a tender voice I had assumed until then he reserved for me. "You need rest. You and Lyman can argue later, I'm sure."

My aunt nodded and looked at Lyman with a scowl, which he returned before he spoke.

"You'll find an empty bedroom just to the right at the top of the stairs. If I can make your stay any more comfortable, please don't hesitate to ask." Though he smiled, his expression was not friendly in the least, making it obvious to everyone in the room that his dislike for my aunt rivaled hers for him.

"A bed is all I require, thank you. Come, Ada." She caught up my hand and squeezed so tightly it hurt, leaving me no choice but to climb with her up the back staircase.

The room was positively garish compared with the simple decor of the bedrooms in Zeviah's house. Bright blue wallpaper with a floral print—I think they were roses—clung to the walls of the small square room. A tall four poster bed stood against one wall opposite a bureau with a wide gilded mirror. Aunt Harriet climbed onto the bed, not bothering to remove her dress.

She lay still for a few moments and I wondered what she expected me to do. I could have used a rest as well, I'm sure, but I remained much too excited for such. Just as I began to believe her asleep, Aunt Harriet spoke. "Do you want to stay here, in New Barker, Ada?"

"I'm not sure," I replied cautiously. "I don't want to keep moving."

"Nor do I, child." Aunt Harriet's words were heavy and slow. "Remember that I am not your enemy. You cannot trust Lyman. And you cannot trust your uncle while he is under the influence of that man."

It was rare for my aunt to consider my feelings. It touched me that she had bothered to ask. Perhaps emboldened by the combination of her fatigue and her concern for me, or even her self-restraint in her recent conversation with Lyman, I chose this moment to ask the question haunting my thoughts since Lyman's arrival in Hartwick.

"Aunt Harriet, why are Papa and Lyman such good friends if you and Lyman hate each other so?" My voice trembled as I spoke. I rarely dared ask my aunt a personal question, and I was never sure how she would respond.

For a long moment she looked at me with tired eyes. Then she turned her gaze toward the ceiling. "Ada, there are some things a child can't possibly understand."

"Please try to explain, Aunt Harriet. You tell me not to trust this man, yet we are going to live in his house."

I knew my questions were a great aggravation to my fatigued aunt, but I pressed her for an answer anyway. I possessed such little context in which to place the life lessons Aunt Harriet tried to inflict on me. Had she put more faith in my ability to understand her warnings, perhaps I would have heeded them.

"I've known Lyman since I was a girl," Aunt Harriet began, placing her hand upon her forehead. She did not lift her head to speak to me, instead remaining flat on her back with her eyes closed. "It was he who introduced me to John. For that I suppose I must be grateful. Lyman and your uncle were in business together, a long time ago now. Oftentimes unsavory business. When John and I married, the partnership dissolved on difficult terms, but John was much relieved, as was I, knowing Lyman as I did. Your uncle is a good man. Misguided, but good. Now go away and let me rest."

Just like that, I was dismissed from the most telling conversation I'd ever had with my aunt. I hadn't gained a great deal of information, but I learned a few things I hadn't known before. I knew now that Aunt Harriet had knowingly married a criminal, that she had loved him anyway, and that she believed in his goodness in spite of evidence to the contrary. Still contemplating this new information and what it meant to my own feelings regarding my aunt, I slipped out the door and down the stairs, free to explore my new home.

I found Papa and Lyman sitting at the kitchen table. I caught only a few words, one of which was "Mariana." I was relieved to see she wasn't in the room when I entered. She'd done nothing to deserve any ill feelings from me, but the thought of her leaning upon Lyman's arm filled me with an inexplicable loathing.

Lyman stopped mid-sentence when he saw me. He stood, pushing his chair out behind him. "Ada, my dear. Come join us!"

As he spoke, he took my hand and led me through the doorway of the kitchen, guiding me to the sitting room and settling me onto a velvety sofa. Papa followed, his flat cap in his hands.

"A change of scenery is in order I believe, John." As he spoke to Papa, Lyman's twinkling eyes never left my face. "It'll never do to have a perfect lady skulking around a kitchen table. We'll have a proper conversation in a proper sort of room. Maybe some tea, my dear?"

I nodded and he hustled out of the parlor again, a flurry of coattails. Papa sat beside me on the sofa, his stiff posture indicating his discomfort. I wanted to assault him with a million questions, but before I had the chance, Lyman returned with a tray that held three dainty china cups and a plate of tiny iced cakes. Our food supplies had seen us all the way to New Barker only because of Mariana's pitiful appetite and Aunt Harriet's careful rationing. I was hungry.

"My goodness, don't you feed her?" Lyman smiled at Papa. Then he added, "I expect Harriet's in charge of that, is she? Probably living on crusts of stale bread, by the looks of her, the poor skinny child."

Papa said nothing, failing even to reach for his own teacup or to help himself to a cake.

When Lyman received no answer from Papa, he addressed me instead. "Does your aunt rage at you, darling? She excels at that."

I looked to Papa. On his face he wore a blank expression, his hands in his lap, engaged in wringing his cap.

"Ah." Lyman looked for just the briefest moment as if he might cry, an illusion he was very gifted at conjuring, I would later come to realize. "Well, don't worry. Uncle John here will protect you from the madwoman, I'm sure. I was just telling him that you will all be very comfortable here. The run of the place and you, your own room, of course, perhaps some pretty new dresses. Would you like that?"

I nodded once again, my mouth full of cake.

"She doesn't say much, does she?" Lyman turned his grin toward Papa. "I have a little project you might be interested in. Both of you, perhaps." He smiled in my direction as he watched me finish off the last cake.

"Lyman," Papa offered cautiously. "Harriet and I, we want to settle into a more stable way of life for Ada. We can't keep moving her around. I don't think I'm much interested in any more of your projects."

"Give me some credit, John. I couldn't agree with you more. The child needs security. This isn't anything that will bring you trouble, I assure you. This is, after all, my home. I'm counting on you not to ruin my impeccable reputation with the neighbors."

"So what is it?"

"It's something I think you'd be better off to see. We'll talk more about it after supper one of these nights. I have errands to attend to this afternoon after such a long absence. In the meantime, make yourselves comfortable. Ada." He stood and bowed. "My home is your home, sweet princess."

16

I located a bedroom that would suit me down the hall from where Aunt Harriet napped. Papa brought up my trunk and encouraged me to rest. I was tired from the hard journey but too excited by the curiosities of my new circumstances to really sleep. I stretched across the large canopied feather bed covered by a quilt sewn with some rich fabric in a pattern of yellow and pink tear drops. Everything glowed more vibrant when Lyman was involved—the colors, the textures, the patterns. To enter Lyman's world was to step into an oil painting.

Unable to close my eyes for more than a few moments, my thoughts wandered to *Manuscript Found* hidden in the bottom of my trunk. I pulled it out and untied the string that bound the well-worn papers together. Flipping through the pages, I examined the neat script.

Under Aunt Harriet's tutelage I had become a confident reader. I craved new books. It's true I had a complicated relationship to Scripture similar to that of the one I had with my aunt herself. The Bible intimidated me with its sheer size, overwhelmed me with its complex language, frightened me with its demands for piety, and yet comforted me with its professions of love.

But oh, how I loved to read, and my desire for reading materials proved insatiable. Zeviah had happily supplied me with newspaper stories and simple poetry on which to practice my skills, and I eagerly devoured any writing that read as speech. When I lost Zeviah, I lost that as well, and I knew I would sorely miss it.

I was anxious to find what secrets were hidden inside the manuscript, written by a man called Solomon Spalding whose name appeared on the front, along with the year 1807. Imagine my disappointment when I read the first few pages and found, instead of the beginning of an engaging narrative in familiar language, an imitation of the Scripture daily forced upon me.

A child can only read so much of "And it came to pass . . ." before she grows weary.

And thus, it came to pass, I fell asleep.

Lyman remained in New Barker for a time, coming and going with Papa, introducing him to the farm and the community, I supposed, and making plans for whatever business they planned to enter together.

I saw little of either of them, as busy as my aunt kept me. There was much work to be done, she insisted. A local farmer rented Lyman's small acreage and we would receive some income for the season, but if we were to survive a New York winter, the household would need to be put into shape. Harriet's determination to do so demanded long hours of labor.

Mariana was little help. At first she remained locked away in her sickroom, recovering. When, after nearly two weeks, she emerged the very picture of health, she made herself scarce. Soon after, Lyman shared the news that the two of them would at last be taking their leave.

The day before their planned departure brought no less hard work for Aunt Harriet and me, but Lyman had planned a special supper, even hiring a cook from town. In the late afternoon Aunt Harriet sent me, dirty from my chores, to wash up and rest.

Once scrubbed raw, I slipped into a fresh brown dress and marched into the kitchen, overflowing with delicious smells. A woman I didn't know, young and pretty, in a crisp gray dress and long white apron stood by the oven, busy with preparations.

I greeted her and rushed into the dining room to find Papa, also looking thoroughly scrubbed and dressed in a fresh suit. Still, he appeared dingy next to Lyman who never failed to cut an impressive figure.

"Just in time, the princess arrives refreshed!" he greeted me with a flourish.

"You needn't have gone to any trouble on our account," my aunt said from the other side of the room. She, too, appeared freshly bathed, but bone tired.

"No trouble at all, Harriet. When one has much to celebrate, one should dine accordingly. Don't you think, Ada?" His attention sent a flush of pleasure through me. He indicated that I should sit beside him, on the opposite side from Mariana, who glowed with renewed vitality. Lyman followed my gaze. "She looks well, don't you think? Thanks to John, of course."

Mariana's cheeks flushed with pleasure as I felt mine drain of color. Lyman showed her to her seat next to him and again beckoned me into the place on his other side. Before I could sit, my aunt maneuvered into the chair instead, I could only assume in order to shield me from Lyman's vulgarity, for I doubted she was envious of his attentions.

The woman from the kitchen began to bring in the food— roasted potatoes and baked chicken, seasoned greens, and several other savory dishes. As I have said, everything was richer with Lyman, and food was no exception. I nearly ate myself sick while the adults made uncomfortable conversation around me.

Actually Lyman seemed perfectly at ease, my aunt audibly disapproving of most of what he said. Papa wisely remained quiet. Lyman spoke of travel mostly, recounting the many scenes he and Mariana had encountered along their travels through southern Pennsylvania before her sudden illness had brought them to us in Hartwick.

The young lady who cooked for us was named Emily. Lyman explained she would be pleased to help with the cooking and the washing if Aunt Harriet had need of her which, we all knew, she would not.

Still, Lyman appeared as taken with Emily as he did everyone around him, and I thought at one point I saw him pinch at her waist as she filled his wine glass, blushing. Mariana's eyes narrowed as she drew a long drink from her own glass.

I don't know when I first noticed, but through the course of the conversation, Aunt Harriet commented less and less frequently and her speech, when she did join in, was slower, more cautious somehow until at last she lay her head on the table, cushioned by her arms, and closed her eyes.

Lyman, who throughout much of the dinner had stopped talking only long enough to take a bite, didn't waste a moment. He flashed his handsome smile and declared, "Good! That's taken care of. Now we can get to business."

I didn't understand the shift in the conversation until Papa, more weary than angry, asked, "What did you give her?"

"Just what are you implying, John?"

Papa, unamused at the little joke, arched an accusing eyebrow.

Lyman continued, "Of course if Emily happened to give her a little henbane, well, I'm sure I couldn't say."

Papa's face darkened, red and angry. "You could kill her with henbane."

"Could I?" His casual inflection frightened and thrilled me. His smile reassured that he only joked, but his eyes spoke another truth, that animosity perches on a fine edge between tolerance and vengeance.

"How much did you give her?"

"Only about five drops of the extract. Emily has quick hands."

The cook grinned at Lyman and curtsied.

Mariana giggled. Apparently she had drunk enough wine to forget any small jealousies. She beamed at Emily with appreciation.

Papa stood, pushing his chair back from the table. "She'll have terrible dreams," he said, rubbing his bearded chin and shaking his head. His anger fading somewhat with Lyman's admission that Aunt Harriet would not suffer permanent harm. "She won't wake very happy."

"Does she ever?" I probably shouldn't have said it, but I couldn't help myself.

Mariana let out a shriek of delight and Lyman reached across Aunt Harriet's slumped form and pointed to me, his eyebrows raised playfully. Only Papa did not smile.

"Help me get her upstairs to bed," he said to Lyman.

Lyman and Papa returned just as I refused cobbler from Emily. "No need to worry, Ada," Lyman joked. "Emily would never drug anyone who didn't deserve it."

Emily nodded, her gentle eyes meeting mine. I decided not to trust the cobbler anyway. Mariana, I noticed, left her portion untouched as well.

Instead, she stood and said, "Lyman, enough with the mystery. What have you planned for us tonight?"

"I thought we'd celebrate your returning health by showing John and Ada your special skill. There's a lady, name of Mrs. Leah Woodruff, who loves a good mystery and always has lots of questions for me when I come around. I saw her in town shortly after I arrived and she spoke at length about her recently married son. I suspect she'd like me to settle down with one of her homely daughters. I was quick to mention my talented new traveling companion and she is anxious to meet you, to see you at your work. Do you feel well enough?"

"Of course." New light shone in her eyes, her jaw set with purpose.

"Let's get this over with, then." Papa turned toward the front door, adding as an afterthought, "Be a good girl, Ada. Look in on your aunt in a bit."

Much to my surprise and delight, Lyman reached out a hand to stop him from leaving the dining room. "No, no, no, John. The whole purpose of this was so that she could come."

"I've been thinking about that." It struck me that Papa sounded apologetic as he spoke, like he was concerned about offending Lyman. "It's not a good idea."

"Harriet will suffocate her. You've said it yourself. Let her have some fresh air, John. Let her come and see what possibilities and wonders the world holds."

I found my voice then. "I want to come with you, Papa." I had never intentionally used that term of endearment in front of anyone else before, and I knew it was unkind of me to do it then. I very much wanted to see what Lyman was up to, but still I understood in some sense Papa was trying to protect me from something. I felt ashamed of my attempt to manipulate him.

Lyman seized his opportunity, as I suspected he would. "Yes, Papa, let her come."

Papa thought for a moment, hesitant to yield his ground, but at last he said, "Okay, Ada, you may come with us, but not a word to your aunt."

I nodded, his warning sending a jolt through me, his words a threat meant for my understanding alone. I could never forget the first time I'd heard those words from him and wound up betrayed, bruised and burned. But I have always found it difficult to pass up an intrigue. Papa's hesitancy only served to encourage my interest.

The four of us walked through the growing darkness, with Papa keeping a firm grasp on my hand at all times. The Woodruffs resided half a block from the town square on a lane of modestly wealthy homes. Flowers lined the front walkway, their petals closed against the night. Before us loomed an expansive porch upon which a woman sat, wrapped tightly in a shawl and awaiting our arrival.

Even from a distance I could see that Mrs. Woodruff was a plump, cheerful woman, deep into middle age, clothed in a fashionable dress and excessive jewelry. She waved, motioning for us to join her. Lyman and Mariana returned her greeting, hurrying onto the porch, but Papa caught my hand in his and held me back.

He stood before me, whispering, "Ada, I'm glad you're with me and I don't want to hide my business from you, but be careful. Lyman is a big thinker, always looking for new schemes and drawing in everyone around him. He cheapens the sacred, Ada."

"I know, Papa." Reminiscent of Aunt Harriet's words, Papa's warning surprised me. "But he doesn't draw in Aunt Harriet."

"You're a clever girl, Ada. Harriet has learned just how far Lyman can be trusted, and so have I. Listen to me, girlie—Lyman can be useful as long as you don't put too much faith in him, and as long as you are of use to him." He looked up toward the porch where Lyman and Mariana stood, already in animated conversation with Mrs. Woodruff. Lyman gave him a questioning look and waved for us to join them.

Papa stepped back and we continued up the walk. I thought of Zeviah, a woman I had trusted completely, until the moment she turned us out of her home, innocent victims of her husband's accusations.

I wondered, too, what Papa could mean, bringing me out here with this man I wasn't to trust, this man I couldn't help but want to trust. Regardless of my aunt's and uncle's misgivings, I admired this handsome, smooth-talking Lyman who couldn't be intimidated or even imprisoned. No warning Papa could have given would have ever changed that. My own complicated relationship with Lyman would have to unfold on its own.

Papa squeezed my hand and together we walked up onto the porch. Mrs. Woodruff stood and looked us over, her mouth forming what I took to be a faint frown. Lyman quickly explained, "This is my new caretaker and business associate and his daughter Ada. They are new in New Barker and I thought I would take the opportunity to introduce them around."

"Of course. I met Mr. Powell on his way into town." Mrs. Woodruff nodded, amiably extending her hand to Papa. I recognized her as the woman who had given us directions to Lyman's farm. "Welcome to New Barker, officially."

"Thank you, Mrs. Woodruff." Papa took her hand. I offered an awkward curtsy.

"John here is a gifted dowser, one of the best I've seen, and little Ada has the gift herself, I hear, though I've yet to observe her in action." Lyman patted me on the head, a gesture I'd outgrown. I tried not to take offense, but it stung me. I wanted Lyman to treat me like a young lady as he often did and instead he'd chosen to present me to Mrs. Woodruff as a child.

"My, my. You always find the most wonderful characters, Lyman." Mrs. Woodruff was plainly as charmed as I by Lyman. "New Barker is mighty dull when you're away."

"Why, thank you. It is kind of you to say so, Mrs. Woodruff. Shall we move inside? I would hate for all of you lovely ladies to catch a chill in the evening air."

Lyman opened the front door and motioned us in with a graceful flourish. I tried not to scowl as he took Mariana's hand, escorting her into Mrs. Woodruff's parlor, where a round table stood right in the middle of the room. It struck me as an unusual arrangement for a sitting room, with a single sofa remaining pushed back against the wall. The only other seating consisted of three chairs arranged around the table.

Lyman appeared completely at ease in Mrs. Woodruff's parlor. As he settled himself onto one of the chairs, he chattered on quite warmly. "Mrs. Woodruff is one of my dearest friends here in New Barker."

"Oh, Lyman, you always know how to make a lady feel appreciated," Mrs. Woodruff said. She turned her smile to Mariana.

"Lyman's wife, Katherine, was a very dear friend of mine, you know."

Papa cleared his throat as though he wished to comment but then thought better of it. I watched Mariana to catch her reaction to the casual mention of Lyman's wife, but if she was surprised, she hid it well. Mrs. Woodruff continued, unaware of any shockwaves she may have caused in the room.

"I knew Katherine all my life, since the two of us were little girls. Of course, her health was always delicate. She lost her first husband not long after they wed. She had a hard time after that. Lyman was a true godsend, showing up with his medicine show. I suspect his handsome smile did more to rejuvenate her than did his miracle medicine." Mrs. Woodruff chuckled and patted the back of Lyman's hand resting on the table. "She was fortunate to have found herself such a charming young man."

"It was I who was fortunate. I only wish we could have had more time together." Lyman looked from Mrs. Woodruff to Mariana. The fine lines at the corners of his eyes deepened and for one short moment I could have believed him to be suffering emotional pain, "Sadly, my bride only lived three short months after we wed."

"Ah, yes, well," Mrs. Woodruff began to tear. Lyman offered her his handkerchief and dabbed at his own cheeks with his folded gloves. His eyes looked dry to me, but his pantomime was convincing. "Sometimes even brief miracles can supply a lifetime's worth of happiness."

*****

"You wish to say something, Reverend?" Ada smiled at the shock written across the old man's face.

"Forgive me, Miss Moses, but I am appalled! He married her for her property, yes? To take advantage of a widow is a terrible sin, you must see."

"I cannot disagree with you, Mr. Rigdon, but Lyman possessed few scruples. I can say this for him, though. He is the only man I have ever known to be truly, undeniably charming. If this widow of his believed that he loved her, it is because he never gave her any reason to doubt it. He doted on her, I am certain, every day, every moment, until he killed her."

The prophet gasped. "You can't mean that he murdered the poor woman?"

"I never asked him, of course. He would have considered the question quite rude. But I did come to know Lyman well enough to understand much about him, and yes, I believe he murdered Katherine."

"And this Mrs. Woodruff never knew?"

"Certainly not. If someone had suggested it to her, she would have adamantly denied even the smallest possibility of it. She trusted him completely and felt honored to know him and anyone he called a friend."

"I see why your aunt and uncle wished for you to remain distant from such a man."

"Yes. I have long since learned charisma does not make one a good person. In unworthy hands it can become the most dangerous weapon in the world."

"I suspect you are no longer speaking of Lyman."

"Mr. Rigdon," Ada dabbed at her moist brow as she felt the familiar flush of illness course up her neck and across her face. "If only Lyman were unique. But, as you well know, there have always been men like him just as there have always been decent people who will follow them. Lyman's own story goes far beyond what I can tell here today, but I will promise you a satisfying ending to his tale, at least."

*****

"Such a charming couple you make." Mrs. Woodruff smiled at Mariana and Lyman in their fine attire. "I am always telling Lyman that he should find himself a nice girl and settle down again."

Mariana returned her smile but did not comment. Instead she sighed and reached into her carryall, pulling out a folded wooden contraption that she placed in the middle of the table. Next, with both hands she drew from her bag a glass ball and set it gently atop the expanded wooden structure, which turned out to be a stand designed specifically for the purpose.

Mrs. Woodruff gasped at the sight of the ball and I could understand why. The tinted glass was a deep translucent blue and when it caught the light of the burning lamps just right, it sparkled like the moonlight dances off ocean waves.

"What can I do for you this evening, Mrs. Woodruff?" Mariana started simply, settling herself in the remaining empty chair at the table. She didn't sound at all mystical to me, getting straight to business like that. As Mariana made her small preparations, Lyman stood, indicating that I should take his place at the table. Papa squeezed my hand to stop me. When I hesitated, Lyman took the chair himself. Papa and I seated ourselves on the lone sofa which remained pushed along the wall.

Wide-eyed, Mrs. Woodruff studied the glass ball for a moment before saying, "Tell me something about my future."

Mariana put on a new expression, one clearly belonging to her performance persona. No longer did she appear flushed with wine and frivolity. Instead, her face became masked in intensity, and I recognized the same wildness in her that I saw the day she grasped my arm on the roadside. A shiver traveled up my spine and my limbs tingled as the memory of it.

Drawing a deep breath, Mariana spread her arms wide while leaning her face close to the glass ball, her eyes narrowed in concentration. A few wisps of hair had fallen from the loose knot she wore and lightly brushed the table as she studied the glass.

When she spoke, it was with a hollow tone of voice—ethereal, haunting. I imagined her breath tinged with the sour smell of the wine she had drunk so profusely at supper, but Mrs. Woodruff, captivated, was either unconcerned or failed to notice.

"I see great joy in your future, Madam," Mariana began. "The birth of a grandchild, perhaps?"

Mrs. Woodruff offered no encouragement and so Mariana deftly revised her course.

"I see reconciliation, a misunderstanding overcome. Your son was recently married, I see."

"Yes." Mrs. Woodruff sounded cautiously interested in Mariana's words. Something about them did not sit well with her. Mariana had begun to lose the woman's trust, but there was no question of the fortuneteller's determination and skill.

"You don't wish to talk about this," Mariana said, quite sympathetic. "I don't mean to pry. If you'll but give me a direction you wish to pursue. That is usually how my gift proves most effective."

"No, dear," began Mrs. Woodruff, her voice suddenly weary. "It's just that George—"

"Your son is happily married," I added before I knew what I'd said. Mariana scowled at me. "Though not entirely happy, I'm afraid. Something feels wrong."

"I'll thank you not to interrupt the reading," Mariana snapped.

I shrank back in my seat, ashamed I had trampled on her routine. I didn't know if Mariana was a complete fraud or if she did, in fact, possess a gift for reading fortunes, but I could sense power in the surge of her anger.

Another sensation emerged, overshadowing any concern over my misstep. My stomach churned and I shifted in my seat. Then I felt it, or rather I realized that I was feeling it, that sickening pulling, tugging, tingling. My body responded to some force, the source of which called to me from across the room on the other side of the table. I realized at once that the source was in fact Mrs. Woodruff herself. Agitated, but attentive, Mrs. Woodruff waited for Mariana to continue with the reading.

But it was Lyman who spoke. "Why don't we let the girl have a go? Sometimes the spirits are more willing to speak to the innocent, yes?"

Mariana shifted in her seat, anger flashing across her face, but she remained silent and so I rose from the sofa and approached Mrs. Woodruff. When I reached her, I placed my trembling hand on her arm. As I did so, the sensation retreated.

"Mrs. Woodruff," I said, my small voice infused with fear. "Are you hiding something?"

To my surprise, the woman laughed, shaking her head. "Ada, you are a wonder!" Then she reached into her skirt pocket and withdrew a ring. Gold and diamonds glinted in the dim light. My heartbeat slowed. Once again I felt as normal as I had when we'd first arrived.

"This is my grandmother's ring," Mrs. Woodruff began. "My son knew I'd saved it because I showed it to him when he was young, but when he wanted to give it to that girl, I couldn't bear the thought. I had another one made up, cheaply and with lesser stones. I presented it to him so he could give it to his bride. I just couldn't stand the thought of a family treasure gracing her stubby hand." She frowned. "Do you think I'll ever survive the guilt?"

I studied her face for a moment and smiled, noting that she had become visibly more relaxed as she'd confessed. Mariana took up the cue. "I think you don't need us to tell you what to do. Confession has clearly been good for the soul."

She sighed, "I suppose it has. Reconciliation, you say?"

Mariana nodded and crinkled her nose, flashing a friendly smile in my direction, sweeping away any animosity between us. I had edged in on her demonstration, stolen attention that should have been hers, but she would forgive me.

Mrs. Woodruff chuckled softly, her chins waggling. She looked at Lyman, gestured toward Mariana, and said, "I'd hang on to this one, I think."

Lyman, suave as ever, stood and rested a hand gently on Mariana's shoulder while Mrs. Woodruff looked on approvingly. Next she turned to Papa and said, "And you, sir, have a very special young lady. I imagine she will make quite an impression in New Barker."

And over the years, I did.

17

That was my true debut, there in Mrs. Woodruff's parlor. Papa had glimpsed my natural abilities that predisposed me to a life of deceit, but in many ways it would always be Lyman who gave direction to those more secretive or useful skills. He was something of a talent scout, I suppose you might say.

That was by far his greatest gift and how he stayed mostly clear of the law. He rarely wove together a scheme in which he appeared, at heart, the true villain. Instead, he surrounded himself with more compelling scapegoats: fortune-tellers, healers, hypnotists, mediums or, when no one of genuine ability was available, confidence men with no supernatural abilities whatsoever.

The life of a burner is risky, as I'm sure you must realize. Most are constantly on the move, from one state to another, outrunning a damaged reputation only to build it up again in a new place. That's where a partner is useful—preferably a handsome slick-talking partner who can easily draw in the gullible. Few would have believed Lyman a mystic, even though he played the part beautifully when required. That he knew a mystic, and unquestionably trusted his instincts, well, anyone might accept that. Gentlemen are known to be sometimes drawn to an interest in the mysterious.

Papa's reputation as a gifted healer first brought him to Lyman's attention when the two were young men, both in their early twenties, if I have accurately pieced together the story. However, it was Papa's skill with the rod that most intrigued his new friend. Lyman knew of successful scams in which treasure hunters searched the New England countryside. Tales abounded, and indeed still do, of secret caches hidden away or abandoned through the years by bewildered Indians as Europeans spread across their native lands. One had only to gather a group of devoted investors, keep them interested long enough to bleed them dry, and then vanish.

All Lyman needed was a man with enough skill to convince the marks that the supposed treasure could be found. What Papa needed was a believable gentleman backer. A partnership was born. Papa played his part well. His elfish features and quiet, thoughtful disposition fed well into his intrigue. Lyman brought him an audience and Papa took their money.

This was before Aunt Harriet of course, that great love affair, or so Papa maintained the few times I managed to press him. Long before I knew them, their unlikely marriage severed the partnership and strained the faith between the two men. But that night, when I discovered Mrs. Woodruff's secret, there passed a shared mischievous twinkle in the eyes of the two old friends.

"Lo and behold, Harriet has saved you at last!" Lyman nudged Papa as we strolled through the dark streets of New Barker. "I never could figure out what you saw in the woman, but maybe you're more insightful than I give you credit for."

"Okay, okay." Papa laughed at his friend, but then his mood became more serious. "Ada is still my wife's niece, the only daughter of her only brother. And we can't drug Harriet all the time."

"Can't we?" Mariana asked, giggling.

Lyman smiled, but said, "No, of course we can't, but there must be some way to use this little talent."

I was very tired by this point. I leaned into Papa as we walked and allowed my mind to drift back over the evening and the other times I'd felt the pull of concealed treasures. Perhaps I did have a particular talent—a gift, if you will.

Papa's voice interrupted my thoughts when we reached Lyman's house. "She's a little girl, Lyman. Let her just be a little girl for a while."

But I wasn't a little girl, hadn't been since the moment I watched the life drain from my mother's face and my father abandoned me to the supposed care of my venomous aunt. I did not know it then, but I believe it was during that night, walking with the three of them back to Lyman's house where Aunt Harriet lay harmless in a false sleep, I began to imagine my life when I would be free of her. I grabbed hold of a secret hope. I possessed a unique gift and with guidance, I would learn to wield it.

The next morning I awoke to shouting. I dressed and hurried down the front stairs, hoping there may be some breakfast to be eaten. I gave up on that thought as I crossed the sitting room and heard my aunt's angry words flying from the direction of the kitchen.

"That woman poisoned me! And I know you are responsible for it!"

"Harriet, I assure you, no one has tried to harm you." Lyman's voice was calm and patient. "Yesterday was a long day. You turned in early, overcome by exhaustion."

"I had dreams, you demon."

"Visions, perhaps? What shall we expect? Locusts? Please tell us, oh, prophetess."

"You dare to mock the Almighty!"

"I doubt I'll hurt his feelings much."

"'Talk no more exceedingly proudly; let not arrogance come out of your mouth: for the Lord is a God of knowledge, and by him actions are weighed.'" Aunt Harriet's loud breaths accompanied each syllable. I pictured spit flying from her mouth. Anyone else would have been afraid. Lyman probably should have been. "I will not allow you to infest my family with your evil."

"I wouldn't dream of it. That niece of yours is something special, I can see."

I heard the crash of a dish shattering against a wall. I was sure Lyman was bloodied, maybe unconscious, but I ran into the room to find him smiling at my aunt, broken china on the floor beside him. Aunt Harriet stood with her back to me, her body trembling with angry energy. "Don't even speak of Ada, you vile man. You know nothing of the innocence of youth."

"That is perfectly true. I don't believe any of us is ever truly innocent." He looked straight at me and my aunt turned. She snatched me into her arms so that I partly stumbled under her fierce protective hold.

"The moment John can arrange transportation, we're leaving."

"Be sensible, Harriet. New Barker is a good place, a real fine community. There's a lot of work for a man like John around here. Maybe even work you could approve. Do you have someplace better to go? You've got a child now, after all."

My aunt said nothing, but squeezed me more tightly.

"Mariana and I are setting out this morning. John says she's well enough to travel and we have business to complete. It would be foolish of you to leave now."

"What business?" I asked, wishing I hadn't. Aunt Harriet clapped a wide hand over my mouth, pressing her fingers into my cheek, the side of her index fingers sealing closed my nostrils. I squirmed, struggling for breath, which only encouraged her to tighten her hold. Panicked, I bit hard on the skin at the base of her thumb. She released me with a swift shove toward the door. I fell against the frame, bruising my hip, and drawing a deep, grateful breath.

Without taking a moment to examine me, Harriet turned her attention directly back to her nemesis. Lyman remained calm, his arms crossed and resting against his chest, an amused arch to his eyebrows. His eyes wandered to me. I so wished to see sympathy in them that I can imagine I did.

"My business often requires that I travel."

"I've no doubt it does." Aunt Harriet's tone carried an implied threat. Lyman was to say no more of his business.

"You and John and Ada can stay here for as long as you like. You'll never even see me."

"Why are you doing this, Lyman?"

"I owe your husband much."

"Yes you do. You've always been his downfall. He's been your scapegoat. You are the sole reason we were run out of our last home. You expect me to believe that you would help us because of a sense of gratitude?"

"I can't be dishonest with you, Harriet, which is perhaps why we've never gotten along." Lyman sighed. His next words seemed to be carefully chosen. "John has agreed to help me with a small project. Of the most forthright nature, of course."

"Of course." Aunt Harriet spoke as though she willed her pinched words out of her mouth against a great force. She did not ask Lyman to elaborate and, after a moment, her shoulders sagged in defeat.

Reflecting back, I can see that this was the moment when I began to doubt her sincerity, began to recognize that she and Papa had come to an understanding in which she did not meddle with his dealings no matter how much she may have abhorred them. For his part, he would not interfere with her religion, no matter what hatred it inspired in her.

This made a kind of sense in the context of their marriage, but of course I only began to realize that later, as a grown woman. At the time, the games unfolding around me left me mystified. Often I felt myself caught between an aunt I hated and an uncle I wanted to love.

Perhaps that is why Lyman began to mean so much to me—because he stood up when Papa wouldn't. In him I saw the potential for affection more real than I otherwise knew.

But of course, his friendship was little more than illusion. He was in the middle, too. He had been Papa's business partner and so Aunt Harriet owed him perhaps some small amount of respect and a healthy bit of fear. But his very presence, the type of life he led, the type of man he was, so offended her religious sensibilities that she never quite knew what to do with him. Tolerance is a difficult thing to pair with open hostility. To her credit, Aunt Harriet sometimes managed it.

I cried when Lyman left that morning without a great deal of pomp. He took Mariana with him, a healthy glow upon her cheeks.

They set out in high style. Lyman did everything in high style. Dressed in his comically tall top hat, and a dark-colored benjamin overcoat under which I could just spot a sunshine yellow waistcoat and matching cravat, he mounted the driver's seat atop the carriage. Behind him perched Mariana who had abandoned her turban for the journey, donning instead a black velvet bonnet and a traveling cloak. Just as Mrs. Woodruff had observed, they made an impressive pair, and I must admit to no small amount of jealousy.

18

Lyman kept his word that he would stay away. It was nearly two years before we saw him again. Aunt Harriet and Papa and I settled into farm life. Never quite pleasant and always somewhat unpredictable, life with Aunt Harriet did improve in some ways over those first years in New Barker. Papa had respectable work to keep him busy and we needn't fear being run from our home.

He was not a brilliant farmer, but he was a quick study, and neighbors were generous with their time and knowledge. He forged quick ties, offering his unique brand of aid to them, helping them to witch wells and providing herbal remedies when no doctor was available or trusted.

Meanwhile, the people of New Barker largely viewed Aunt Harriet with suspicion, though rarely open disdain. Not without its share of Godly people, the town boasted few citizens who wore their faith with quite the fervor she did. Still, she performed her Christian duties of attending worship, ministering to those she felt misled, and raising me to fear both her and her god.

Mrs. Woodruff tried to behave as my ally, as did Papa at times, but I fear my aunt had begun to break me. By the time Lyman returned to New Barker, any secret hope I'd harbored that my gift would somehow liberate me had become buried under layers of Scripture and despair.

I spotted the carriage approaching, kicking up swirls of dry summer dust. He pulled to a stop in front just as Aunt Harriet and I rounded the side of the house, having finished hanging laundry to dry in the sun.

"Who on earth?" Aunt Harriet paused, recognition flooding her face, accentuating the lines of her sharp features.

His identity dawned on me more slowly, but as soon as I knew him, I ran toward the carriage, nearly tripping in my haste.

The carriage was itself the most unusual I'd ever seen, the entire back portion draped in a tarp that Lyman pulled back at my approach. There I found a sign, painted in gold letters, taking up the entire side of the wagon:

Dr. Rudolph's Traveling Medicine Show!

Featuring
The newest in medical miracles, straight from
the healing waters of the Nile,

Available for the first time on this continent
Dr. Nassar's Famous Egyptian Remedy!

"Ada!" His smile warmed me, as did his arrival unaccompanied. "You've grown in height and beauty, I see. What do you think of the wagon?"

"What does it mean?" I asked, flustered and breathless.

"I am returning to what I do best—selling cures and restoring hope."

"Peddling poisonous swill, you mean." Aunt Harriet had caught up and now stood, arms crossed, shaking her head at Lyman.

"Harriet. Lovely as ever," he said with a smirk.

"You'll find John in the barn." She grabbed my hand and turned toward the house, looking back over her shoulder at Lyman. "I'm sure you'll want to be on your way soon."

That was all she had to say to the man who'd graciously given us his home to call our own. She made no offer of refreshment, nor did she give him any sign of welcome at all. I caught his eye and tried to convey that I, at least, was pleased to see him, this champion who stood up to my aunt with sharp-tongued wit. That I loved him could come as no surprise. It would be years before I could look beyond the illusion I had created for myself and recognize him as a brute.

Lyman let the tarp fall across the sign. "Good to see you, too, dearest Harriet!"

I walked behind my aunt, my hand still firm in her grasp, but watched Lyman disappear around the side of the house, sauntering toward the barn.

Two hours I spent working alongside Aunt Harriet, kneading dough and setting it to rise before scrubbing at floors while reciting, memorizing, and generally despising the Word of God.

At last satisfied with my work, she handed me a dinner basket with instructions to take it to Papa and Lyman if they could be found. Without hesitation, I walked straight for the barn. The mumble of their voices reached my ears just outside of the small shed built onto the side of the barn that Papa used to store his herbs. I did not knock, but let myself in as quietly as I could.

"What are you doing here, girlie?" His back to me, Papa stood busy at his work table, his hands busy stripping leaves off the limb of a bushy plant.

Lyman, facing the door, leaned against the work surface, his jacket draped over his folded arms.

"Aunt Harriet sent me with dinner for both of you."

"That was surprisingly thoughtful of her." Lyman reached for the basket, which I gladly let him take. "I am rather hungry." He set the basket on the work surface and began to rummage through it.

"Thank you, Ada. Go on back to your aunt now." Papa still hadn't turned to face me. He busied himself pulling various jars and small wooden boxes from the shelves lining the shed—his store of herbs and medicines.

"John, that's too harsh." Lyman smiled at me, pulling salted pork, bread, and cheese from the basket. "Let her stay for a while, see what it is you're up to."

My heart fluttered, anxious as I was to know what the two of them were doing. Papa seemed to have placed nearly all of his stores on the work surface now and had picked up a freshly cut forked branch from the corner of the room. Grasping it in both hands as I had seen him do so many times, he hovered over each ingredient, watching for the bobs of the divining rod. When he got to one that moved the rod, he set it aside.

"What are you doing?" I ventured.

"The master is at work in his laboratory, Miss Ada." Lyman's eyes grew excited as he explained. "The market is ripe just now for something called patent medicine, and John here is making a special healthful brew."

"Dr. Nassar's Famous Egyptian Remedy," I said.

"Exactly. We're going to make a fortune with it."

"What does it do?"

"It restores health, prolongs life, and promotes general good feeling. It's also quite an effective treatment for lumbago and constipation, whatever ails you, really."

"Nothing can do all of that."

Papa grunted. "Better work on the sales pitch, Lyman. Ada's not buying."

Lyman laughed. "She's a particularly discerning customer. With luck, I'll not encounter many of those."

I watched, fascinated, as Papa continued to find the proper ingredients and the amounts he would need of each. This was the method on which Papa always relied when mixing elixirs and healing potions. He knew no definite recipes, something I lament because for all my skill with the rod, this I am unable to duplicate. Though I have a vague notion of which types of natural ingredients made up many of his remedies, I can only guess at the proportions, if they were consistent at all. Papa's unique knowledge of elixirs died the day he did.

As for Dr. Nassar's, which Papa made in large quantities exclusively for Lyman's traveling show, the proclaimed secret ingredient was crocodile oil, purported to be good for your heart and lungs.

I honestly don't know whether crocodile oil can truly boast such powers, but what I can say for certain is that there never was any in Dr. Nassar's concoction. What it did contain was opium, beef fat, camphor, red pepper, mineral oil, and a few other assorted herbs that I doubt ever did anyone much good.

Nor did I know who Dr. Nassar was meant to be, but I supposed the imaginary Dr. Rudolph would be best served by an imaginary partner. My aunt soon pulled me away from the men, greatly displeased by my curiosity.

The two worked the rest of the day, locked away together in the shed. Lyman pulled box after box of brown glass bottles from the wagon, each to be filled by Papa's elixir. They did not come to supper, and Aunt Harriet did not send me to fetch them.

They must also have worked late into the night because by the time I saw Lyman the next morning, he and Papa had already loaded the strangely painted wagon in preparation for Dr. Rudolph's departure.

I begged my aunt to at least let me bid farewell and she grudgingly allowed me to do so after I cleaned up the breakfast dishes. I couldn't stand for Lyman to go when I hadn't seen him in so long.

"Why must you go again so soon?" I asked, running my hand over the gold lettering.

Lyman pulled a knot snug on the ropes that held the stacked cargo in place in the wagon before turning to look at me. He wore his sleeves rolled up to his elbows and his shirt untucked, more casual and disheveled than I'd ever seen him. I was at once both smitten and embarrassed.

If I blushed, Lyman was kind enough to pretend not to notice. He looked me full in the face, his sharp eyes searching me. "Ada, you know I cannot stay here. Harriet would never allow it."

"But it's your house." I sounded like a child.

Lyman smiled and mussed my hair, freeing curls from the loose tie at the back of my head. "It is, but if I stay, then you will have to leave, and you need it far more than I do. You're a special young lady."

I stood straighter, thinking myself taller, wishing myself more grown up. "Will you come back?"

"I may." He frowned. "But I think it best if I don't. At least not for a while."

Papa approached from the house carrying a covered basket. "Harriet sent some food for the road."

"That's twice she's fed me now. She must really be grateful I'm leaving. If she's not careful, I may start to think she likes me." He smirked as he reached for the basket.

"Not sure I'd count on that," Papa said.

As I moved to leave, Lyman caught my arm, "Wait, princess." He leaned toward me and whispered, "I left something for you behind the house. I'm guessing you won't have any trouble finding it. Don't let Harriet get wind of it."

The feel of his warm breath against my cheek as he spoke sent a thrill through me. I wished I could hug him, beg him to take me and Papa with him—a childish wish. Instead I whispered, "Thank you," and returned, teary eyed to the house, hand-in-hand with Papa.

Lyman took his seat, urging the horses forward. Then Papa, Aunt Harriet, and I, strange family that we were, watched in silence as Dr. Rudolph and his medicine wagon disappeared down the road.

Lyman's departure that day is an image that has been forever burned in my mind. Some moments matter profoundly as we grow. Perhaps it is what we choose as significant in our own minds that truly shape us. But I am growing philosophical now. All I really mean to say is that the moment Lyman left was a moment of significance in my life. Had I listened to the warnings of either Papa or my aunt regarding that slick-talking man, my life would have turned out quite differently.

I watched until I lost sight of the wagon and then ran around to the backside of the house, determined to hide my tears. My aunt did not bother to follow me and neither did Papa. They had better things to do than run after a sniveling child. Their indifference afforded me the time I needed to grieve the loss of my friend,whose shady business dealings intrigued me and whose kind words boosted me.

I sprinted across the yard as fast as my legs would carry me, slowing only as I felt the familiar magnetic pull. The sensation directed me to a large oak that stood almost at the back edge of the property in the corner opposite the barn and shed where Papa and Lyman had concocted the Dr. Nassar's elixir. Despite the intensity of my grief at watching Lyman vanish down the road, I had not forgotten his mention of a gift. My heart pounded as I scampered around to the back side of the tree.

It was a good hiding place, large enough to comfortably accommodate reaching arms but facing away from the house and garden just in front of a slight upslope in the ground so few were likely to pass directly by it or notice it if they did. I stretched out on the grass and peered inside, surprised to discover quite a large hollow beneath the otherwise unremarkable tree. Set in almost a foot from the opening, I could see the outline of a white box bound with a ribbon.

Drawing the gift out from the hollow, I loosened the bow and lifted the box flaps to find an envelope with my name written across it in neat letters. The envelope rested on top of a ball made of blue glass similar to the one I had once seen Mariana use. My fingers trembled as I opened the envelope to read the letter it contained:

> My Dear Ada,
>
> What a pleasure it was to see you again. How I wish I could stay and come to know you better. I see so much potential in you. Please do not let Harriet bury it with religious fervor the way she has done to poor John. You see things others miss. Never stop seeing! Maybe this will help, but hide it well. Your aunt will not tolerate finding you with it. Hoping we will meet again before too long!
>
> Lyman

In the midst of a terribly dark life, Lyman served as a shining star and, as I read his letter, something in me awakened, or perhaps it was a reawakening. I would not have an easy, traditional path toward adulthood and it would be up to me to make what I could out of the supplies I had been given which, at this point, were an over-zealous aunt, an uncle of sometimes questionable loyalties, and a crystal ball presented to me by a distant guardian angel.

I tucked the note into a pocket on my dress, stashed the box back under the tree, and turned to the house. I wasn't sure how long I could put off Aunt Harriet, who likely waited to begin my lessons, her patience wearing thin, but I needed to visit Papa first.

He'd just walked from the house toward the shed when I found him. The skin beneath his eyes drooped with fatigue and I wondered if he'd gotten any rest the night before. Papa was certainly not new to late night work, but the strain of his days as a respectable farmer was taking a toll.

He altered his path to meet my approach. "Your aunt is expecting you, girlie. You better go on in."

"I know, Papa. I will, but Lyman left me a note."

His eyes narrowed, his attention sharpened. "What kind of note?"

I pulled the paper from my skirt pocket and held it out to him.

Papa looked at the letter, but did not take it from me. "What's it say?"

I read it to him, leaving out the bit when Lyman implied that Aunt Harriet had stifled Papa's potential in some way.

"What might help? Did he leave you something?"

"A tinted glass ball, like the one Mariana used at Mrs. Woodruff's house." I held my hands cupped, about eight inches apart to indicate the size.

He nodded, "Call it an orb."

"But what do I do with it exactly? Why would Lyman give it to me?"

Papa took a deep breath, apparently mulling over his answer. "How did it feel when that stick moved in your hand, back on that farm in Hartwick?"

"I was surprised." I had been surprised, to be sure, and relieved that I'd discovered some use for a sensation that had long plagued me.

"I don't mean how you reacted. Surprised me, too, girlie. I mean, how did it *feel*?"

Only one word came to my mind. "Heavy," I said. "Really heavy, like the earth pulled at me and I couldn't stop it, like maybe I'd get sucked into it and buried right there on the spot."

Papa nodded encouragement. I added, "And then the stick moved."

"There's what you do with it." He glanced toward the house and then quickly back at me. "There's some folks that feel things other folks never can. You understand?"

I nodded.

"I've been witching most of my life and I'll tell you, the rod never talked for me the way it did for you. I only ever heard one person describe it the way you just did, and that was my grandfather who taught me how to do it.

"He always talked about that heavy pull. The rod works for me, but I never felt that, not like you describe. It was like the old man didn't even need the rod at all. Like that was just for a show."

"But what about this orb?"

Papa smiled and shook his head. "Ada, at Mrs. Woodruff's that night, when you sensed the ring in her pocket, I haven't ever seen anything like that. Did it feel the same way as when you found the water?"

I nodded, remembering the other times I had felt the same sensation at Zeviah's house before I snatched *Manuscript Found* and when searching for the gift Lyman left me.

"Like I said before, my grandfather didn't truly need the rod. It was as if he could sniff out water. He just used the rod because he said people would think he was crazy if he didn't. Lyman thinks you can use the orb for the same purpose. No one wants to believe you can sense their secrets without the aid of some mystical device. That'd make them too nervous and they'd run you off just as fast as they could."

"If I need the orb, though . . ." I was beginning to understand what he was saying to me. Papa was revealing to me a trade secret. He spoke of the delicate line that the truly elegant confidence man had to walk, that line between mysticism and mistrust.

"It sure is a lot flashier than the forked stick. More Lyman's style."

"But it's just a glass ball, then?"

Papa sighed, "A *crystal orb*, girlie. And that witching rod that tried to pull itself out of your hands was just a stick cut out of a cherry tree, too. I don't know, maybe Lyman is on to something." He smiled, wringing his hands together, his excitement mounting.

I wanted to catch hold of his enthusiasm, to make it my own. "What do I do, Papa?"

"Leave that to me. We'll have to practice a little, get it right before we try it for real, but it's never too hard to find the right folks for this sort of thing. I'm sure your old friend Mrs. Woodruff would be pleased enough to help with that. But Lyman was right. Harriet's the real trouble."

Papa rubbed his fingers over his beard, mumbling more to himself than to me. Finally, he looked me square in the face and said,

"Ada, your most important job right now is to study and work hard. Make your aunt a happy woman. Can you do that?"

I wasn't sure I could. My aunt never was a particularly happy woman, but I shrugged and said I'd do my best.

"That's my girl."

What Papa did over the next few weeks, I wasn't entirely sure, but I think he mainly sowed rumors. He'd gained a reputation throughout the county for his talent with the rod. Aunt Harriet did not approve. She considered the use of the divining rod as forbidden by Scripture, but she chose not to fight that battle.

Papa used the connections he made through the various farmers and landowners for whom he provided witching services to find potential customers for me. As he encountered farm wives of the county, he began to subtly mention me, his young niece who had a touch of the gift herself and was said to occasionally see things others could not. What he meant by this exactly, no one knew, including himself, but it was enough to start whispers, which led to curiosities, and added legitimacy to the tale spread by Leah Woodruff.

Now on somewhat better terms with her new daughter-in-law and happily anticipating the arrival of another grandchild, Mrs. Woodruff began leading the ladies of New Barker to me, the youthful seer who could answer all of their questions with her mysterious ways.

For my part, I threw myself into my lessons with a new sense of purpose. Aunt Harriet could not have been more thrilled with my increased receptiveness. In a few months, I had gained a new level of her trust, though time to follow my extracurricular pursuits proved more difficult. Aunt Harriet, too, threw herself with renewed vigor into the life of New Barker, confident that at long last she had set me on the path to righteousness.

She forged closer relationships with the few circuit ministers that came through the community on a rotating basis. With their encouragements she organized a ladies Bible study and aid society to relieve the poor. My newfound zeal brought out the best in Harriet, whose heart, I learned, was not entirely calloused. Her fanaticism, though it isolated her in many ways, also equipped her to serve. Theologically, she was a Calvinist with an unwavering faith in a vengeful and angry God who would sweep over the land with righteous fire at the impending millennium.

Fortunately for me, many of the good people of New Barker still paid her little attention, even those ladies who joined in the aid society and her Bible study. In fact, some of those same women became my best clients. I served by Aunt Harriet's side, spouting her angry prophecies while at the same time engaging my more spiritual side by honing my skills with the orb.

Papa carefully limited my exposure. Still, my business grew. At the high point I had half a dozen clients in and around New Barker for whom I performed a crystal reading on a biweekly basis, and many others who wouldn't dare make an important decision without consulting me. As a teenage girl, I offered the deciding advice on major land purchases, cross-country relocations, and even once on an offer of marriage one local woman was considering.

Through all of this, and even to this day, I can confess that I possess no psychic ability. In fact, as far as I can tell outside of my affinity for treasure-finding, there is nothing about me even remotely supernatural. I cannot speak with spirits, hypnotize a crowd, or heal with incantations, despite Papa's great efforts to teach me. I often find it difficult to believe that to others I might even look the slightest bit transcendental. I inherited height from my father's family I can assume because, as much as it pains me to say, I resemble Aunt Harriet. Perhaps that lends me some sort of otherworldliness.

In those early years, I was just this sad girl, made strange by isolation and by the excessively formal language patterns that leeched into my speech from my intense Biblical study. I think initially people sought me out less for serious spiritual guidance than for entertainment, which gave me time to practice the illusion of my supposed skills. I became in those years a great student of people and of the human condition. I found there were only a few very particular types of personalities that would seek wisdom from one who claimed psychic abilities, and none of them is difficult to manipulate once properly identified.

My customers ranged from the highly superstitious and little educated, who readily believed anything I cared to say, to the curious skeptics out to disprove the existence of the supernatural. The latter, though never entirely satisfied after meeting with me because they had failed to disprove my abilities, did not really ever pose much of a problem as long as they left with their egos stroked and their purses still fat. At Papa's suggestion I only ever accepted payment at the end of a reading if the performance had gone well.

My loyal customers remained satisfied, and easily forgave any mistakes, attributing them to some communication failure of the great unknown or to the inexperience of youth. Some days were better than others.

Through it all, Papa and I managed to keep our side business from Aunt Harriet's watchful eyes due, in no small part, to the fact that as my reputation grew, so too did her notoriety as the town zealot. As such, anyone likely to be familiar with my services, with the notable exception of those few like Mrs. Woodruff who helped to mask my activities, was just as likely to avoid interaction with my aunt.

19

"What you say is true, you know, Miss Moses." The old man's interruption surprised Ada and she fidgeted in the uncomfortable chair. "You do not possess true psychic ability because that would imply an inexplicable origin. Clearly you have been blessed with the gift of divine prophetic revelation."

Ada laughed out loud, stifling a cough. "I appreciate your confidence in me, Mr. Rigdon, but I doubt your God has much to do with my gift."

"But you are misguided. God has revealed in quiet moments that you were to come to me and to be ordained a holy prophetess unto the Children of Zion. For I am the father of Zion in the same way that Abraham was a father to the faithful in ancient times. The Almighty has led you here in the last days. He is gathering together His faithful. You must see that."

Ada sighed and gazed at the aged prophet. "You remind me so of Harriet. Perhaps I was wrong to come here. Whether led by God or not, I want no part of your Zion just as I wanted no part of my aunt's delusions. Thank you for your time, Mr. Rigdon." Ada stood to leave, the manuscript clutched tightly in her hands.

"No, please," the old man attempted to reach forward as if he possessed the strength to physically detain her. "Please stay."

"I will not be converted."

Sidney Rigdon lifted his head, studying her with a disquieting intensity. Her thoughts wandered to Silas Allen, his blood spilled for his final act of apostasy. Ada had been outrunning dangerous theology for nearly her entire life, and she would not suffer an old man's attempts to push her toward it. But at last he spoke.

"Of course, Miss Moses. We all must choose our own fate."

Ada lowered herself into the chair once again. Looking at the man seated across from her, she tried to process her feelings. A cloud hung over her mission here now—a cloud of delusion, pity, and fear.

*****

I couldn't blame the citizens of New Barker for avoiding my aunt, as I would like to have done the same, but she was still very much a part of my daily life. As I grew older, her lessons became more intense. In the year 1840, shortly after I turned seventeen, when many young women think of marriage, of establishing a home of their own, I thought instead of the end of the world.

Aunt Harriet pushed me to study Revelation, a book we had only ventured into a few times before and never with great attention to detail. When I was very young, the imagery had haunted my nightmares. In many ways, it still does.

My aunt must finally have believed me old enough to comprehend the unnerving visions, because she threw herself with great furvor into the eschatological writings in Revelation and later Daniel. And she began to speak to me of the teachings of William Miller. You may recall he was the farmer and amateur mathematician who predicted the end of the world and, in so doing, captivated the imaginations of thousands.

Miller's argument entirely convinced Aunt Harriet of the nearness of the rapture and the end of days. Consumed as she was by this revelation, her determination to preach at anyone who would listen grew to a furious pitch at the approach of the fateful day.

Under Aunt Harriet's tutelage, it is true that I became a great reader with remarkable recall for long passages, but that was not the most valuable lesson she taught me. I have found more usefulness in the manner in which she spoke by manipulating the structure of the conversation in such a way that she could directly quote as much scripture as possible. In this way, her words evoked a supernatural power that communicated an authority beyond mere mortality.

I studied her increasingly for this skill, practicing to develop it in myself for use in my own area of expertise, longing for the day I would escape her.

Of course, I could never accuse my aunt of deliberately affecting others in such a way. That would imply she was much cleverer than I believed her to be. Then again, I have feared few people in my life as much as I feared my beastly aunt, the effect of which was obedience.

"Again!" She shouted as I spoke the words of St. John.

And again, I read:

And he said unto me, "It is done. I am Alpha and Omega, the beginning and the end. I will give unto him that is athirst of the fountain of the water of life freely. He that overcometh shall inherit all things; and I will be his God, and he shall be my son. But the fearful, and the unbelieving, and the abominable, and the murderers, and the whoremongers, and the sorcerers, and idolaters, and all liars, shall have their part in the lake which burneth with fire and brimstone: which is the second death."

My aunt's eyes glazed over when listening to this passage and often her arms reached, involuntarily it seemed, toward the heavens somewhere beyond the kitchen ceiling or the tree tops. Sometimes she lost herself in thought for more than a minute after I reached the end of my reading.

Then, like the crack of a whip, "And what does that mean, Ada?"

By now I knew the response she expected. "The evil people of the earth will be thrown into hell and burned in a lake of fire."

"Not the evil people, Ada." My aunt lowered her voice, bringing her face close to mine, grasping both my hands in hers so that I could not escape the importance of the moment. "The unbelieving people." She paused for effect. "Those who do not accept the truth of Scripture and its meanings on the earth. Those who reject enlightenment, who reject God. Will you be one of those people, Ada? Will you experience a second death in that fiery lake, or will you rise in glory, purified by God's refining power?"

She held me, spellbound, in her searching gaze. My mind raced through several thoughts at once. Obviously I had to respond appropriately to her question or risk her dangerous wrath. What occurred to me even more urgently, however, was that of all the characteristics I shared in common with this woman—my tall lean form, my wide shoulders and saucer-like hands—what I really wanted from her was this power. With just the right words and that fiery tone, she'd managed to mesmerize me with the magnetism of her own fanaticism.

Even as she held me there, her eyes betrayed a sort of distant otherworldliness, some madness washing over her, consuming her. Probably because a part of me feared it would consume me, too, I answered her.

"I am going to rise in glory, Aunt Harriet."

Her frightening lips stretched from ear to ear across her face. I lost all focus on the rest of her and saw only the wide grin overwhelming her expression. Then she did something I never would have expected from her. She clapped her enormous hands rapidly together, giddy with the flush of a new revelation, like a grotesquely overgrown child.

"'I thank thee, O Father, Lord of heaven and earth, because thou hast hid these things from the wise and prudent, and hast revealed them unto babes.' Ada, you make me so happy. In two days there will be a great revival in Nineveh, up the Susquehanna River. William Miller himself will speak, and you will be baptized!"

I had seen many baptisms, often wondering why Aunt Harriet would not encourage me to participate, but then her standards of Christian righteousness always struck me as more particular than others. Until that moment, reading Revelation, she'd not thought me ready.

As a young woman who spent much time in the spiritual realm, I admit, I had no desire for baptism. Perhaps I even feared it, but seeing my aunt so unexpectedly delighted, I readily agreed. Despite her many abuses toward me, I did not wish to begrudge her happiness if I could help it. Not only did her elation offer me the promise of greater opportunity, but also in some very real ways, she was the closest thing I knew to a mother.

And so I basked in her joyful exuberance, allowing her to fawn over me for a time before making my way out of the kitchen across the yard and into the shed where I knew I'd find Papa at work.

"Ada! I thought you'd be at your lessons. Daniel and Revelation today, is it?"

I blinked, surprised. Did Papa and Aunt Harriet discuss my lessons? I rather doubted it. "I think I met the expectations of the day already," I offered. Then I added, "How did you know—"

"What you were studying?" he finished for me. "It's a big house, Ada. Easy to sneak around and hear what you want to hear, yes?"

I had to laugh at his reference to my own habits of eavesdropping, made more difficult now by my size, though I was no less likely to engage in it.

He shrugged. "Harriet loves those books. Ever since she heard that Miller man preach years ago, she's been obsessed with them. She wasn't always like this, you know."

"I know you married her. And you're the wisest man I've ever met."

He didn't speak for a moment. His eyes grew misty. I meant what I said. I mean it still. Without Papa's wisdom and guidance, I could not have become the woman who sits here today. In fact, were he still alive, it would be his wisdom I seek today and no one else's.

"You flatter me, girlie." His eyes met mine as he handed me a stack of herbs and a knife. I began to chop against the wooden table. "So, I imagine we are to attend a camp meeting. Your first?"

"That I know of. What's it like?"

"It's like a feast." His eyes danced.

"A feast?"

"Picture hundreds of people absolutely convinced of the certain truth of their convictions, reveling in the fact that they alone are truly righteous. They may say they've come to learn, but anyone can see that's not true."

"So why are they there?"

"To eat, for one thing. And to celebrate. To steal a few days from working and to be surrounded by likeminded people. To delight in not having to defend their religious fervor for just a little while. Really I don't know how your aunt does it most of the time. I'm exhausted watching her." He leaned across the table and met my eyes again. "People come to the revival to let their guard down."

I understood well his meaning. People with a tendency toward religious fervor, gathered together and relaxed their inhibitions. "You're going, too, then?"

A knowing smile crossed his face. We were of one mind. "I wouldn't miss it."

"I'm getting baptized," I blurted. I'd been holding back that information, wondering if he'd be disappointed in me. Perhaps my willingness to participate in baptism meant that I was one of the foolish crowd, ripe for the picking by a clever huckster. "Just to make Aunt Harriet happy. I don't believe in it or anything."

"Belief in itself is never a bad thing, Ada, and a little religious ceremony never hurt anyone." His voice contained so much. I had trouble understanding his meaning, though he apparently thought we shared a great secret.

"Have you done it, then?"

"What, Christian Baptism?" He laughed when he said this. "Oh, I don't think I'm the sort they want. But you go ahead, girlie. Maybe something good'll come of it for you."

"Don't you believe in it, then?" All I had heard, it seemed, since coming to live with my aunt was God's plan of salvation through Christ and about how all the truths anyone ever need know were bound up in the Holy Bible. That dusty old book contained, according to Aunt Harriet, countless secrets locked up in its old language, revealed only to the most deserving. Papa's belief system proved more elusive and, in fact, I had never given it a great deal of thought, assuming that he mustn't have either.

I could see now that I had been wrong about that. Papa's respect for the belief of others was not merely a façade, and I began to wonder to what exactly he chose to cling. He lived with Aunt Harriet so could not escape the influence of her Christian fanaticism, his understanding of which made up only a small part of his system of belief. Like me, Papa faithfully studied the human condition. I had often felt his curious eyes on me and wondered what he thought about me in those moments. Still, I had never considered that his deepest interest in the beliefs of others might have less to do with how he could take advantage of them, than with how it might inform his own understanding of the greater world.

Genuine intrigue lined his sun-worn face as he studied me, taking a minute or two to consider, it seemed, how he would answer my question. Finally, he rubbed his dirty palms on his pant legs and leaned against the table. "What I believe, Ada, doesn't make a difference in what's true and what isn't."

20

As the gathering at Nineveh would be my first experience with a camp meeting, I didn't know what to expect, and though I have attended many since, none has ever quite compared to my first.

I'd simply never seen so many people gathered in one place before. And all kinds of people, too—old men and women, young children, some of whom laughed and played while others remained still and attentive by their parents' sides. Most attired in working clothes, others were ladies in fine dresses, too, and gentlemen whose appearance made them shine like diamonds in the dirt. I saw many colored men, women and children as well, each person as happy as the next to be there.

Men set up canvas tents. Women tended fires. The aroma of food wafted from every direction. Small groups, maybe long-time friends but just as easily new acquaintances, laughed together. Others argued, loudly, generally without malice, urged on by small audiences. My favorite groups were the singers gathered around fire pits. One person hummed a melody, and the others joined with their various harmonies until the parts of the hymn came together and the singing swelled.

It's a special place, the camp meeting. Everyone loosens, allows himself the space to stretch out and feel at ease. There's a power in it, far beyond the preaching and praising. Pull all those people together in one purpose, of one mind, and suddenly the world of the camp opens one up to all kinds of new possibilities. That's the purpose: the feverish, joyful, ecstasy of revival ensnares even the most graceful of ladies and the most proper of gentlemen.

Papa found a good location to set up our camp. As he pounded wooden stakes into the ground and fussed with the canvas, Aunt Harriet and I gathered kindling. Before long, our site felt almost like a home, and the three of us relaxed around a modest fire, the aroma of our roasting rabbit mingling with delicious smells floating through the air from neighboring campsites.

As the nighttime settled in around us, I expected to retire to bed on a makeshift mat in our little canvas tent. Instead, Aunt Harriet surprised me by grabbing my hand and leading me away from our campsite toward the middle of the celebrating throng until we reached the very center. There we found rows and rows of wooden benches facing a raised platform. Between the front line of benches and the platform remained a wide empty space, guarded by a hip-high wooden barrier.

Hundreds of people moved through the bleachers, rustling about as they settled into the seats. We followed along, climbing to the very top before finding space only a few minutes before the first speaker took his place on the ground below.

A seemingly coordinated hush fell over the crowd as a preacher, whose name I can't recall, launched into an enthusiastic sermon on the enormous mistake we would be making if we were to, for even one moment, misunderstand the absolute torture that is Hell.

Actually, I think that might sum up nearly all of the preaching I heard during the many days of the revival. The words changed, as did the faces of the preachers, all with slightly different backgrounds, affiliations, and theologies. The only thing that never varied was that they were all convinced that Hell was not a place one would wish to go, and I saw no reason to disagree with them.

Though most of the specific sermons have not endured in my memory, the ecstasy that accompanied the meeting has. It began with those simple hymns, the ones that repeat the same phrase over and over so that one need not think hard in order to join in. Words like "I am bound for the Kingdom; Hallelujah, Praise the Lord!" or "On Jordan's stormy banks I stand; I am bound for the Promised Land!"

I remember these not because they were so compelling or moving to me, but because they frightened me or, more precisely, the response they elicited frightened me. After each sermon, throngs of penitent souls marched forward in a communal trance, swaying to the nearly wordless tunes until they reached the empty space beyond the barrier.

There they convulsed and threw themselves to the ground until the whole group of them formed one pulsating pile of moaning, wailing, shrieking bodies. For hours this lasted—women, red-faced and raw from lying prostrate on the earth, shouted phrases eerily echoing the choruses the rest of us sang.

Aunt Harriet and I finally walked back toward our campsite well after midnight that first night. For hours I had stood by her side on a narrow wooden plank, my arms raised in sanctimonious worship, my muscles aching with exhaustion. In contrast, Aunt Harriet appeared radiant. We passed tent after tent from which issued the sounds of continued worship and fervent prayer and I watched her reactions, fearing I would be made to stop.

At last she turned to me with a look of wild fire in her eyes. "Ada, can you find your own way back? I feel compelled to stay here for a while." We weren't far now from our tent, and all I wanted to do was to sleep and try to block out the images of the convulsing worshippers. I also understood very well what she meant—the sensation of needing to respond to a stimulus, to follow its urgings. I nodded, grateful she hadn't insisted I remain with her.

She spun on the spot without another word and disappeared into a nearby crowd gathered at the outside of a large tent from which drifted numerous hallelujahs and amens.

I continued my walk to our campsite, about to fall prostrate myself but not for the purpose of worship. As I approached our tent, a campfire, still crackling even at the late hour, caught my attention. The flames danced, some distance beyond any tents, surrounded by six or seven shadowy figures. As I moved closer to it, I began to make out some of the features of the figures, both men and women, with bowed heads, mumbling some incomprehensible words, and then I realized that Papa was among them. He mumbled, too, but more loudly than the others, and he held his head upright. In fact, that is how he held his entire body. Normally somewhat bent, now he sat on the dusty ground, with his upper body perfectly erect, his clear eyes wide open and focused on the center of the fire.

"Papa." I approached him cautiously, speaking in a whisper. I thought it best to alert him to my presence without disturbing the others. A familiar scene to me, this trancelike capnomancy was

Papa's favorite method of gathering signs from the spirits. Privately he admitted to me that in his experience, it had always proven more showy than reliable.

Papa smiled and beckoned me to him. I leaned close to his bearded cheek. "What's going on?"

He didn't answer my question, instead mumbling, "Where's your aunt?"

"She stopped at some crowded tent on our way back. Sounded like an all night church meeting. I doubt she'll be back anytime soon."

He sighed in obvious relief. Then I noticed a young man, probably only a few years older than I, stretched out on a blanket on the ground between Papa and the fire.

"Who is that?" I asked, forgetting my fatigue.

"Ah," Papa said, his eyes shining with excitement. "That is a young man who found himself overwhelmed by the spirit earlier this evening, speaking in tongues and convulsing. All of that was fine, you see, but then he got violent, shrieking obscenities and attacking his companions."

"So why is he here?"

"Because I was in the right place at the right time to convince his family that I could help."

"And can you?"

He shrugged. "I've given the whole lot of them plenty of soothing tea to calm them. The young man first, a larger dose of course. Then I put them all in a hypnotic trance. I mumbled a few holy-sounding words and they picked up the chant. The whole lot of them will wake up a little stiff and confused in the morning, but the incident will be well behind them."

"And you charged a good price for your services?"

"Healing never comes cheap at a camp meeting, girlie." As he spoke, he stood and stretched. "How was the preaching?"

"Disturbing."

Papa laughed. "These traveling preachers. They stir everyone up into a frenzy until they're ready to devour them. Too much hard work, if you ask me. I'll take their scraps, though." He looked back at the fire where the family still chanted. One woman had now slumped over onto the shoulder of the man next to her, asleep.

"There's nothing more to be done here tonight. Let's get some sleep. Morning comes early at a camp meeting."

I followed Papa back to our tent. Tired as I was, I doubted I would sleep. One of these sadistic preachers would dunk me in the river at some point in the next few days, and I wasn't convinced I would ever come up for air.

"Are you sure you should just leave them there like that? Will they be safe?"

"Can't think about what should be done, Ada. Trust me, that's a road you don't want to go down. They'll be fine by morning. And with any luck, they won't remember much."

We awoke the next morning to a bugle call. Aunt Harriet had arrived in the tent at some point in the night because she was there, still fully dressed and curled next to Papa. She rose bleary-eyed but happy and fetched together a simple breakfast of rough bread and jam before rushing me toward the preacher's circle again for a morning sermon. Papa stayed behind, though I knew he would be on his way soon, circling the crowd, a watchful vulture.

The camp meeting gave me the impression of a circus, where everyone was delighted to be there even though it was dirty and crowded and one could find any sort of character if he searched hard enough. The excitement of the affair bubbled up inside of me, but at the same time I grew frightened of the grotesque piles of writhing bodies in ecstatic convulsions—a large, Christian orgy.

Equally strange were the exorcisms, which turned out to be Papa's specialty. Almost every night he could be found among a group of wailing and chanting people, sharing with them his· "gift of healing"—for a small donation to his ministry, of course—and then slipping into the crowd.

Aunt Harriet managed to disappear night after night into some tent or other for furious worship and Bible study. Thankfully she still considered it inappropriate for me, a young unmarried lady, to be out too late. I wasn't sure my aunt was entirely comfortable sending me back to the tent alone either, but the draw of the religious throng was too much for her to resist and, I suspected, she could not bring herself to face the truth of Papa's routine. More than once it occurred to me that I should have brought my orb.

There were whispers of other seers at the camp practicing hydromancy as darkness fell over the baptizing waters of the Susquehanna. I wanted to see them at their work, learn their secrets, but Papa insisted I resist the temptation, convinced that to implicate myself with dark practices at the revival, if discovered by my aunt, might endanger the business we had so carefully built together in New Barker. Instead, I would have to be content with distant observations of Papa at work.

I never knew if Aunt Harriet truly believed that if she ignored his dealings—the ways he found to supplement their living—that she could never be implicated in his sins, or if she suspected that her god would call her to confront her husband at the right time to really convict him and win his soul. Either way, I both appreciated that she left Papa to his own business and thought her a coward for her inaction.

There is no question, looking back, that I never truly understood Aunt Harriet and what drove her until the third afternoon of the revival at Nineveh, when William Miller took to the pulpit.

Aunt Harriet quaked with excitement as we made our way toward the speaking circle and found places on the women's benches, only a few rows back from the anxious seats. Papa disappeared, as always, into the outskirts of the crowd, to watch unseen and to scan the swollen mob, searching for an easy mark.

The singing started with just a few voices at first, and soon the whole clearing filled with simple melodious praises to God. Aunt Harriet always sang loudly, but on that particular afternoon, her voice stood out as never before, above all the others, her mouth open as wide as the heavens with which she conversed. Her head swayed back and forth as she lost herself in worship, her palms uplifted to the sky.

Next to her, I quietly sang along, watching her hypnotic motion. She closed her eyes. Teardrops trembled on her eyelashes. I'm not sure when I first noticed it, but at some point she had ceased using the now familiar words of the praise chorus and instead belted out clearly formed words in a language I did not recognize.

The chorus ended, and the preacher took the stage motioning for the congregation to sit. Aunt Harriet remained standing, singing, more quietly than before, the same simple tune. More and more strange words poured from her mouth, more and more worshippers turning to watch her with rapt attention.

I scooted away from her, the few inches I could manage on the crowded bench, and tried to melt into the faces of the gathered. A man pushed into the seating area, gently taking my aunt by the elbow to lead her to the anxious seats. Once there she fell prostrate, and I noticed for the first time that she was not alone. At least five other women and one exceptionally petite man had also become overwhelmed during the singing.

The preacher smiled his approval at them and began his long sermon on the imminent end of the world. I did not take my eyes off my aunt, broken under the stress of little sleep and too much religion. Still I listened to the words that poured out from the preacher. I have since revisited the sermons of William Miller, those popular enough to have found their way into print, and I have pieced together his words that had such a profound effect on my life.

> *See, see! the heavens to shake! the clouds, the light, the air, are trembling yet…And yet the light rolls on, the clouds grow brighter, and the rays diverge from yonder point. An eye! An eye! How like the All-seeing Eye! I will not tremble yet.*

The gathering of the anxious grew as he spoke, and a low mumble rose from them, the same strange language I was unable to identify, now swelled with many voices speaking in unison as Aunt Harriet and the rest of the overcome rolled blindly across the dusty ground.

> *Another sound! A dreadful blast, a hundred-fold more loud than former trumpets! This shakes my soul; my courage, too, has fled. What bit a Gabriel's trump could give such sounds—so loud, so long, so clear?*

The words bounced around inside my head and mixed with the otherworldly tongue of the anxious. I was trapped, both penned in by the crowds around me, but also suffocating in my own confusion. Aunt Harriet, whatever she had been—quick-tempered and dangerous—always displayed some logic, no matter how warped, in her actions. Yet here she writhed, on the ground before me, sobbing and beginning to shake. First just her hands and feet, but then her whole large frame began to tremble, tapping out the strange rhythm of the mumbled chant.

I could see the blood then, a vision from my childhood. That was the only time I can recall truly associating Aunt Harriet with feelings reserved for my own mother, though it would have displeased her greatly to know it. The red fluid swam before my eyes, my aunt drowning in the blood of Christ, submitting completely to it, beyond reason, beyond consciousness, as my mother had submitted to death. All the while the preaching grew more furious with increasingly terrifying imagery.

And, O my soul, what do I see? A great white throne, and One upon it. His garment is whiter than the driven snow, and the hair of his head is like pure wool. See fiery flames issuing from his throne, rolling down the vault of heaven like wheels of burning fire.

The anxious rose, Aunt Harriet with them, and slowly they pushed their way, moving both with and against one another as their eyes remained closed. I felt the crowd around me begin to push, too, the momentum building until the whole throng surged from the benches beyond the preaching circle, past the ring of tents, circled wagons, and tied horses. The anxious continued their chant as others in the crowd picked up the praise melody again. Above them all, I could hear the preacher, his voice unnaturally magnified among the chaos of the moving crowd.

The earth now heaves a sob for the last time, and in this great throe her bowels burst, and from her spring a thousand thousand, and ten thousand times ten thousand immortal beings into active life. And then those few who had looked on the scene with patient hope, were suddenly transformed, from age to youth, from mortal to immortal; and thus they stood, a bright and shining band, all clothed in white, like the great throne which yet appeared in heaven.

At long last, the pulsating crowd stopped moving forward. We had reached our collective destination at the river's edge. This, I sensed, was a moment to dread, but one from which I could not escape. I heard the splashing, the wailing, and the fervent prayers and knew my time would soon be upon me. Even so, it startled me when Aunt Harriet appeared beside me, with tear-streaked cheeks, recovered from her spiritual seizure.

She gripped my elbow and pulled me toward the water where a man in just trousers and shirt with no overcoat stood in the shallow river. She walked me to him. He took my other arm and, with Harriet's help, pulled me into a deeper portion of the river where the water flowed more swiftly.

My skirt clung to me and I shivered. I offered no resistance to my escorts. Then before I was expecting it, two large hands belonging to the coatless man pushed my head down toward the water. I closed my eyes tight and, I am not afraid to admit now, screamed some very unchristian words in my mind. When I broke the surface again, I shouted in relief and then found myself immediately dunked again, with a mouth full of river water.

By my third trip into the river, I'd managed to prepare myslf and submitted easily so that I was allowed to rise again on my own with only a hand on my arm for support. And so I rose Ada Moses, drawn up out of the waters of baptism, filled with righteous anger against the god to whom I'd just publicly submitted.

21

Ada sat back in her chair, exhausted from the memory she had shared and curious how the prophet would receive the news of her baptism. Perhaps it would be a relief to him as it had been to her aunt, or perhaps he would find it offensive that she could have received Christian baptism and yet expressed no true faith. To her surprise, he appeared disinclined to comment and only pondered over her story.

Disappointed, she breathed deeply and continued, "1844 was a big year for both of us, Mr. Rigdon. A prophet murdered, his church divided, and according to the calculations of Mr. William Miller, time itself drew to a close."

*****

I was 21 in the fall of that year, a woman grown, washed in the waters of baptism, and making good money as a seer. Still, I hid my earnings, along with my glass orb and a few treasures I'd chosen to keep along the way, and wondered when I would strike out on my own. A part of me wanted to make my own way in the world. Papa encouraged me to do so, but I could not yet bring myself to leave him.

I had only a vague notion of what life might hold for me away from New Barker and my childhood tormentor. My aunt had a much clearer picture of my future, though I did not know it at the time.

Have you ever watched anyone go mad, Mr. Rigdon? It's a quieter process than I would have imagined, a slow, steady increase in unusual behaviors starting with the silent withdrawal from those things which mattered absolutely before and then cease to matter at all.

That's the way Aunt Harriet's mind slipped. Since the moment I submitted to baptism, I believe she saw me as an adult. Her anger still swelled at times, but her expectations of me changed. Rarely did she call me to study anymore, and when she did it was only to pore over a passage I already knew well. She addressed me at those times almost as an equal, seemingly eager to hear my thoughts as I listened to the words spring from her lips, but then never really wanting me to offer my own opinions at all. I served instead as a sounding board for her disturbed thoughts.

I became concerned less because of my observations of her unusual behavior than because of the unique insight with which I have been blessed. I have called myself a discoverer of treasure, though maybe that is not precisely the right way to describe the scope of my gift.

I do have a strong reaction to the intentionally hidden around me. I know, for instance, Mr. Rigdon, that you keep a copy of the manuscript I hold, tucked away in the roll top desk in the corner of this very room. That is bold, I must say. You must have had that in your possession for many years, yet you have never revealed it. Nor have you destroyed it.

That decision—or rather that indecision—speaks volumes, Mr. Rigdon. Is it the action of a man who does not fear being caught in a deception? Or are you afraid, I wonder, that if you let it go, you might deceive even yourself?

But as I was saying, my aunt's sanity, such as it was, slipped by tiny increments, and though I did not at first see them, I felt every one. In the same way that I am drawn to secrets, I felt an increasingly intense physical need to retreat from my aunt, as if she repelled me with a growing, invisible force. That, more than anything, is the reason I stayed. I could not leave Papa, and he would not come with me. My greatest regret is that I could not convince him.

I should have tried harder to make him understand. Looking back, I realized he must have sensed the change in her, too. He chose to rent out the farmland for the first time in many years and though he still practiced his healing arts and brewed his elixirs, he rarely strayed far from the house as the fall settled in that year.

Had it not been for the constant ominous feeling, I might have thought Aunt Harriet much improved the morning of October 23rd. Happier than I'd seen her for a long time, her wide lips curled into a scarecrow smile as she prepared breakfast. She wore a white gown, simple as always, but crisp and fresh in a way her clothes usually were not. She had bid me sew a new white dress for myself as well and I wore it to please her.

I knew the occasion, of course. This was the day the world would end. I might even have believed it, given the dreadful tugging at my gut warning me of danger. As Aunt Harriet set about her daily tasks, scrubbing and dusting away dirt no human eyes could have seen, I watched, silent. And I listened to her mumble as she worked, oblivious to my presence.

"The son of man shall send forth his angels, and they shall gather out of his Kingdom all things that offend, and them which do iniquity. And shall cast them into a furnace of fire: there shall be wailing and gnashing of teeth. Then shall the righteous shine forth as the sun in the Kingdom of their Father."

She rushed from room to room, throwing back curtains to let in the fall sunshine, straightening and polishing as she went, in a kind of frenzied trance. Her eyes focused not on her task, but on some distant and invisible point. It was the strangest behavior I had ever witnessed. I couldn't tear my attention from her.

"The Heavens and the Earth are kept in store, reserved unto fire against the Day of Judgment and perdition of ungodly men. But the day of the Lord will come as a thief in the night; in which the Heavens shall pass away with great noise, and the elements shall melt with fervent heat, the Earth also, and the works that are therein shall be burned up."

All day, I followed her. Papa left. I knew not where he went. I had seen the pain written upon his face and couldn't blame him for going. He had loved her once, I knew. I didn't understand, but I knew. And he loved her still. It broke his heart to see her in this state the way I hoped it had destroyed my father to watch my mother's life slip away.

So I stayed because if he could not, I would. I worked alongside her, as I had always done, until every inch of Lyman's house—our house that had felt almost like a home—was polished to a shine and put into perfect order. The sky grew dark and the house took on a chill. Aunt Harriet, grimy from her hard work, turned her eyes toward me, seeming to see me for the first time that day.

"Ada," she said in a sweet voice that struck me as false. "There is a chill in the house. Would you be an angel and build the fire in the sitting room? I think I need to rest for a moment."

"Yes, Aunt Harriet." I walked through the kitchen and out the back door to the high stack of firewood, selecting several pieces. The bark caught on the fabric of my new dress as I shuffled the logs in my arms. I looked over to the shed to see the flicker of a lamp. I thought then that I might call to Papa, report on my aunt's strange behavior, but I did not. If he wanted to know, he would come into the house.

When I returned to the sitting room I knew something was wrong because my legs resisted carrying me into the room. That was the first thing I noticed—the heaviness in my limbs. The next was the smell of kerosene.

Then she grabbed me.

My aunt and I were of similar height and build, but her attack caught me surprised. I could not defend myself against her violent grasp. Her deranged state had served to increase her already freakish strength. She forced me onto the floor, releasing my arms as she pressed her knees into my chest, pinning me in place.

"What are you doing?" I tried to force calm into my voice, though my words were surely tinged by the panic I felt.

"Can you recite Leviticus 20, Ada?"

I knew much of Leviticus, but my mind had emptied of all except dread.

When I did not respond, Aunt Harriet pressed on, her voice eerily calm. "Leviticus 20:6 says: 'the soul that turneth after such as have familiar spirits, and after wizards, to go a whoring after them, I will even set my face against that soul, and will cut him off from among his people.'"

I felt the pounding of my heart under the weight of Aunt Harriet. She smiled at me. I knew she could feel my fear. She savored it.

"Did you think I did not know? That I could not see you and John, scheming right in front of me?" She lifted her eyes toward the ceiling, her balance shifting on my chest. I thought for an instant that I might throw her off, but before I could try, she looked back down, this time leaning lower and pinning my wrists to the floor with her hands. When I met her gaze, I was astonished to see that she was crying, and it stilled me.

"God has given you many gifts. I should have done more to protect you, Ada. I'm sorry I failed you. It is the Day of Judgment and I will atone for my sins. God will 'thoroughly purge his floor, and will gather the wheat into His garner; but the chaff he will burn with fire unquenchable.'

"He will not allow you to suffer the fires of Hell, you innocent child who has risen from the waters of baptism. He will 'burn away the chaff and gather you to Himself in glory. And God shall wipe away all the tears from your eyes; and there shall be no more death, neither sorrow, nor crying, neither shall there be any more pain: for the former things are passed away.'"

As she spoke these words from Revelation, Aunt Harriet released one of my arms and reached to something on the floor next to me. Drawing her arm back up high over her head, I only just recognized what she held before she let the dense log drop.

I woke with a searing pain in my head. I saw only blackness and struggled to find my breath. With each attempt I could hear the strained, rumbling sound of my inhale forcing itself past damaged tissues. My skin screamed in agony, and I felt my flesh as it scraped against the littered floor. I was vaguely aware that I was being dragged and then the air grew cold. My hip bumped something—a doorway perhaps—and then my memory is blank again.

When I regained consciousness the second time, what I remember feeling is wetness. I awoke drenched, in fact, and lying in a muddy puddle of cold water. I was not panicked, though the sounds around me were. Shouts filled the night air, as did the roar of a raging fire and the crash of a building unable to stand. Next I heard him whispering.

It was faint, very faint, but as I focused on the words, the rest faded into the background and I heard only Papa's soft utterings:

"'…there lay St. Laurence on a fire grate. Came to help and comfort him; He lifted up his divine hand and blessed it, the fire; He signified that it must burn no deeper and eat no further round about. So blessed be the fire in the name of God the Father, the Son, and the Holy Ghost.' Amen."

"No!" I tried to yell and threw myself toward him along the ground, managing to roll to firmer, dryer earth. At my movement the pain soared to new heights, coursing through my body like the flames even then destroying our home. I knew somewhere in my mind he was trying to help, but I could not stand for him to call upon the same name that had plunged me into the river and caused my aunt and so many like her to lose their minds, to relinquish control of their bodies.

I would not lose control. I would not submit to a god who would take the lifeblood of a young mother and throw her child to his wolves. I writhed on the muddy ground, trying to break free from the demons closing in on me.

Papa enfolded me in his arms to prevent my continued movement. His touch comforted me even as my charred flesh screamed in agony. I would not be still.

"Stop it, girlie!"

I willed my movement to slow and listened. His words carried with them the edge of danger they had the first night I met him when he pulled me from the woods, a scared runaway. There was something else now, too, in the tone of his voice—a terrible, unnatural gruffness that caused me to pause and to think not of myself, but of him. Fear gripped my heart and I focused my eyes on him, seeing him, seeing anything, really, for the first time since I'd regained consciousness.

His face was red and wet with blood that seeped from beneath badly charred skin, his beard black with soot and burned away completely in large patches. His suit hung on him in blackened rags, and I couldn't imagine how he had managed to speak at all as I listened to his labored, rasping breaths.

My own lungs felt heavy, my breathing slow. I knew in my heart, however, that it was not for myself I should fear. I let him hold me and, as I calmed and his grip loosened, I wrapped my arms instead around him, letting him rest the weight of his upper body against me.

We remained there on the ground for what must have been hours. Someone brought us blankets and water to drink. Papa swallowed little, choking with the pain of the effort.

At some point in time, the town doctor arrived and tried to convince us to leave with him, someplace we could rest, he said, and recover. Papa refused. He mistrusted doctors. Always said he'd seen them kill too many people.

I hoped he would at least take the medicine the physician offered, but he became more agitated at my suggestion, so to keep things as peaceful as possible for him, I refused it, too. If I could have offered him some of his own remedies, perhaps it would have helped, but as much as I had tried to learn from him, healing had never been my gift. That was always his. I couldn't recall what he had used for burns, but that wasn't his most immediate problem anyway.

He couldn't breathe without an immense effort and I feared that if he fell asleep, he might simply stop. He'd taught me that the cure for most breathing problems was found in the musk of a skunk, but I couldn't have harvested any even if I had known how. The skeletal remains of Papa's burned shed were revealed by early dawn light. Any healing stores he may have had on hand had long since turned to ash.

With little hope, I began to whisper the words he'd said over me, adding my own to them, focusing entirely upon Papa, blocking out the terrible scene around me. From him, I'd learned healing was less about reciting the right incantations than expressing true emotions. I envisioned him whole and well again, picturing the precise look of his eyes in those shared moments in which I'd been his daughter in every way that mattered.

Aunt Harriet's Bible insists that the gift of healing comes from God and is given to only some. I recognized truth in St. Paul's claim, but if God was merciful—and I was by no means convinced He was—then I knew He could grant me that gift in my moment of need.

And so I uttered that night undoubtedly the most genuine prayer ever to pass my lips. I fervently begged for healing in the name of the Father, the Son, and the Holy Ghost, for whom I had no love. Perhaps the outcome would have been different if I had studied Papa's methods more diligently, or if I had been more worthy of speaking to God at all.

Hatred washed over me as I watched him slip away—anger at him for dying and for not teaching me how to save him, anger at myself for proving a hopeless student of his healing arts. And most of all, anger at the god who would let him die when he had given himself to pull me from death's edge. This was the same god who had inspired the insanity that bound me in the hands of my aunt as she sought to destroy the world's sin with fire, and who had taken my mother from me when I was so young that I found myself here, on this scorched ground, staring up at the ashen remains of all that had come to mean anything to me.

Papa died cradled in my arms. As I had feared, he went to sleep and his body failed to make the effort at breath. I would have died with him. Such was the intensity of my grief. Once again, God proved unmerciful.

22

I can't remember if I cried then or if the tears all came later. After a time I allowed myself to be led away. By then the fire had long since burned out with little of the house still standing and what was left blackened beyond recognition.

Mrs. Woodruff, that dear lady who had launched my clandestine career, finally managed to collect me. She took me to her own home and dressed my burned arms and legs with some salve I'm sure would have made Papa scowl, but I did not resist.

The doctor arrived shortly after ordering strict instructions for rest and a laudanum regimen to soothe my nerves and promote healing. Dulled as my senses remained, the full weight of my grief didn't descend on me until more than a month later when Mrs. Woodruff finally called me back amongst the living.

She helped me dress. I recall standing in front of the window glass to inspect my appearance. I wore a long sleeve dress designed to be snug at the waist. Thankfully it hung loosely on me, barely brushing my most damaged skin. A delicate lacy trim graced the collar that struck me as so out of place against my plain visage that I might have laughed had I not been heartsick.

"I thought the sleeves might be good for covering your scars." Mrs. Woodruff, normally boisterous and overbearing, spoke gently, apologetically. I believe she thought I might shatter if she raised her voice above a whisper. In truth, I might have. For the second time in my life, I found myself in the position of having no family to call my own. Though I had no illusions about their faults, Papa and Aunt Harriet had been of central importance in my life and I had depended on them.

"Such a shame." Mrs. Woodruff clucked as she fussed about me, adjusting my borrowed dress that must have belonged to one of her own daughters before they married.

I studied the embroidered flower pattern on the long skirt and took little notice of the plump woman as she rattled on. Old fashioned as I knew it was, the dress was still the prettiest thing I had worn in many years.

Mrs. Woodruff tied a limp ribbon around my waist and stood to look at me. "You are such a pretty young lady." She smiled as she spoke. "With your fair skin and sandy curls, you'll catch the eye of a fine husband. I can tell. I always thought it was unfortunate your aunt hid you in that awful, rough homespun." As soon as she'd spoken the words, she gasped and brought her hands to her mouth, shaking her head. "Oh, Ada, forgive me. That was a horrible thing to say at such a time."

"No. There is nothing to forgive. My aunt never spared a thought for outward appearance. She possessed far worse qualities than that," I whispered as I stared at the faint image of myself in the glass. I pondered Mrs. Woodruff's words. I'd never considered that I might be pretty. My mother had been. At least I remembered her that way, but then I suppose all little girls think their mothers are beautiful.

My coloring came from my father and I had been beginning to think I resembled Aunt Harriet. Standing there in Mrs. Woodruff's home, in a much more fashionable dress than I would normally have been allowed to wear, I assessed my tall, lean figure. I stood straighter, conscious of my breasts and hips. There was still a youthful fullness in my cheeks. I tried to imagine Aunt Harriet at my age and it struck me that perhaps I had been unfair to think her strictly homely. There had been a certain beauty to her, as there might have yet been to me.

I took great comfort in that realization. Once again alone in the world, I was not entirely helpless. I did not have to rely on God to deliver me into caring hands. I could care for myself and seek out the company I wanted rather than what others assigned to me. I would no longer have to try to craft a parent from an unworthy or unreliable substitute. I was Ada Moses, passably pretty and seer of great truths and hidden secrets.

"Ada?" Mrs. Woodruff's voice broke into my thoughts. "May I ask what happened?"

I took a deep and still slightly labored breath, not sure what I should say. In the end, I decided there could be no harm in the truth. "Harriet tried to kill me."

The rosy glow drained from Mrs. Woodruff's face. She lowered herself onto a cushioned chair beside me, her mouth hanging open. "Why in Heaven's name would she do that?"

I knelt beside the older woman, my tender skin complaining beneath the loose fabric of the dress. "Dear Mrs. Woodruff," I began, feeling more at ease as the comforter than as the recipient of condolences. "My aunt was unwell and was a devotee of William Miller, that man who predicted the end of the world. The day of the fire was to be the Day of Judgment. She fell prey to her wild imagination. Overwrought with her disappointment as the day drew to a close with no trumpet blast from Heaven, she took it upon herself to rain down judgment through fire."

"How could anyone be so foolish?" Mrs. Woodruff had begun to cry and, in her sad disbelief, I found the strength to remain objective.

"I think she honestly did not intend me harm. Her last words to me were an apology for failing to protect me from sin."

Mrs. Woodruff reached out toward me but stopped short of resting her hand on my damaged skin. "You're very brave, probably in shock over it all. Your poor uncle, too."

"He saved my life, didn't he?" I knew the answer. The images returned to me in my drugged stupor. He had pulled me from the fire and died in the effort. I asked only because I needed someone else to acknowledge his heroism.

She nodded. "He was trapped in the shed when it caught fire. I suppose Harriet set it ablaze as well. Neighbors saw the smoke and heard him pounding on the walls. They helped him out and he stumbled into the house after you. The fire was already well established, but there was no stopping him. He was determined to get to you. He dragged you out onto the front lawn, collapsed beside you, and started mumbling incoherently." She lowered her voice. "No one found your aunt."

"She died in the house." I knew it was true. She would not have wished to live on after judgment day had come and gone.

"Ada, you will stay with us. Mr. Woodruff and I have plenty of room and our children have grown and gone. We would be honored to have you with us. You don't have to be so brave." Mrs. Woodruff stood then and guided me up and into the seat. "I'll take care of everything. We buried your uncle, of course. The doctor thought it best not to burden you with that in the beginning. But we could have a memorial, however you wish. And your aunt?"

I nodded my consent. I had no idea how to memorialize my tormentor, but I thought of Papa and knew he would have wanted her to have a proper send off.

"Lyman came, of course. We sent word about the fire and he arrived to help bury your uncle."

In the previous weeks, I'd forgotten about Lyman's role in all of this. The farm was his. True to his promise to Aunt Harriet, he'd remained away while we occupied it. Though I was disappointed I'd missed him, just the thought of him now comforted me.

Aunt Harriet's mental collapse and treachery would not surprise him. He had known my father—been a boy with him. He knew Papa, and he'd encouraged the development of my secret gift. I knew I would find in him a sympathetic ear. I had been warned not to trust him but wondered if perhaps Lyman was the last true friend I had in the world.

I remained with Mr. and Mrs. Woodruff through the winter. Grateful for their kindness, I hoped not to offend them by refusing their hospitality, but I was anxious to begin my new life. I saw the town doctor regularly for some time and found that established medicine had something to offer after all. Under his care, my burns healed with little scarring to show for them. My breathing difficulties gradually eased as well and I weaned from the laudanum, accepting what disturbing thoughts and restless nights may yet come.

I whiled away my time with Mrs. Woodruff whose household tasks we shared with hired hands. Life with her was much different than it had been with my aunt.

At last, on one of the first sunny days of spring, we sat in the cool breeze on the front porch of the grand house, and Mrs. Woodruff's prattling turned to the news I longed most to hear. "A man was in town yesterday to see about the farm property."

"Lyman was here?" My heart raced as I thought of it, my rescuer coming to carry me away into my new life.

"No, I'm afraid not. Just a lawyer, here to set the property straight. The word is that he's going to cut his losses and sell the land. Not that I can blame him. Never was much here for him after Elizabeth passed on."

Her words were undoubtedly true. With Papa gone and the house in ashes, Lyman had no reason to return to the farm. His business interests lie elsewhere and he hadn't made use of the property in years. He would not be coming for me. My body grew cold with the realization as Mrs. Woodruff chattered on.

"Where is Lyman?" I interrupted her in the middle of a sentence, but she seemed not to mind. I half suspected that Mrs. Woodruff had a bit of the second sense herself, which she expressed with an uncanny ability to disregard the commonplace in favor of the significant.

"Oh, that's always hard to know, now, isn't it?" She chuckled. "Never stays anywhere very long, that man, but I know he has a little shop—curiosities, I believe—up in Utica. That's where I've been able to contact him in the past. Couldn't say if he's there now, but he has a partner."

That was all I needed to hear before I made up my mind what to do.

*****

I didn't tell the Woodruffs I was leaving. They surely worried when I left, but they can't have been surprised. No matter how kind they'd been, I didn't belong to them. I didn't belong to anyone. Left behind by a dead mother, abandoned by a spineless father, and now barely escaped from a murderous aunt, I determined to make a home for myself, to which I could belong.

I retrieved my treasures from the woods. My cache included a good deal of money, for over the years, I had spent none of my earnings. There was nothing on which I could have spent it that would not have been viewed with suspicion by my aunt.

I purchased a fine dress, finer than any I had ever worn, complete with a high fashion corset and a new petticoat with delicate embroidering along the hem. Paired with fancy boots, the kind I had seen on the women whose secrets I manipulated, and a wide brimmed hat, I believed I made quite the image of a lady.

Next, I bought a ticket for the stagecoach. I stuffed my remaining treasures into a travel bag and, without a word of thanks or even a goodbye to Mr. and Mrs. Woodruff, I climbed into the coach heading for Utica where I hoped I might find a friendly reception.

23

Utica was a beautiful place, just starting to come into its own when I arrived in the early spring of 1845. The population had begun to boom on the heels of the completed Erie Canal and new businesses lined the streets. The city sprawled in a mismatched, haphazard way from numerous hubs, each sprouting tentacles of streets that snaked off toward the Northeast. In that way it mirrored my own emotional growth. I, too, had evolved under various influences, never quite sure what to look to as my center but nevertheless fiercely determined to wind my own way to some sort of life.

Not a large city, Utica couldn't have had a population greater than 15,000 people by the time I arrived, but collectively I believe we all felt we were heading somewhere as fast as we could go. This was just the sort of place I would find my Lyman who was himself always in the center of everything and headed off as fast as he could be in the direction of his latest fancy.

I knew only that he owned a curiosity shop on Genesee Street. Whether he still traveled hawking patent medicine or not, I didn't know, and it didn't matter. I felt certain if I could find the shop, I would eventually find Lyman himself.

I searched storefront after storefront, finally lighting upon a sign printed with the word "Curiosities" and beneath that in green script: "Dealers of unique items that mystify and delight." In my mind I could hear Lyman saying those very words in that smooth inflection of his, and it made me smile. The building was far plainer than I would have imagined. A long window on the door provided the only possible glimpse into the shop. One had to descend three steps that led to the entrance set just below street level, making it difficult to peer inside without committing to entering.

A bell tinkled above my head as I opened the door and received an unpleasant greeting from a man leaning over the counter. My eyes were slow to adjust from the bright sunshine to the dim light of the shop, but something struck me as familiar about the man.

"Morning. And just what do you want?" He flashed me a large smile full of crooked, rotting teeth. He wore a dark overcoat that was too large for him. Long, black sideburns in need of a good trim covered the better part of his cheeks, and the corners of his smile drooped as he took in the sight of me.

I shrunk under his scrutiny, lowering my gaze from his face to the countertop. Spread across it was a newspaper page of death notices glowing in the flickering yellow light spilled from an oil lamp—entire human experiences condensed into small rectangles of newsprint.

"Perhaps young miss is lost?"

"No," I quickly replied, attempting to sound brave despite my jittery nerves. "I was hoping to find a Mr. Lyman…um… Durand." It occurred to me I did not know which of Lyman's many aliases this man might know. "He is the proprietor of this store, I believe?"

The man shifted his weight behind the counter, his jaw muscles clenching at the mention of Lyman's name. "And what would the likes of you be wanting with him?" he asked with a slight German accent, his voice tugging at my memory.

I wasn't sure what to make of this man and I suddenly worried that Lyman would not be pleased to see me. After all, I'd been only a silly little girl when we'd last spoken. He had always been very kind. Still, I didn't know if he would willingly invite me into his life.

"I knew him when I was a child," I offered.

"Oh, when you was a child? What, last week then?"

"I'm not so young. I'll be 22 soon." I threw the words at him, hoping they exuded a confidence I did not feel. "I am his niece, Ada."

There was perhaps a small bit of truth to my claim. Lyman had once told me of his closeness to my father's family. He was like a son, he'd said, to my late grandmother.

My lie must have satisfied the man behind the counter because he straightened and strolled out from behind it, stopping directly in front of me. The top of his head stood barely above my shoulders and I wondered at his nerve, assuming I was too young to be a legitimate customer.

"Okay, Ada," he said, rubbing his hand over his scrubby whiskers. "Your uncle's out right now, but I'll tell him you called."

"Thank you." I offered a small curtsy. I suspected that this was a mere dismissal and that Lyman would hear nothing of my visit. I needed to extend the conversation, to improve the odds that he would. "And may I ask your name?"

His eyes narrowed in suspicion, as though no one had ever cared to know his name before. "Name's Ben, Ben Seymour," he offered as he turned his back to me and worked his way back behind the counter.

"But wait. I know you. You're Mr. Seymour. We've met before."

The man turned and searched my face. He laughed and said, "That don't seem likely."

"I was a little girl traveling with my aunt and uncle." I shrugged. "That is, my real uncle. You helped us."

His eyes widened in surprise and recognition. "You little swindler, all grown up." He grinned. "I knew you were no niece of Mr. Durand's. 'Course, that wasn't hard to figure since it ain't Mr. Durand these days. Been using the name Robard lately. Not many 'round here ever known him as Lyman Durand. What are you doing here anyway?"

Suddenly I didn't know how to answer. Truthfully I hadn't really thought this through, I suspect because I knew that if I did, I would have to conclude that it was foolish to come. It would have been much smarter to remain with the Woodruffs, who would have provided a home for me until I was established in one of my own. They treated me as if I were their own daughter. My life would have turned out very differently if I had been able to bring myself to adopt new surrogate parents, worthier ones than I had previously known. But no matter how much it might have made sense to do so, I could not.

"My uncle is dead. Aunt Harriet, too. Lyman always told me I had potential. I hoped—"

"I was sorry to hear about John's death. Truly." Mr. Seymour's face fell into a somber expression and he slumped against the counter.

"Thank you, Mr. Seymore."

"John was a good man. Deserved better than what he got." He locked eyes with me, a tear threatening to tumble down his cheek. "Did she kill him?"

I nodded.

A low, mournful whistle came from Mr. Seymour's lips. "Come back tomorrow, Miss Ada. Lyman'll want to see you."

On four different mornings I returned to the shop. Each time, Mr. Seymour informed me that Lyman was out. I didn't like to stay for more than a few minutes under his partner's peculiar stare. Then, on the fifth morning, I walked into the store to find someone else standing behind the counter.

He had the friendly handsome features I remembered, now lined faintly with age, but was not as tall as I had pictured him, for I had grown several inches since last we'd seen one other. Even so, he cut a dashing figure in a double-breasted suit coat of brilliant, deep black over an emerald waistcoat. His dark hair, flecked now with silver, fell just over his ears and across his forehead. His eyes sparkled when they met mine.

"My dear lady, welcome to my emporium of all things mysterious," he said with a flourish and an exaggerated bow. "May I help you find something today? A beautiful crystal to catch the enchanting radiance of your aura, or a healing balm? Perhaps a love potion, if I may be so bold."

"Lyman." It was all I could do not to cry out, I was so moved to see him again after so many years.

For a moment, confusion clouded his fine features, but it left as quickly as it had arrived. "Why, can it be that this beautiful lady is dear little Ada?" His arms opened wide and I ran to him as if I were still the small child he'd met years before. Always the gentleman, he smelled fresh and clean with a trace of musky cologne.

He released me from his embrace and clasped my shoulders, looking me up and down. I gazed at him, awash with emotion. It didn't matter that I had grown to the same height as he. Everyone looked up at Lyman. Somehow he always managed to appear larger than life, with his fancy colored waistcoats, fashionable suits, and winning smile that could draw in even the most skeptical.

"Whatever are you doing here, princess?"

My limbs tingled when he called me that. "You came to help bury Papa and I just . . . wanted to see you."

He nodded, his smile fading only slightly. "And I'm so pleased you did. The fire was a terrible thing. But you're here and safe. That gives me great comfort in my grief."

"Lyman, did Mrs. Woodruff not write to you?" I asked quietly, daring to reach out to him, resting my hand gently on his arm. "Aunt Harriet set the fire. Papa pulled me out, but he couldn't breathe. I didn't know how to save him." My eyes welled up with tears. I'd had months to come to terms with the deaths of my aunt and uncle, but I had not yet had to describe it to another soul for whom it might have some impact.

Lyman handed me a delicate handkerchief and clasped my hands in his. "Don't cry, princess. Ben," Lyman said to Mr. Seymour who at that moment coughed, drawing my attention to him for the first time since my arrival that morning. "Be a good man and make us a pot of tea, would you?"

Ben grumbled a response and disappeared into the back of the shop.

Lyman tenderly brushed the tears from my cheeks with the backs of his soft fingers. "You don't need to cry for him, Ada. John wrote his story years ago when he saddled himself with that woman. There was always madness in her. I think John believed she would save him in the end. Who knows? Perhaps she did. She did one good thing for him anyway."

His hand moved to lift my chin, ever so delicately, a gesture that reminded me so of Papa I could barely breathe. "He loved you like his own daughter."

He planted a soft kiss on my cheek and it was as if our shared grief, as brief as it had been, were erased. We took our tea in a back room of the little shop. Shelves lined the walls and held all manner of objects, only some of which I could identify. Small, dusty bottles of oils cluttered one long, low shelf.

It looked not entirely unlike the shelves that had held Papa's collection of remedies in his shed, but the bottles bore foreign names paired with the words *potion*, *oil*, or *powder*. Other shelves contained irregularly shaped rings of carved wood, polished stones of all sizes and colors, engraved amulets, and even a few glass orbs similar to my own.

Lyman watched me as I looked over the objects, stretching my fingers toward them, not daring to touch. "What do you think of my collection?"

My skin tingled as I looked and I felt a familiar stirring in my stomach, a weightiness in my arms and legs. I smiled. "What are they?"

"Items having to do with the occult are our specialty here. I can't even tell you what all of them are, or, for that matter," He leaned close to me as he spoke, a mischievous glint in his eye. "If any of them are what they claim to be."

"They are real." I knew this for a certainty. The items in this room held power.

Lyman's lips curled into a smirk. "You think so? Well, I certainly charge a good price for them. I am almost a gentleman of leisure these days, Ada. I've been on the road a good many years slinging snake oil, but I'm finally getting out of that business." He showed me a seat at a circular table in the middle of the room, a dark blue table cloth spread across it and a single glass ball in the middle. Next to that sat two cups of steaming tea.

"I'd been telling John for years that folk remedies and treasure hunting weren't going to get him ahead, not that those aren't useful skills to have." He nodded at me and my face flushed with guilt.

I hadn't held a witching rod in years. As for herbal remedies, I knew how to cure a fever or how to cause a deep or deadly sleep. And like so many frauds and false prophets, I knew where to harvest the liberty cap mushroom to produce angelic visions. But none of this trivial learning had proved useful when I needed Papa's skills most. I did not allow myself to linger long on these thoughts lest I crumble beneath the weight of my remorse. Had I spent more time studying remedies at Papa's side, he might have been still alive. Instead, his love and his knowledge were lost to me forever.

"But this is where the money is, Ada." Lyman, oblivious to my sorrow, was giddy with excitement. I sipped my tea and tried to hide my anguished thoughts as he spoke. "Spiritualism is sweeping across the country. I saw it everywhere I went. People clamor for a taste of the beyond, tired of the grim preaching they're being fed at those camp meetings of which John was always so fond."

A pain pierced my heart at the mention of camp meetings. I hadn't been to another since the revival in Nineveh. Lyman could not know, I thought, of the business Papa had been up to, inducing his own version of religious trances, offering a way to those who believed the salvation of their souls depended on some sacred involuntary act of devotion. I'd felt sorry for them. So had Papa, in his way, though his pity was motivated by a desire for wealth, as was Lyman's. They were not as far apart in their thinking as Lyman assumed. But then, of course, his perceptions of his recently deceased business partner likely remained tainted by his hatred for Aunt Harriet.

"I devised a new business strategy. I gained a lot of knowledge in my travels, from Indians and Gypsies and what have you. I thought that if there was a way I could sell people magic, then they would do anything to buy it." He smiled, leaning back in his chair, and took a sip of his barely cooled tea.

"So you let just anyone buy all of these things?"

"Ah, yes. But the trick is to make each customer feel as if I don't. That's the real magic of this place. It's the reason that when you enter the store you see healing herbs and elixirs, candles and incense. The most wondrous objects are all in the back room where only the worthy may enter. I find if I can convince a customer that he is the true mystery, then I am more effective at separating him from his money."

"And that's why your assistant seems to disdain the customers as they come through the door and why the proprietor himself is rarely here."

Lyman laughed. "Ben's certainly less than charming, but he's a good man to have around. You're a perceptive one, Ada. You know, I realized that when you were just a small child. John wouldn't let himself see how much potential you had."

"He did." I sounded more defensive than I'd intended and so I quickly added, "I've been using the orb you left me."

Lyman's well-manicured hand slapped the table as his mouth broke into a wide grin. "Have you, now? That was good business for a while until my seer and I went our separate ways."

"Mariana?" I offered, shamefully relieved to know that she was no longer in Lyman's life.

His jaw clenched for the brifest of moments and then he said, "I think that was her name. I'm surprised you remember. A fraud, I suspect, though she'd never admit to it." Lyman took another sip of tea, casually wiping away any memory of the woman I had loathed for years. "Tell me about you, though. Does it work for you?"

"In a manner of speaking," I admitted. "I see things. Not exactly future things. It's more like seeing secrets."

"That's even better." His eyebrows arched as he seemed to lose himself in thought for just an instant. The corners of his mouth twitched as an idea took hold. "Do you need the orb, do you think?"

I shrugged, unsure how much I wanted to tell him. I'd never revealed the full nature of my abilities even to Papa, but I wanted to trust Lyman with my whole heart. I suppose that was always his power. Everyone wanted to trust him, often against their better judgment.

"I think it's kind of like the witching rod," I began. "I get this feeling, like there's something tugging at me, waiting for me to reach out and grab it. I honestly don't know that it has much to do with the rod or the glass ball."

Lyman put down his teacup and rubbed his hands together in his excitement. I swear I saw the shadow of a demon sweep across his visage.

"I think we're going to make lots of money together, princess."

24

Lyman invited me to move into the apartment above the shop. It was larger than it first appeared and ostentatiously decorated, with all of the modern conveniences. He sent Mr. Seymour to bring my things from the inn where I had been staying since my arrival in Utica and showed me to a lavish airy room with tall windows overlooking the street below and then into a beautiful bedroom.

"My home is, as always, your home," Lyman said with a bow.

"You live here?" My face grew hot with a spreading blush.

"Oh, no." Lyman shook his head, chuckling softly. "No, I fear I do have some notion of propriety after all. I lived here for a time, when I traveled with the medicine show and was rarely here. Now that I've given that up, I have taken a house in town."

"And Mr. Seymour?"

Lyman let out a rich, deep belly laugh. "I think he would prefer it if you would call him Ben. Too much formality makes the poor man nervous. Don't worry about him, though. Every night he crawls back to the same little hovel he crawls out of each morning. Believe it or not, he's a family man with a wife and a little son. Since most of what he says is merely indiscernible grunting, I really couldn't explain how that might have happened, but who's to say when and why love may bloom."

"Indeed," I offered, thinking of Aunt Harriet and Uncle John, as unlikely a pairing as I could imagine.

Satisfied that it was mine alone, I looked around at the room. Velvet drapes blocked out much of the afternoon light. Oil-filled sconces evenly spaced along the wall would serve as the main source of light for the bedroom, casting shadows across thick rugs that spread over the open spaces of floor. An intricately carved frame held a high featherbed, and matching chests of drawers stood along one of the papered walls.

"It's beautiful," I said.

"A beautiful room for my beautiful princess." Lyman brought my hand to his lips and offered a gallant bow.

Again I felt myself grow hot and I very nearly giggled at his flattery. Had I been wiser in the ways of the world, I might have left again that night, disappearing under the cover of darkness. I knew the stories of this man. I had seen firsthand the way he seduced women with his eloquence and understood very well that once he had obtained his end goal, he would inevitably cast them aside. But I was so very young and he was so very handsome, and I was his princess.

The next morning, I dressed quickly before the sun had fully risen and hurried down the stairs, letting myself though the door into the little shop. I had hoped to spend some time looking through the cluttered shelves of oddities without interruption. When I opened the door, I found not only Mr. Seymour, but also Lyman in deep conversation with a woman I assumed must have been a customer.

Tall and slender, the woman wore a long, dark cloak. She did not turn her face toward me, but Lyman looked up the moment I entered, his sparkling eyes meeting mine. "Ada, my dear, I hope you slept well?"

"Yes. I was very comfortable."

"Excellent! I'd like to take you to breakfast. We have some business to discuss. Ben, would you mind finishing up with Mrs. Smith here?" Then to the woman in the cloak he added, "You can trust Ben to get you what you need. He's wonderful with potions, though I do recommend the amulet we discussed as well."

Ben grunted and led the woman to the back room while Lyman walked to me, a spring in his step that I found suspect for so early in the morning.

"You are certainly ready to meet your day." I blushed, embarrassed at the familiar tone in my voice. I knew Lyman from my fantasies rather than from any substantial experience with him, but I could not help myself. I found his presence intoxicating.

"Ada, this business often requires that I'm here at odd hours. My day is well begun. Our Mrs. Smith is an important customer, as are all of the Smiths who come into our store. Discretion is often a necessary part of this business," he explained. "Names are guarded when required. Shall we breakfast?"

He offered his arm and ushered me out the door of the shop. We strolled along the nearly empty street where windows revealed hints of activity as businessmen began their days. After several blocks we stopped at a remarkably well-lit storefront. Lyman opened the door for me to enter. The aroma of fresh baked bread wafted over me, warming me and making my stomach growl in anticipation.

"I love bakeries," Lyman said wistfully. "Not only do they smell glorious, but they keep strange hours, too, baking through half the night. I'm a regular here. I often stop for breakfast on my way home."

"That's why I had such trouble catching you in the shop. You are there all night."

Lyman's head tilted in a slight nod. "As required. Ben can manage in the day when the curious come through, gawking at our peculiar stock. For our more serious clientele, I prefer to tip my own more fashionable hat. But that's not what I wanted to discuss with you this morning."

An old woman from behind the counter broke into our conversation with a cheerful "Mr. Robard! We missed you yesterday."

"And I you, Mrs. Howe." He removed his hat with a flourish and inhaled slowly. "And I missed that sweet bread. We'll have two of those famous buns your husband makes. And two cups of coffee as well, if you would."

He took the warm rolls, wrapped in paper, and our cups, and led me to a seat at one of four wrought iron tables that stood next to the front window. The sun had fully risen, and there were more signs of life on the street. The baker's wife busied herself extinguishing lamps. Despite the warm air inside the bakery, filled with the heat from the baking ovens, a chill seeped around the window glass. I was glad for the hot coffee cup in my hands.

The sweet bun was the most delicious thing I had ever tasted, practically melting on my tongue. "This is good," I said, forgetting my manners and speaking with my mouth full of roll.

Lyman only nodded, taking a sip of his coffee. "If only I could have been a baker. A much simpler life to be sure, but I lack the talent, and I'm sure I would grow bored without the intrigue." He took a bite of his bun and chewed slowly.

Three well-dressed men walked into the shop then and the baker's wife rushed to fill their order. In fact, in only minutes it seemed the little shop was filled to bursting and the low rumble of chit chat offered a kind of privacy to our conversation. Only then did Lyman begin to tell me his grand plan.

"Have you heard about these sisters over in Hydesville? Fox I think their name is."

I shook my head, still enjoying the last few bites of roll and wondering if I might get another one. After surviving so many years on Aunt Harriet's practical but bland porridges and stews, I had recently discovered that I possessed a more sophisticated palate, as well as a greater appetite than a lady ought.

"They claim to talk with spirits and they hold these meetings, these spiritualistic sessions. The French would call them séances. It's small right now, but people are starting to come from all over— important people sometimes—and pay big money to have these girls talk to their dead for them."

I took a sip of the bitter coffee and nodded encouragement for him to go on.

"If I've learned anything traveling, it's that there's not near as much magic as there is belief in magic. They're frauds. I'm completely convinced they're frauds. I saw them myself and they sell it well. You ask them a question and they get the answer in this series of noises, like clicks. I don't know the source of the clicks. I don't believe for a minute they are caused by spirits.

"But plenty of people do believe it. I've traveled all over, to much larger cities than this, but I am convinced this is the place to be. We could do this, Ada. You have some sort of a gift for secrets, right? Is that how you put it?" Lyman spoke with passion, forgetting to keep his voice low, but as customers continued to stream into the bakery, it didn't matter.

"So you want us to hold these séances?" I asked, trying to capture his vision.

"Something like them, yes. We'd make it your own and be careful about who we invite. People with money, of course, and those whose minds might be a little more open to that kind of thing."

"So you don't think any of it is real?"

"You mark my words, these girls will be undone. They're too flashy. Too high profile. That's where most of those types make their mistakes."

"We're those types, Lyman. You and me and Papa."

"John got sloppy. He married himself a conscience and it burned him up."

His words stung me, but he had a point. Papa would still be playing at mysticism, a happy oracle, if not for his desire for something pure and noble. In the end, Aunt Harriet couldn't give him what he sought, but he'd never stopped looking for it. I wouldn't make the same mistake.

*****

"Tell me, Mr. Rigdon, what choice was ever given me? A young single woman, without family, without a true home, without prospects. All I had was this sense maybe given to me by God. I don't know. Possibly I could have used that gift for good somehow, but then I've always found the line between goodness and deception isn't as thick as we would all like to think."

Ada's voice grew louder as she spoke in defense of the foolish decisions of her youth, but she soon discovered that her insistent justifications were unnecessary. The old prophet, with unmistakable sympathy in his clouded eyes, sat patiently across from her, sipping thoughtfully from a cup of cold coffee delivered with a plate of salt pork and potato cakes, by his silent wife as Ada had prattled on. Caught up as she had been in her own memories, Ada had failed to notice at the time that a plate had been brought for her as well.

She was touched at the thoughtfulness of Mrs. Rigdon, who had initially been reluctant to even allow Ada into the home. Tears threatened to squeeze out of the corners of Ada's eyes as she reflected on this unexpected hospitality in a time when she once again found herself in the process of reinventing her life.

For many years, Ada managed to live quietly in the city, reading fortunes and attracting little notice. Still an avid reader, she had followed the stories in the papers. As the nation continued to try to heal from the devastation of civil war, one story, little more than an undercurrent, always captured her attention.

The Mormons of the Utah Territory had been accused of terrible crimes against strangers passing through their lands and, even more disturbing to Ada, against each other. The Prophet Brigham Young preached the doctrine of blood atonement, an idea which suggested that the only way to find forgiveness for one's sins was through the spilling of one's own blood upon the earth. If a saint would not seek absolution for his own sins, Young suggested that his brethren perform the task for him.

What the police hadn't yet discovered Ada had understood the moment she read the description of Silas Allen's ritualistic murder. The apostate Allen had been blood atoned, with Ada's name in his notes and on his lips. It mattered little that she herself was not a saint. Ada had no doubt that if she did not act, she would be next.

She took a sip from her own cup before continuing, relieved for now to be in this hospitable place. In truth, she was awed by the lack of judgment issuing from Mr. Rigdon, for though he was her chosen audience for her painful story precisely because of his devotion to his own deceptions, Ada couldn't help but crave his approval. Whether her diseased body finally gave up its fight for survival, or whether atonement caught up with her at long last, Ada's days grew short. She intended to purge herself of her darkest secrets before her time ran out.

"So" she said, lowering her voice to a calmer volume. "I told Lyman I would be his partner in crime. I sold my soul to a slippery snake charmer of a man."

*****

It only took a few weeks to work out the details of our ruse. Lyman's connections to the occult underbelly of Utica proved useful in spreading the news that we had ourselves a genuine medium who could talk with the spirits.

We held our first séance in the back room of the shop in the middle of the night, with the only light coming from three tall candles set up in the middle of the round table where a crystal orb once sat. Like Papa, I had learned to trust darkness and allow it to bolster my confidence. I found as I began to speak, I could soothe the tremor from my words by remembering how nearly invisible I was.

I spoke slowly, my tone deep and ethereal as I had practiced with Lyman, instructing the participants—all older than I by at least ten years—to clear their minds of all preoccupations. Six of us sat at the table, clasping hands around the circle. Lyman had insisted upon a number divisible by three so as to evoke the mystery of the trinity, which he thought lent authority to our claims. I readily agreed, recognizing one of Papa's signature tricks. With which of the two men the idea had originated, I couldn't be sure.

Lyman himself did not participate, but rather lurked outside the doorway of the back room, listening and watching to see how I would do. He had first wanted to find a way to open the mind of our clients with vision-inducing substances, as Papa had also been known to do, but I have never been competent at hypnotism as Papa was, and without the combination, I feared any intoxicating effects would be too suspicious to the gathered.

I would be alone with my gift for this enterprise, either in success or in failure. As the tension in the room subsided, I drew out my words, peppering my speech with nonsensical syllables until the language spilling from my mouth was barely English at all. We had practiced that, too. It was important, Lyman explained, that the participants could follow my meaning, but at the same time believe I ventured into another realm they were not permitted to enter, only to glimpse. What we settled on was a hybrid of English, Latin, and German. Aunt Harriet had taught me a small amount of Latin as part of Biblical history lessons and Mr. Seymour supplied the German phrases, snatches of his own religious Dutch upbringing.

I intertwined the phrases as we'd rehearsed. My voice swelled and receded in a lulling rhythm. My body began to rock back and forth carrying the suggestion through my limbs to the others in the circle, who swayed in sync with me unaware, most likely, of our movement.

The next phase was simpler because it was my part of the plan. I'd asked Lyman to instruct each participant to bring an object that bore some meaning to the deceased they wished to contact. They were each to carry that object somewhere on their person. When all began swaying, eyes closed and minds opened, I turned my attention inward, to the sensation in my gut, calling each participant to concentrate on his or her chosen treasure in its specific location, as though it were the dead themselves calling for their hidden treasures.

As I called out the treasures by name and location, Lyman began to stir the air currents in the small room by fanning the door on its newly oiled hinges. The candle flame flickered in the breeze as I cautioned the participants against opening their eyes and risking that our spirit visitors would retreat as quickly as they had arrived.

To my surprise, one of the participants, a young woman of maybe twenty five years, began to moan, low at first and then to call out the name of her deceased sister, talking to her as if she were in the room. Others followed her example and soon the eerie space, filled with their voices mingling together and bouncing in strange echoes off the walls lined with occult artifacts.

More than an hour passed before the chanting subsided at last, as did our rhythmic swaying. I offered a Latin blessing and told the men and women around the table they could take back their hands and open their eyes. As I lit oil lamps around the room, the features of exhausted faces emerged from the shadowy darkness. There was little talking as chairs scraped the floor and one by one the participants got to their feet to make their way out the door, stopping to thank me on the way.

The woman who had begun the moaning held my hand in hers and looked at me with moist eyes, her cheeks streaked with tears. "Thank you, Miss. I know now that my sister rests in peace." When she pulled away from me, she left a tinkling silver charm bracelet in my hand. "I can let go of that now. I think she would be pleased for you to have it."

I thanked her and watched her go, following the rest out the front door of the quiet shop and onto the dark street. Examining the bracelet in my hand, I dropped back into my chair and sighed heavily.

Lyman locked the front door behind the five customers and came to the back room. Kneeling beside my chair, he gently lifted my chin, looked deep into my eyes, and kissed me. This was not an innocent peck on the cheek from an older relative to a favorite niece. His warm lips moved against mine and a tingle danced up my spine as he lifted me, sitting me on the table edge. His fingers deftly undid the strays on my corset and he buried his face in my bosom as his hands reached under my skirts.

After that first brush with success, we hosted frequent séances in the back room of the curiosity shop, maybe as many as two or three per week. And after each, Lyman returned with me to the apartment to that high feather bed, any semblance of innocence I ever had, officially behind me.

*****

The old man cleared his throat. Ada stopped, flashing him a mischievous grin, pleased to see she still wielded the power to hold him at a distance, even in this state of emotional vulnerability in which she had placed herself.

With his acceptance of her darkness thus far, as a product of a disturbed childhood, she now wondered how far she might push his sympathies, for that knowledge alone would reveal to her his true nature. And learning the prophet's true nature was, for Ada, at the very heart of her mission.

Foremost in her mind was the question of motivation for all of his careful illusions involving the manuscript. She desired, more than anything, to know what type of man he really was, and she hoped he would understand that she knew enough about him to judge him fully.

"I can see I am making you uncomfortable, Mr. Rigdon. Forgive me. My relationship with Lyman is an important part of my story, but I understand that you have rejected the notion of the spiritual wifery preached by other prophets of your faith. I will spare you the details."

25

Lyman credited me with our first successes. Stroking the egos of his most valuable partners was a particular skill of his. I was a natural, he claimed, at helping the grief-stricken to heal. That's how he liked to explain our fraudulent séances, but I was no longer an innocent. I knew exactly what we were doing. We were taking advantage of overly trusting people at the most vulnerable point in their dreary lives. I would be lying if I told you I felt good about it, just as I would be lying to tell you that a part of me didn't enjoy it.

Most of the responsibility for our continued success, however, fell to Mr. Seymour, who implored me to call him Ben. Despite his preference for rough manners, Ben's keen eye for useful detail was unparalleled, and he could rise to the occasion when necessary.

His tireless research led us directly to our most lucrative clients. Daily he scoured *The Observer* for promising obituary notices, paying the closest attention to those that mentioned a surviving spouse with little family nearby. Often he donned a good black suit that I am sure Lyman chose for him and attended family wakes posing as an obscure friend to the deceased and, with his peculiar manners, planting suggestions of supernatural communication with the dead.

As I have mentioned, Ben was a man of few words, but he was not a simpleton as he often projected. Night after night I had a table full of the gullible and the heartbroken mostly found by this man I was only just coming to know.

I suppose he reminded me of Papa a bit. Papa had been a man of few words, too, making what he did say all the more important. But Ben never struck me as dangerous the way Papa often had. From Papa I had learned the art of listening when no one thought I was, gleaning information to file away for later use. I was eager to know this Ben Seymour better and wanted to discover what, if anything, he knew about the relationship between Lyman and Papa, which both men had been reluctant to discuss with me.

I seized what opportunities I could to question him. One morning I received just such a chance as Ben and I stood alone in the shop. Lyman left for his own house to freshen up and get some much needed rest. He had entertained a customer until the wee hours of the morning, even after a séance earlier in the night. I leaned over the counter, a bakery roll in hand, tired from my nighttime activities. Ben stood behind the counter scouring the obituary section and trying to avoid my eye.

"How did you know my uncle?"

He set down his paper and stifled a cough before raising his gaze to mine. "I met John when I was not much more than a boy. He was good to me when not many were. Taught me a lot. He was like my brother." He looked back at his newspaper, offering no further explanation. I could see I wouldn't get more from him with this line of questioning and changed the subject.

"What do you look for in the notices?"

"Widows and widowers without family." Ben relaxed, visibly relieved at the turn in the conversation. Then he added, "Or sometimes the mostly grown children. If they've lost both parents and don't have someone to help 'em finish growing up, they're so desperate they'll fall for just about anything."

I studied his sallow, unshaven face. His eyes locked with mine, offering, for a moment, a glimpse into the sharp mind he kept hidden behind low manners and poor hygiene. I wondered to whom he was truly referring. I reflected that he could have been continuing his own story, a young man alone, desperate enough to attach himself to a treasure hunter. But of course, he could have just as easily been referring to my situation, implying not altogether incorrectly that I had been taken in by a slick confidence man.

I found myself wishing I were anywhere but in the shop and feeling suddenly very young and foolish. I hadn't decided yet whether to rage at him for his judgmental attitude or to politely excuse myself and retreat to my apartment with my misery, when the tinkling bell of the shop door interrupted our conversation.

I turned to see a girl, not more than fourteen, wearing a simple yet stylish gray dress with puffed sleeves, a wide brimmed hat atop her head.

Ben grumbled a surly greeting to her, suspicious of one so young walking unaccompanied into a shop such as this one. Perhaps the girl questioned her own judgment because she looked at Ben with wide eyes and her face paled. I decided to be more tactful.

"May I help you, Miss?" I asked in the kind of sweet voice one reserves for frightened children.

My kind tone apparently helped to strengthen her resolve. Timidly she removed her hat and smiled at me. Pretty curls of yellow hair escaped the loose bun at the back of her head and pooled on her shoulders. It occurred to me that she was dressed much older than her age, an attempt, I assumed, to appear more confident.

Her voice quavered as she spoke. "I was led to believe I might be able to find help here. My father has been ill for a long time and we had hoped there might be a healer here who could offer him comfort."

"S'no healer here. Try a doctor." Ben sounded gruffer by the moment, intentionally I had no doubt. I shot him an angry look and tried to shoo him into the back room. He refused to take my hint.

"I'm afraid you've been misinformed," I offered. "We do have many herbal remedies in the shop and you are welcome to browse them, but we do not employ a skilled healer."

The girl looked at her feet in disappointment. She drew a deep breath and said, "Doctors cannot or will not help now. My father once knew a healer by the name of John Powell. He believed he might have been connected to this shop somehow. Perhaps he was mistaken."

My breath caught in my chest at the mention of Papa's name, his real name as I understood. "Miss, I…" I didn't know what to say and when I needed him, Ben didn't make any effort to take over the conversation. Perhaps her words had shocked him as well.

"I'm sorry. The man you seek is deceased." It chilled me to speak the words.

"Oh no, I'm so sorry to hear it." Tears had begun to spill onto her youthful round cheeks.

"T-thank you." I stammered. "I am sorry that your father is unwell. May I ask how he knew Mr. Powell?" It felt strange to refer to Papa so formally.

"They were brothers through marriage. My father remembered that Mr. Powell was a healer and had once been in business with the proprietor of this shop." She glanced nervously at Ben as she spoke.

I nodded, unable to speak. Papa had possessed no other family I knew of and, as I studied the girl's face, I could clearly see in her many of my own features. I was looking at my sister, unknown to me until that moment, speaking to her about her ill father, the father we shared.

"He was indeed a gifted healer and a good friend to the owner of this shop," I tried again to subtly shoo Ben to the back room, but again he refused. It was important to me, somehow, to indicate that he was not the owner of whom I spoke. "Mr. Powell was my father." It surprised me how easily the lie tripped from my mouth.

"Oh, then we are cousins!" The girl's face lit up at this new false discovery and she rushed forward to embrace me. "I am pleased to have found you. My name is Clara. Have we met before?"

"No." I returned her hug, choking back tears of bitterness. I felt no joy in discovering my little sister, but rather intense jealousy at this young girl who had been my replacement in my father's affections. "I don't recall meeting. My name is Ada."

I released her from the hug and studied her face. Nothing changed in her expression when I told her my name—no flash of recognition nor nagging memory. She had never heard of me. Anger surged through my body and I said, too harshly, "Take me to your father."

"Oh, yes," she responded, clasping my hand in hers. "I know he will be delighted to see a long-lost niece."

I excused myself to put on my own hat and shawl while she looked over the cluttered shelves in the front room of the shop. When I was ready to go, she asked, "Is there anything here that might help?"

Truthfully, as much as a part of me resented this girl, I did feel pity when I saw the desperation in her eyes. I must have worn the same expression upon my own face so similar to hers as I held Papa dying in my arms nearly a year before. "I'm afraid I am not as skilled at healing as my father was. I'll see what I might be able to do. I can make no promises, but I can try."

She hugged me again. "Oh, thank you, dear cousin. You are an answer to prayer!"

Hand in hand, we walked out of the shop into the breezy summer morning, leaving a dumbfounded Ben grunting behind us.

"Have you always lived in Utica?" I asked as Clara led me out of the business district and down a tree-lined street full of small, well-kept houses. I didn't like to think my father had lived so close by, remarried with a new family and never came back for me, but I had to know before I came face-to-face with him.

"No." Clara shook her head. Her pace quickened as she spoke. "We came here seeking Mr. Powell. We arrived quite recently. Father has been ill for so long. Travel is difficult, but he and my mother thought this would be best. He wrote several letters to your last known location but received no answers. Of course, we were not aware that Mr. Powell had passed on. I am truly sorry to hear your sad news. When did it happen?"

"Oh," I said, trying to fit the pieces of my missing life together. "It's been nine months now."

"And your mother?"

I shook my head, unable for a moment to think how to respond to her question. I rarely thought of my mother anymore, but then, that was not who she would be referring to. "There was a fire."

"You're all alone?" She stopped, facing me and reached for my free hand with hers.

"I have Lyman." I shrugged, trying to sound older than I felt.

"The man in the shop?" Clara eyed me, her expression one of disbelief.

"No, that wasn't Lyman. Lyman owns the shop. He was Papa's friend. He's *my* friend. He's become very dear to me." My voice began to trail off at the last words, the guilt of my layered lies and indiscretions nearly causing me to choke.

"Well, you must think of us as family, too." This girl, my sister, had not seen my discomfort, or she had been too well-mannered to remark upon it. I reflected that Clara had grown up with a mother and would have been thoroughly instructed in the rules of polite society, I assumed with much more clarity than Aunt Harriet had ever bothered to teach me.

"So where were you before you came to Utica?" I asked, desperate to change the subject.

"Nauvoo, Illinois. We moved there when I was very young and much of it was still swamp."

"I'm sorry, I'm not familiar with it," I said, mystified. She had a faraway look in her eye and spoke as if I should know the place to which she referred.

"You've never heard of Nauvoo? Oh, I wish you could see it. It's the most beautiful place—neat clean streets with pretty little houses and up on the bluff, the temple sits overlooking the whole town."

"Temple?" The color must have drained from my face for concern flashed in her eyes as we walked on. She could not have known that the mere mention of religious fanaticism would fill me with dread.

"The Temple of the Church of Jesus Christ of Latter-day Saints," she continued. "You do know about *The Book of Mormon*, don't you?"

I shook my head.

To my surprise, Clara squealed in delight. "Oh, Ada, God has surely brought us together today so that you might come to know Him."

"I've been baptized," I offered, hoping this might calm her and prevent her preaching to me. It didn't.

"But not in the true church. I can't wait to introduce you to my parents. This will bless Father so much. Nothing could be better for his health than the opportunity to bring his niece to true faith in Jesus Christ!"

By now I had serious doubts about my purpose in visiting my estranged, ailing father, but we had at last stopped at a small, neat house reminiscent in some ways of the home I first shared with Papa and Aunt Harriet just after my mother died. I could not think how to excuse myself from the situation now. I allowed Clara to lead me into the house and directly into the bedroom where my father lay dying.

"Father!" she called, her joy-filled voice barely above a whisper. The curtains were drawn tightly over the room's windows and the low light added a cheerlessness to the room in which Clara's youthful exuberance felt out of place. I could see his outline, propped against his feather pillows, this man who had been my father. I could not distinguish his features.

Kneeling at the bedside was the figure of a woman who rose, offering Clara a stern reprimand as she approached us. "Be calm, Clara. You are disturbing your father." The woman looked at me, curious. Her face was drawn, her dress rumpled. Clearly she could have used a good, long rest. "And who are you?" she asked, offering only a small nod of her head by way of greeting.

"Mama, this is Ada," Clara spoke for me. "She is Father's niece."

"My goodness," the woman smiled, her face softening, giving way to kindness. "I didn't know Harriet had a daughter. Welcome. Albert will be delighted to see you."

I nodded, looking over her shoulder at the man on the bed who struggled to pull himself higher up onto the pillows.

"Ada?" Though he spoke in a low rasping murmur, I could hear that it was him. I could not bring to mind my father's voice today, nor could I have done it even a moment before he spoke on that day of our reunion, but I knew it certainly when he uttered my name. Its innately familiar tenor filled my ears and my heart with longing. I fought the urge to run to him, hardening my heart with a crust of unforgiveness. "Come closer."

I went to him as slowly as I could make myself go. As I approached, the door closed behind my sister and stepmother, leaving me alone with the man who was once my father. I knelt beside the bed in the position I had first seen my stepmother in and looked at his face for the first time in more than a decade.

He was thinner than I recalled, ravaged by a terrible illness from which I had little doubt he would die. His hair, much too long, fell in limp curls over his ears. A wild beard covered his sunken face, but the features, I recognized. His eyes were the same cold gray Aunt Harriet's had been, and he shared her long nose.

I stared at him, listening to the labored rasping of his breathing, thinking of all the things I would like to say and not saying any of them. He seemed to be feeling much the same and neither of us spoke.

At long last, he broke our silence. "How old are you?"

Of all the ways I had imagined this conversation may someday begin, I admit this question had never occurred to me. "Twenty one," I answered, angry that he would need to ask.

He nodded with great effort, stifling a cough as he began to speak. "You are beautiful."

"Thank you," I whispered, fearful that somehow if I spoke loudly, the shock of it might kill him before I'd had my chance to ask him any questions. Perhaps it was that fear that drove me too quickly to the question I needed answered most. "Why did you leave me?"

He drew a labored breath before he spoke. "Ada, please do not judge me too harshly. Your aunt is a good woman and I knew you would be safe with her, safer than you would be with me. I was so lost after your mother died. If God hadn't found me, I don't know what would have become of me. Forgive me."

"How can you ask me to forgive you?" My voice shook but I continued, gaining more control over my emotions as I spoke. "Harriet was a monster. She's dead. Did you know? She died in a fire that she set in an attempt to kill us both. She killed Papa, too." I admit I enjoyed the hurt in his clouded eyes when I referred to my uncle with that familiar term.

"This supposed good woman crushed my spirit every day of my childhood," I continued. "It should have been your job to protect me from such bile. And now I'm alone with no one but an unscrupulous criminal to care for me."

"Ada," he said, his voice was stronger now, fueled with emotion, but just what emotion, I could not as yet tell. He made me feel, for a moment, like an unruly child about to be deservedly scolded. "The prophet Nephi, son of Helaman says plainly, if you forgive the sins of men, the Father will forgive you, but that if you fail to forgive, then your sins won't be forgiven."

"Are you lecturing me with Scripture?" I could hardly contain my fury. It boiled up within me, and I felt the need to escape the air of this stifling sick room with its diseased odors. Then as I thought about what he had said, something occurred to me, a familiarity that I couldn't initially place. "Did you say Nephi?"

"From the *The Book of Mormon*." He responded in an eerily calm voice, his attempt, I assume, to soothe me. "It's the truest testament of Jesus Christ, as revealed to the prophet Joseph Smith."

I shook my head in disbelief. Of course I knew the name Nephi very well, but that my father would invoke it while scolding me was as strange as it was infuriating.

"You're as mad as she was." I placed my palms on his bedside and forced myself to a standing position, sending shock waves through his mattress that I hoped would cause him pain. Without another word, I rushed out the door.

Outside my father's sick room, my supposed cousin and aunt waited anxiously for me in the tidy front room. "It was good of you to come!" exclaimed my father's wife. Now in the brighter light I could see that she was remarkably pretty, even with streaks of gray in her hair and small, cheerful wrinkles around her mouth and eyes. She almost danced in eagerness to speak with me. In her excited movements I could see much likeness between her and her daughter. She hugged me, saying, "My name is Margaret. And you are most welcome here any time."

"Will you be in Utica long? Clara tells me that you have only just arrived."

"Yes, that's true, and now that we've discovered you, I doubt we will be going anywhere else again until . . ." She trailed off and her face fell, yet somehow her eyes remained joyful. "It's just such a blessing God has brought you to us at this time."

"Yes, well, I am glad to have met you, but I must be getting back to the shop. Lyman will be wondering what has become of me." I knew Lyman would not be at the shop and if he were, it would not likely occur to him to care where I had gone, but I very much wanted to leave these people.

"But you'll come back, of course."

"Yes, of course," I lied.

Margaret's giddiness returned, as did that of Clara, who jumped up from her seat behind where her mother stood talking with me and walked briskly out of the room, only to return seconds later carrying a small black book which she handed to me.

"Thank you," I muttered, looking at the book in my hands, the words *The Book of Mormon* embossed in gold on the front.

"Please take this with our warmest regards, dear Ada," Margaret said with a flourish and Clara nodded her agreement. "Read it. It will change your heart."

"I will," and I would, I knew, for my love of reading and for the sake of satisfying my curiosity. I bade them farewell and hurried out the door as quickly as I felt propriety dictated.

26

Ben was in the back room of the shop when I returned. At the tinkling of the bell, he peered around the corner of the door frame, but as soon as he realized it was only me, he went back to his work without a word. I was grateful to him, as I especially did not wish to describe the details of my morning's adventure.

I offered a stiff nod in his direction, though I doubted he would notice or care whether or not I acknowledged him at all. Only when I closed and locked the apartment door did I allow myself to truly consider my encounter with my father and his family.

I don't believe I had ever, nor have ever since, cried as I did that afternoon. Even as I said my final farewell to Papa dying in my arms, I did not grieve so fiercely. Always, it appeared, in the back of my mind, my father had somehow been a different kind of man, one who was strong, individualistic, ambitious, a man who would want his daughter to become the same. I often dreamt that I would one day meet him again. When I did, he would explain how he had always known I would rise above adversity, that I would learn and grow to be a young woman he and my mother would be proud of if given the chance to experience pain and discovery on my own in the world. He would hold me in his powerful arms and explain everything to me—what to truly believe, how to live a life of contentment and grace.

This was a childish fantasy, I know, but if rather than abandoned I were simply a baby bird nudged from the nest in order that I might fly, then I could still be beloved. Heartbroken, I had to admit when the day of reunion finally arrived, that secret hope was shattered by a bedridden zealot who had never bothered to tell his new family about his old and who had the audacity to scold my unwillingness to absolve him of his sins.

It was nearly an hour later that I rubbed my eyes dry and remembered the book dropped on the floor. My sorrow momentarily spent, I was both fatigued and hungry. I prepared a light meal, looked over my growing collection of books, and decided to peruse the copy of *The Book of Mormon* given me by my half-sister.

*****

"I wonder, Mr. Rigdon, if you can imagine my astonishment when I realized that I had read this great work before. I suspected a connection when my father mentioned the name Nephi, which I soon located in my memories. But the similarities went significantly further than the mere coincidence of a name. In fact, though this book departed somewhat from the manuscript I had stolen years before from Zeviah's wardrobe, those places in which it did so were quite reminiscent of, if not directly quoted from, the one book which, thanks to Aunt Harriet, formed the cornerstone of my childhood."

The old man's body became rigid. Veins throbbed visibly in both temples and his face had become quite red. Ada would have begun to be concerned about his health were it not for the agitated tapping of his foot on the hard floor.

The prophet appeared eager to speak, to defend himself against a perceived threat. Ada had observed this reaction more times than she could count in the bodily postures of her customers. Those who felt somehow pressured to justify the secrets Ada uncovered in their lives. Truthfully she enjoyed their discomfort, though it mattered little. For Ada never revealed secrets only for the sake of the secret itself, but to make accurate interpretations and predictions that mattered in her customer's lives. Even if they were bad people—and some of them were very bad people—Ada's purpose was not to judge, but to guide. That was how she remained in business.

Sidney Rigdon now wore this same expression. She knew he sought her understanding but did not yet know how to earn it. Ada soaked in this feeling of power over a person more vulnerable than she, reveling in it for a moment before she would offer him relief from it.

"It is truly a work of genius, you ought to know. I can see that you wish to interrupt my story at this point, but I beg of you to indulge me just a while longer. I have nearly reached the culmination, which I feel I must do, before the tale of the two of us can find its own conclusion."

*****

Captivated, I read all the afternoon, through the supper hour and well into the night, ignoring several knocks on my door. Finally, as the hour drew very late, the scattered attempts to reach me gave way to frequent and more urgent poundings upon my door. I yelled out that I was engaged and wished not to be disturbed, but I should have known that Lyman would not be a man who would easily come to accept such a statement.

He let himself into the room and found me there, at my reading table, poring over *The Book of Mormon*. It lay open, illuminated by a single oil lamp, this forming the only light in the room outside of the cloud-filtered moonlight shining through the windows.

"Princess, are you feeling ill? You haven't been answering." Lyman always sounded sincerely concerned even when he wasn't.

"I am well enough." I didn't look at him as I spoke, engrossed as I was in the newly revised teachings of Jesus.

He placed a tender hand on my arm as he leaned over my shoulder to glimpse the book. "What is this you're reading?"

I sighed and looked into his eyes, dog-earing my page before closing the book. "It's *The Book of Mormon*. Have you ever read it?"

"Oh, I've thumbed through it once or twice," Lyman admitted with a casual shrug. "Dreadfully boring."

"It is that," I agreed.

"And what, may I ask, has prompted you to read the Golden Bible?"

"Is that what they call it?"

He nodded in the shadows. "I've heard that. A few years ago it was discovered by, or rather revealed to, an otherwise unremarkable treasure hunter named Smith."

"Joseph Smith," I added. "I have my doubts about heavenly revelation, though."

"Well, he certainly became successful for a while after that." Lyman chuckled. "I unloaded some mummies on him once over in Ohio, along with some papyrus. Claimed he could read the Egyptian. His people just loved it.

"He kept trying to establish himself a town—the great Zion or something. A good cover for criminal activity, if I had to bet. Surround yourself with enough religious fervor and you can do just about anything without too many questions coming your way. Not a bad plan, I should think."

"Did it work?"

"You have the book."

I shrugged. "So that's it, then? This Smith suddenly has a new Bible and then people flock to him and he grows rich off them? Sounds like you could use one."

"More trouble than it's worth. Smith got himself shot by an angry mob not too long back."

I vaguely remembered reading something in the newspapers about the murder of the leader of a great religious movement in Illinois. Then I thought of something Clara had said. My father and his new family had lived in Illinois.

"What happened to all of Smith's followers?" I asked, turning in my chair to fully face Lyman in the semi-darkness.

"Scattered, I suppose. I don't really know." Lyman had grown bored with the conversation, examining his fingers in the low light. As important as this information felt to me in this moment, it all meant little more to him than any missed opportunity or perhaps bullet dodged. Clearly he saw Smith as a member of some imagined fraternity of swindlers. After reading much of *The Book of Mormon*, I can't say I disagreed with him.

Still, he obviously knew more than I did of the strange sect, and I craved information. I continued to press him. "Does the town name Nauvoo mean anything to you?"

Lyman rubbed his smoothly shaved chin and shook his head. "It's familiar, but I can't place it. Why do you ask?"

"It came up in conversation today."

"When you went for a walk with your sister?"

A shiver ran through me.

"Ben mentioned you stepped out for a bit. That's why I came to check on you. I was worried."

He didn't worry for me. He worried about losing me when we were just beginning to make some real money with our séances. Lyman, I knew, never seriously considered the emotional state of anyone else unless it impacted him. He frequently reminded me that total objectivity was the key to a good venture and that nothing but trouble came from scruples.

My next question I designed to help him become more invested in my story. Worthy or not, Lyman represented the best source of guidance available to me, and I meant to use him to the fullest. "I saw my father today for the first time since I was small. You used to know him, right?"

Lyman didn't respond right away. Instead he took a candle from the table, lit it from the lamp, and proceeded to make his way around the room, lighting the sconces. The tiny flames danced, painting the walls with their flickering glow. When he finished, Lyman blew out the candle and sat sideways on the sofa so that he looked at me over the back of it as I remained seated at the table.

"I knew your father Albert when we were both boys in the city. He was a little younger than I. Harriet had to have been older than him by maybe five or six years, I'd say. Your grandfather was a musician, and your grandmother a French beauty he'd picked up along the way. She spoke almost no English, but she had this way about her. Even those that couldn't understand a word she spoke longed to listen. She was a medium, too." He winked at me.

I didn't know what to do with this new information. Of course, I had wondered about my grandparents before, but never had I given any serious thought to them. Now, suddenly I was discovering a deep connection to a grandmother I had never known. I wasn't sure whether to feel pride in that or not.

"Was she like us? Like me, I mean?"

Lyman smiled in the dim light. "Oh, yes. She was the real deal. Except, unlike you, she knew it. I think I fell in love with her. My own mother was ordinary next to lovely Annette. So I pursued Harriet—the next best thing, I thought."

I smiled, remembering that Harriet had once claimed the same thing in an argument with that Mariana woman Lyman ran with for a time. I hadn't believed it possible then, but listening to Lyman now, I could hear the truth in it, and I craved more of the story.

"Their children couldn't have been more unlike them I don't think. Albert and Harriet were both going places, off embracing a new world lifestyle and finding it, or maybe themselves, lacking. Harriet had no interest in me. She wanted to be part of high society in Christian America but, unfortunately for her, she lacked the grace of her mother and found the life she thought she wanted unattainable.

"Eventually, as you know, she left the city and ended up with John, a man who could offer her a life not so different than what she had known growing up, where she could lick her wounds and grow increasingly bitter.

"Albert was more successful. He started small, as an apprentice in the printing business. He distanced himself as much as he could from his humble beginnings, married himself a pretty little actress, and started a family. They moved to a small town where he could set up his own business. She died and he, well, you probably know the rest better than I do."

"He moved to Nauvoo, Illinois and joined the radical Joseph Smith. He remarried, had a daughter, and failed to mention to either of them that he had a living daughter from his first marriage."

The news seemed not to shock Lyman. "So that explains your sudden interest in *The Book of Mormon*. What are they doing here?"

"Albert's dying. They came to find Papa. They thought he could help."

"So he didn't come looking for you at all, then?" If I hadn't known Lyman better, I might have thought he felt sorry for me, but I could hear the subtle relief in his voice.

I shook my head. "It doesn't matter. My papa is dead."

"Are you going to see them again?"

"I don't know."

"Ada, my dear." I could sense much of Lyman's intention in his tone, and it frightened me. That he could respond to my obvious grief with blatant opportunism was not as surprising to me as was my disgust. "What you have here is a chance to get what's yours. You can't just leave that alone."

"What are you talking about?" I asked, dreading the answer.

"If Albert's time in this world grows short, then his grieving widow will be left to search for connections to him. That just happens to be your area of expertise, does it not? And the best part is that you *are* the connection. You can probably even get a share of the inheritance out of this!"

"What makes you think there's an inheritance?"

Lyman looked truly shocked when I asked this. "Ada, what kind of gentleman would I be if I didn't even look out for the best financial interests of a young lady under my protection?"

"Is that what I am?"

Lyman stood and walked to me, taking my hand gently in his. He whispered, "What you are, princess, is beloved. And Albert has had his share of successes. He will leave his family well provided for, I am sure, and you are, after all, his family."

Warm tears spilled down my cheeks. Lyman pulled out a silk handkerchief to wipe them away. His tenderness was calculated, as was his every action, and as he wrapped me in his arms, a sense of foreboding gripped me.

"I'm going to try to help him," I said.

"As any devoted daughter would. Just remember that devotion, no matter how pure, is always bought. Albert has not yet paid."

27

I awoke after only a few short hours of sleep, tangled in Lyman's arms, in need of both a bath and a cup of strong coffee. My sleep had been fitful at best and as Lyman snored beside me, I drew several conclusions. The first was that I was most certainly not Lyman's beloved, nor cared to be. Secondly, I realized if I had learned to fly, it was not because my father had pushed me out of the nest, but because I had found the love I needed to nourish my soul despite his abandonment of me. And thirdly, I very much wanted to claim what was rightfully mine.

With all of this in mind, I bathed, dressed, and breakfasted before the sun had fully risen in the sky. From a trunk I kept, locked at the foot of my bed, I retrieved Solomon Spalding's bundled manuscript from a small pile of found or, rather, claimed items. Slipping the pages under my wrap, I descended the stairs and let myself into the dark curiosity shop. Ben would likely arrive soon, I determined. Through the slats of the closed shutters, dawn light began to slip into the shop, illuminating the bottles and jars of the shelves nearest the windows. It was to these I went, searching for the herb I knew I would need.

I sighed as I looked through the rows of labeled containers, many of which bore Papa's own careful lettering. Over the many years I had known him to be in business with Lyman, he had not only continued to brew the elixir that Lyman sold indiscriminately through the countryside, but had also collected and dried medicinal herbs both for use in his own healings and at his business partner's request.

Since my arrival, I had often seen Ben returning from treks into the wood to collect plants to replace the stock. With just my limited knowledge, I knew on sight that many of them were wrong. It didn't matter. Even with the proper ingredients, healing took place in direct proportion to the talent of the healer. As I took hold of the bottle for which I had searched, I said a silent prayer to some unknown god that I would possess the skill I needed to see this medicine effectively administered.

A bell tinkled behind me. I turned to find Ben closing the front door. Suspicion settled across his hard features when he caught sight of me. I offered him no explanation, choosing instead to slip silently past him toward the exit. To my great surprise, he caught my wrist as I passed.

"What do you think you're doing?" he said.

I cried out in surprise, too loudly for the small space in the shop.

He dropped my arm and stammered out some sort of apology, followed by these words I will never forget. "Ada, Lyman is no one's friend."

"Pardon me?"A warning was the last thing I expected to hear from this man who was apparently so devoted to his unscrupulous friend, watching me, reporting my every move. "What do you mean?" I tried to narrow my eyes and stare him down. I was painfully aware that a young lady attempting to intimidate a much more seasoned and criminal man was vaguely ridiculous, but I have always possessed an unusually strong ability to manipulate others, and possibly an overinflated sense of confidence.

His next words he spoke so carefully, so precisely, that I imagined he must have practiced many times just what he wanted to say. "Ada, you remember when we first met, when you were just a little girl, all bruised up from your aunt?"

I nodded, intrigued. This man had barely spoken more than a few words at a time to me since my arrival in Utica even as I peppered him with questions. He'd volunteered almost nothing in the time I had known him. I couldn't imagine he had anything useful to say now.

"John was a good man. I always thought so. And he loved you like you were his own. You know that, right?"

"Yes," I whispered, my throat tightening.

"He never would've taken up with Lyman again if he didn't think it was the best thing he could do for you—to provide you a home."

"What happened between the two of them?"

Ben shook his head. "John never would've wanted you to know all of it, and I sure as hell don't want to be the one to tell you, but seems to me if you're mixed up with him now, you'd better know some of it.

"The two of them used to work together in some of the big cities down south peddling miracle cures. Lyman got greedy, started working over the desperate families. It was a little like he does now. That wasn't so bad, offering a few weeks or months of hope to folks when there wasn't any.

"I think John could stand that, but where he drew the line was this scheme Lyman got going that made him into an angel of death for hire. Families that stood to gain a fortune from the death of a rich family member got Lyman to recruit this miraculous medicine man who could keep the 'em alive just long enough to throw off any suspicion and then kill them when the time was right."

"Papa was an assassin?" I knew that Papa had done some unsavory things in his life. I had even witnessed a few of them myself, but this new information didn't fit with my image of the man who had been the only father I'd ever known.

"Not a willing one. I mean, he was no angel, but John always had a line he didn't like to cross. Lyman was the one with the sweet setup. He liked to remind people he had no skills in the healing arts. His hands remained relatively innocent since all he'd done was acted as broker for the deal to find the family a healer, or so he'd claim when a deal went bad. Set himself up real nice for blackmail on both sides. John could stay and get rich along with him, or Lyman could let him get strung up for murder."

"I don't understand." My mind reeled. I felt as though I would be sick. Papa's and even Harriet's warnings about Lyman came rushing back into my mind. "How did Papa break free from him?"

"Don't know that he did entirely. He always seemed to be outrunning his reputation. They worked over the south pretty good and moved up north, settling into New York for a while while Lyman worked his magic, made his contacts. John, in the meantime, made a few contacts of his own. He started getting to know some of the local mystics, including this old French woman who used to tell fortunes on the waterfront."

"My grandmother. Lyman knew her, too."

Ben nodded and continued. "That's when he met Harriet—younger and gentler, before she turned zealot. Harriet had an unfailing sense of good and evil, but given her family background, mysticism for her fell somewhere in the middle of the two. What she saw in John was a chance to escape a city that refused to let her rise above her station. What he saw in her was an escape from Lyman."

"They fell in love?"

"John sure played it up that way to Lyman. He knew that if he had a pious wife in tow then he wasn't much use to Lyman anymore. He knew, too, by attaching himself to this family, who Lyman had grown up thinking of as his own, that if there was an ounce of sympathy in Lyman's body, he'd let it go."

"And there was."

"I don't know about that. But one thing I do know is Lyman's always got something else cooking up." Ben shrugged. "He's not one to tread the hard path when there's an easier one to follow. And, I always thought if Lyman really believed love had blossomed between John and Harriet, he might just be smart enough to fear for his own life. Love might've given John enough reason to finally just kill his old, slippery friend. He certainly had the means to do it. Whatever Lyman's reasons, he never told me, but he kept his distance from John and Harriet for a few years. Until he needed him."

"Why didn't Papa ever tell me any of this?"

"Maybe he should have, I don't know. But I was there through most of it, and I think when he married Harriet and moved to the countryside, some small part of John believed her virtue could save him. By the time he figured out it couldn't, you'd come along. In your eyes, he could finally see something in himself worth saving. I don't think he wanted to risk that."

When Ben finished his story, he moved, without ceremony, toward the shop counter. My hand still rested on the door handle, but I couldn't leave. Not yet. I stared for a moment at the thinning hair on the back of Ben's head, his stooped shoulders as he reached for the business ledger below the counter.

"Why did you tell me all of this today?"

Ben turned to face me but wouldn't meet my eyes. "I didn't know it was up to me to tell you. When that girl came looking for him yesterday . . ." Ben's words trailed off as he wiped fresh tears from his grimy face. "John was the best man I ever knew. I couldn't let Lyman ruin his daughter."

"Thank you."

There was nothing else I could say to this man of few words who had solved so many mysteries in my life. I could forgive him his rude manners toward me and his reports of my whereabouts to Lyman, a man whose charms I myself found difficult to resist. I could forgive him because he had loved Papa. I turned and left the shop, leaving Ben alone with his grief.

My mind abuzz with Papa's story, I walked briskly through the streets of Utica, away from the business district. I paused neither to enjoy the cool freshness of the morning nor to listen to the song of birds greeting the new day. All faded into the background. Despite the distraction of a hundred new thoughts swirling through my mind, I easily retraced my steps to the house where my father lay dying, attended by the family he preferred to me.

I expected little activity in the house at this hour, but I had not yet arrived at the door when Clara burst through it, smiling, arms open to embrace me.

"What a beautiful morning, dear cousin. I'm so happy to see you again. Mr. Moreau said you might not come."

"Mr. Moreau?"

Margaret stepped out of the house then to join her daughter on the steps. She appeared fresh and calm, with an apron tied around her waist. She must, I thought, have been a very early riser. "Oh, Ada. Thank goodness. Yes, Mr. Moreau called on us last evening. Thank you for sending him. We are so grateful for your help, for both of you."

"Of course," I recovered, determined to find out what they were talking about.

Margaret placed an arm lightly over my shoulder and pulled me close directing me into the house as she whispered, "He is most certainly an older man, but I think you could do worse than that handsome gentleman of yours."

She squeezed my arm and I felt myself blush, anger rising in my cheeks. I remembered Aunt Harriet once referring to Lyman as Moreau. Likely it was his true name, but then I had heard him use so many, I couldn't be sure even of that. The sound of it now brought to my mind the truth that I found Lyman nearly as distasteful as had Aunt Harriet.

"How is my uncle this morning?" I asked, anxious to turn the subject away from Lyman and whatever this family of mine might think was our relationship to one another.

"He looks to be improving a little," Clara spoke up. "Mr. Moreau administered some of his rare medicines. He does have a way about him."

"Oh, yes." I tried not to express the growing disdain I felt. "Did Mr. Moreau discuss the necessity of more treatments?"

"He said he would be able to return with more in two days time," Margaret explained. "It is difficult to procure the ingredients, I understand. And an expensive venture, but whatever we can do to ease Albert's sufferings. We pray over him almost constantly night and day."

"I'm sure that is a blessing to him. May I see him?"

"Yes, of course." Clara crossed in front of me to the door of the sickroom. "Your visit yesterday seemed to be just what he needed. He even mumbled your name in his sleep."

She showed me in, gave my father a gentle nudge to alert him to my presence, and then exited again, closing the door behind herself.

"Ada?" he whispered. "You came back."

"You're surprised?"

He managed to pull himself to a semi-sitting position against the pillows on the bed. I made no move to help him, once again absorbing the sight of his emaciated frame. "I am surprised. And pleased."

"Your wife tells me Lyman came to see you yesterday."

I couldn't be sure, given the general deterioration of his body, but he appeared to tremble slightly at the mention of Lyman's name. "Ada, please. He said he had learned some of John's skill, that he could help me, and would, but he made threats. He is not a good man. Margaret and Clara were so hopeful after his visit, but I don't believe I can trust him."

I shrugged, keeping my tone casual in my response. "No. It would be unwise to trust Lyman. What kind of threats?"

"He knows you are my daughter and not John's. He has asked for money in exchange for silence."

"Do you have money?"

He nodded slowly, as though he were in a great deal of pain. "But I have decided I do not wish to die with this great secret. I want to tell them myself."

"Thank you." This small act of repentance did little to assuage my fury.

"They are lovely, Ada. Just like your mother was lovely. I am a sinful man and could not give you loveliness in life, but in death perhaps I can. They will be your family and will be good to you. I know it in my soul."

"The way you knew Aunt Harriet would love and protect me?"

"I didn't know her as I know Margaret. Harriet was misguided by her blind religion."

"I know a great deal about blind religion, as it happens. I'd like to tell you, if you'll allow me."

"Anything, my Ada."

I reached for an empty glass next to a pitcher on the nightstand. I poured what I took to be a dark red wine into the glass, adding to it the crushed herbs from the jar I had brought. My father eyed it suspiciously.

"Do you think you could drink?" I asked him.

"What are you giving me?"

"It's an herb from my papa's stock that I have learned to use. It will help you to focus. And what I have to tell you is of great importance." I lifted his head gently from the pillow, feeling the clammy loose skin on his neck. He dutifully swallowed as I lifted the glass to his lips.

"Thank you, my dear."

I settled him back down on the bed, pulling the covers around him, and then slipped the manuscript from the folds of my cloak which I had removed upon entering the room. "I have something I wish to show you, Father."

"What is it, child?"

"It's a story written by a minister by the name of Solomon Spalding. I found it when I was a little girl and read it diligently. I'm afraid it is dreadfully dull in parts, but I think it is a story you will like. It's a fictional account, written many years ago, as the date on the manuscript suggests, and I think, given the state of the paper itself, we might easily believe that to be true.

"The story follows the plight of a people, previously unknown in history who, being descendents of the twelve tribes of Israel, have somehow, through a series of persecutions, come to live in a new land. There they developed into warring nations, some great and some small, and shared great prophesies that were then lost to history. Is it a familiar story to you?"

"Yes, but, I don't understand."

"You see," I continued, "it was a familiar story to me when I read much of it yesterday. It seems Margaret and Clara had a copy of it as well, though more polished, I'll give them. And it was attributed to a very different author, if that is what we might call him, created at a much later date than was my manuscript."

I relished the confusion on the dying man's face as it dawned on him what I suggested. "It's important to me that you know, before you die, that this faith which has meant so much to you and which demands that I forgive you for your wretchedness has been fabricated. If there is a god in some heaven awaiting the arrival of his faithful, it is not this god you claim and you are not the faithful for whom he awaits."

I stared long and hard into his watery eyes, yellowed with disease. He did not respond to me, could not at that point, I imagine. I held his fearful gaze until at last he slipped into a haunted sleep, plagued by the horrific dreams that would accompany him into death.

28

Ada leaned back in the chair, allowing silence to fill the room and signal the end of her story. She wanted to give the old prophet a moment to think about what she'd told him. How exactly he would react, she could only guess. But it was his reaction that was of greatest importance to her because from it she might better understand what kind of man she had just laid her burdens before.

Sidney Rigdon only looked at her expectantly. He had once been an opinionated and commanding speaker, Ada knew. Now he only fixed her in his sideways stare, revealing nothing of what he thought of her after her tale had reached a murderous conclusion.

Grasping for a response, she continued, "My father is the only other person to whom I have ever shown the manuscript, and he died shortly thereafter as a direct result of the large dose of henbane in his wine."

"You did not show your family?" Mr. Rigdon asked. Ada detected a faint undertone of menace in his question. She did not fear this man in his aged and withered state, but she still held a kind of respect for what he'd accomplished in his long and complicated life.

"Have you ever shown your copy, Mr. Rigdon? I rather doubt it."

"But why not?" It was not a mere question of curiosity. It carried with it an accusation, astounding coming from the man responsible for perpetuating the lie revealed by the existence of the manuscript.

"Why, you ask, would I not reveal to them that their religion was based upon false Scripture and the ravings of a lunatic confidence man?" The old man's complexion darkened. Anger filled his clouded eyes, his only response to her mockery of the man he himself had presented to the world as a true prophet.

She could understand why people would choose to listen to Sidney Rigdon, would cling to his theologically complicated ramblings. He had a gift, one she assumed Joseph Smith must also have possessed. Rigdon listened, as Ada herself did. Before he spoke, he listened in order to discover what the speaker most needed to hear.

Ada smiled at the thought of their similarities. She continued, "That is a reasonable question and one I have asked myself on more than one occasion. The motivation for my silence came from my sister and stepmother's responses to my father's death."

*****

When I left his sick room, the scene I found on the other side of the door bewildered me. Both Margaret and Clara knelt on the wooden floor, hands raised toward the heavens, eyes shut tight, mumbling fervent prayers. I closed the door to my father's sickroom a little harder than necessary, causing an audible thud. Both the woman and the girl opened their eyes and sprang up to greet me.

"How does he seem to you? Better?" Clara was the first to question me.

I shook my head, forcing meaningless tears. "I'm sorry. He's gone." I expected their optimism to fade into despair. Perhaps that's what I'd hoped to see. I'd pictured myself delivering the terrible news and then dealing a crushing blow by presenting them with the manuscript. I would rid the world of my father and also his remaining family of a poisonous faith in one swift stroke. I'd been determined to come to the house that morning in order to allow my anger to roam free. Certainly I'd received my share of heartache and more than my share of religious fervor. It was time to pass on my pain.

But whether I thought of my actions truly as an act of revenge or an attempted rescue, I can't honestly say even now. Perhaps it was both. Either way, I never could have anticipated their responses.

At my words both my stepmother and half-sister relaxed, previously unnoticed tension draining from their expressions in the way I often see in the faces of my customers when peace finally comes to them after a long search.

216

Margaret let out a deep sigh, though not one of mourning exactly. She stepped toward me, took my hands in hers, and smiled. "You are an angel, Ada. I am so thankful you came into his life at the end."

"Are you well?" I myself did not feel sorrow for my father's death. Still, Margaret seemed to me remarkably composed for one so recently widowed.

"My husband has been restored to full health this glorious day and we will see him again in Heaven, sealed together as we are for eternity." Her genuine and unwavering expression of faith overwhelmed my senses, causing true tears to spill down my cheeks.

Margaret wrapped me in her arms. "Ada, I'm sorry you couldn't know him longer and that you have had so much loss in your life already. Please understand there is no need to cry for him."

*****

"As I'm sure you understand, Mr. Rigdon, it was not for my father that I wept. My tears were for me and for the little girl I had once been. I had no faith with which to cope when faced with the death of my mother or the sudden disappearance of my father. Even through the promises of love and fulfillment in the Bible, all I was ever offered was a form of cold religion at the hands of a cruel woman. It couldn't help me.

"What did help was discovering this unique gift I possess and learning to use it. Like Papa, I had a knowledge for which people longed. Lyman didn't see it that way, of course. He saw my gift only as a way to make money. I knew it was more than that.

"When people come to me to seek advice or, more often, to resolve some personal grief, I offer them a type of faith. You see, what I came to learn was that when one's life is full of little certainty it is then that the supernatural steps in to offer hope.

"I don't pretend to know Aunt Harriet's god, nor that of my father's family. As I looked at Clara, though, I wondered if her religion, her Scripture, provided her with the peace that had eluded me as a child of a deceased parent. I couldn't take that away from her. I couldn't inflict the world upon her the way it had been thrust upon me.

"To this day, even as the news of Mormon treachery spreads across the nation, I can't be the one to take her faith from her."

"So you never told them any of it?" asked the prophet, tears on his trembling lashes.

"What would I tell them? That I murdered Albert? That he was my true father, making them my stepmother and half sister? No. I never told them. I never saw them again after that day."

"What happened to them?"

"I've never known for certain. I assume they moved west with the larger part of your church."

The old man responded to this with a sharp intake of breath. This western church, Ada knew, grieved the old man, once a leader, second in command some would have said of this so-called Church of Latter-day Saints.

"Margaret encouraged me to go with them, but I explained I could never leave Lyman, and whatever charm he had worked on them was enough to convince them of my sincerity.

"Of course, I couldn't remain with Lyman once I had seen him for what he really was. I took supper with him that night. I discussed with him the declining health of my father and we laughed at the vulnerability and gullibility of his new family. We toasted to our nefarious successes and he drank deeply from his wine glass after which he slept, falling into his own frightening eternal dreams.

"I cleared the shelves of Papa's few remaining herbs and remedies. Those I packed into my travel bag. The rest of the oils and potions I smashed against the floors and walls of the shop before I took a candle and set it ablaze.

"I fled Utica that night, headed once again for a different life, this time in New York City. Much of my life has been spent as my grandmother's was. I have been the fortune teller on waterfront, a diviner of all things unseen." Ada fell silent, taking a moment to catch her now labored breath, her chest tightening from the effort of confession.

The prophet spoke next. "And you've had the manuscript all this time. What is to become of it?" This was the question the old man clearly had been waiting to ask, wondering if the life he had built, had known, and had loved would be stripped away from him now as he stood at death's door.

Ada paused, allowing the suspense to build as she gathered her thoughts. Words, she had found, carried greater significance when anxieties ran high.

The old man would not tolerate the silence. As if to slash through it, he asked, "Why do you bring this all to me? I have no money. I am a broken man. If you had gone to Brigham, perhaps—"

"Surely you can't be naïve enough to think I could have made that trip with the manuscript, if even a whisper of its existence had reached Utah before me. And if I had, Utah is a long way to travel only to die, Mr. Rigdon. As it is, I believe that Brigham Young's assassins search for me."

"If that is true, then I fear you are in terrible danger, Miss Moses."

"Yes. But I've been in terrible danger before. I came to you, Mr. Rigdon, because Zeviah was right. Dark secrets do make us miserable and when we bring them to light, we are able to move on."

"I may well be moving on toward my own death, but I'm unwilling to take these secrets with me. Mr. Young could not be trusted with my story, as I have trusted you. It is not money I seek, but rather a sympathetic ear."

"And you believe you have found that in me?"

"Let me ask you, what do you think of my story?"

The old man took a long time to gather his answer. Before he spoke, he raised his head up and to the left as though he was looking past her, but Ada knew this was the best way he could make direct eye contact with her, trapped as he was inside the narrowing prison of his aged body. What for some might be a handicap, however, Mr. Rigdon used to his advantage. Ada had the distinct impression that while he looked at her, he also stared into the beyond where he alone could grasp at threads of deep spiritual truths.

"I believe you are a remarkable woman, Miss Moses. You have overcome intense struggles, borne enormous burdens, and here you are. You have sinned greatly, but then, so have we all."

"If I believed in sin, I doubt I could climb out of bed in the morning."

"What is it your uncle said to you, 'What you believe doesn't make a difference in what's true and what isn't?'"

"Yes. But then what of your sin, Mr. Rigdon?"

"Is it my sins that mainly interest you, Miss Moses? I doubt that, or you would have delivered that manuscript into the hands of the enemies of the Church, for it has many. Instead you have chosen to bring it into my home. You do not believe in sin, you say, and yet you want some absolution for the way you have lived, using the vulnerabilities of others to feed your own sense of importance with this gift of yours. You freely admit to me not just one, but two vengeful murders. You are hoping I might help you feel less guilt. Is there truth in what I say?"

The old man spoke with a calm that Ada found frightening. She could see in the withered body now before her, the shadow of the man who many once held to be a prophet of God.

"Do you judge me harshly, then? You, who are a false prophet of the god you claim as your own? This," she shook the bundled manuscript, ruffling its worn pages. "Is nothing more than the imaginative work of Solomon Spalding, at best an unskilled writer of historical romance. This is no true history of the people of this continent and you know it. How you attained it I can't say, but as a woman quite skilled at exposing long-concealed items of power and intrigue, I know there are ways. Be they the hidden streams below our feet, ancestral intrigues, or the basis for false scripture, secrets rarely remain obscured forever."

Sidney Rigdon merely sighed at the accusations Ada flung at him. "I am the true prophet and revelator who speaks with the authority of God Himself, as was Solomon Spalding before me, though he may never have recognized his gift. These words that you attribute to him came directly from God, I have no doubt. God delivered them into my hands."

"And you handed them to Joseph Smith? I can't understand why."

"I couldn't make the people hear me. I'd been speaking so loudly for so long. God's church fell into ruin all around me, His people behaving abominably and my brothers of the cloth allowing it to happen. I needed to reach them. No one would hear me.

Joseph understood his role. He was the figurehead. I was the prophet."

The old man's tone was edged in bitterness. It seemed to Ada that he spoke more to himself than to her.

"Brigham knew it, too. They all knew it. I am the one mighty and strong who will set in order the house of God. But they pushed me out, abandoned God's true prophet and revelator."

"Why did you not reveal the truth yourself?"

"I have very nearly done so on numerous occasions, but it is bigger than I."

"On that much we can agree. I put no faith in this book of yours, nor do I need absolution from you and this god you pretend to serve. I only wish for the burden to pass from me. I have held onto it long enough and it is yours to bear." Ada stood, smoothing her skirt. "I thank you for indulging me, Mr. Rigdon. Here is your great revelation from God." With a flick of her wrist, she tossed the bundled pages onto his lap. "Do with it as you will."

The old man let his head drop to his chest, shifting his eyes downward toward the precious stack of papers he must have feared for so long. His throat constricted against the force of a moan as it threatened to escape and then at last erupted out of his lips, an expression of release from long-harbored anxiety.

At the noise, Phoebe Rigdon burst through the door, moving more nimbly than her seventy-two years should have allowed, and rushed to her aged husband's side. As she did so, Ada stepped, all but forgotten, out the door of the room and made her way across the tiny kitchen to the front door, slipping out into the chilly evening air. Ada shivered and took a slow, painful breath. Her task completed, she walked out into the dim light of the lamps lining Depot Street with empty hands, yet exhausted by the burden she had carried for so long.

She felt the men's footsteps before she heard them, tiny shockwaves tickling the bottoms of her feet, entering her body, feeding her a premonition of death. Ada paused at their approach, at least two distinct sets of feet, not turning to meet the men to whom they belonged. She tightened her grip on the handle of her bag and addressed her pursuers in the darkness.

"I no longer possess what you seek."

The footsteps halted. A throaty baritone replied. "And just what is it we seek, Miss?"

Slowly Ada spun toward the voice. In the dark street she could only see the dark shapes of the men, looming, terrifying shadows.

"You want the manuscript," she ventured, her voice steady. The men frightened her, but there was hesitation in their actions, hesitation that hinted at doubt in their mission. "Do you know why you were sent to intercept it?"

A second voice, this one warmer than the first, answered, "We know it contains spurious material designed to defame the teachings of Brother Smith."

"And if the basis of your prophet's teachings could be shown false, would you still take my life?"

"We are not interested in your false claims, only that you may not use your sinfulness to lead others astray."

"For many long years I have possessed the key to the undoing of your faith and yet only now, when I have returned it to your greatest defender, do you wish to spill my blood. I'm no apostate. I have never shared your faith, nor have I pursued a life of service to your god. If you spill my blood, it is you who sin far worse than I."

They were on her before she could think to scream, a firm hand clapped across her mouth, one arm twisted behind her. Ada's captor forced her to her knees, a sharp pain exploding up her thighs as she hit the earth. Her heart thumped wildly in her chest as panic consumed her. Aunt Harriet had performed a great service, Ada realized, by knocking her unconscious before attempting murder. Death would be welcome compared with the fear and anticipation of it.

The other of the two shadows crouched in front of her and Ada saw the glint of reflected moonlight off the edge of a thin blade.

"Do you know how this works, Miss Powell? I take this very sharp knife and slice from one ear, down across your neck, just below your chin, and up again to your other ear. And as I do so, both you and I offer up a prayer for your immortal soul, begging God's acceptance of your final sacrifice. And then you die."

When he finished speaking, the timbre of his eerily calm voice still ringing in the air, he reached toward her, resting the point of the cold knife against the base of her ear. The second man removed his hand from Ada's mouth. The knife blade pressed into the loose skin beneath her jaw. She closed her eyes, felt the first trickle of blood warm against her neck and in that moment, she heard clearly Aunt Harriet's voice. In her fear, she cried out, "If thou, Lord, shouldest mark iniquities, O Lord, who shall stand? But *there is* forgiveness with thee, that thou mayest be feared."

A sharp shove at her back knocked away her breath and with it her words. She fell onto her face, the skin of her forehead torn against the cobblestone street. Her hand, now free, she brought instinctively to the wound in her neck. Sore to the touch, it was little more than a nick one might receive from a shaving razor.

Ada lay on the street for a long while, too frightened to move. When at last she arose, her would-be assassins had gone. Whether her words convinced them their quarrel was not with her, but with the doctrine that compelled them to kill her, or whether they were moved by the words of the Psalms, she could not know.

She'd demonstrated that she was not their enemy and they left her alive. Ada had returned the darkest secret of their religion to its most faithful guardian, the ousted prophet who'd never betrayed them in his years of exile. Neither would Ada in hers.

Epilogue

July 24, 1876

No one was present to take any notice of Phoebe as she slipped out the back door that still summer morning. It was the first time since Sidney's death that she had been alone without the overbearing, if well-meaning, presence of her children and grandchildren. Not that they could have swayed her from her task. She had promised upon the risk of eternal damnation that she would carry out his wishes. Such a threat was hardly necessary. She would have readily agreed to anything he asked of her, knowing his instruction to be of divine origin.

Her children did not understand their father as she had. They would wish, she knew, to preserve his words, to learn all they could of his final years when he had kept so much from them. The Rigdons' grown children had no knowledge of their father's church, his few but mighty faithful followers, most of whom knew him only through his letters. But she would not let her children see. As painful as it may be to begrudge them this opportunity, she would not fail the prophet. Not now as he made his glorious ascent into Heaven to finally receive the rewards he most certainly deserved as God's anointed.

And so Phoebe Rigdon moved as deftly as could a woman of seventy-six, bent with age, filled with prophetic determination. Stack after stack of papers she carried faithfully in her arms to the pit in the back of the house where countless brush piles had burned.

She did not need to look at the papers she held. As a prophetess at the head of The Church of Jesus Christ of the Children of Zion, she alone had been privy to all of Sidney's collected writing in the last, tortured years of his life. Stephen Post would carry on his calling to lead the church in Zion in the

Canadian wilderness, and all he required, Sidney had already sent to him.

After nearly ten trips to and from the little house, the pile of paper had grown to a height of several feet. On the very top, Pheobe gingerly placed the second copy of *A Mansuscript Found*, the one that had been delivered to them by a previously unknown woman Sidney had later understood to be a holy messenger of God, sent to relieve him of anxious thoughts. These thoughts, he had insisted, were given by God to His prophet so that he might suffer in his earthly life and in that suffering come to a fuller understanding of the coming of Christ unto the newly established Zion.

Phoebe had not shared that vision with her husband. She had told Sidney as much, though he would not heed her in this. Ada Moses was not sent of God. What the widow most assuredly did know was that this messenger had brought no peace to the already heavily burdened prophet. Instead, after the day of her visit, Sidney declined rapidly, suffering one attack of the spirit after another, the attacks eventually leaving him paralyzed.

It was after the Moses woman's visit when Sidney shared the revelation that Phoebe must burn all his writing immediately upon his death. The aged prophet had also written to Stephen Post, cautioning him that he must never identify Sidney as the source of the many recent revelations, but that Post must instead claim the revelations as his own. No, her Sidney was never himself after the arrival of that demon woman, sent as she was from the depths of Hell.

Phoebe sighed as she lit the fire, watching the orange flames lick the sides of the tower of papers containing the revelations of the Heavenly Father through the insights of her beloved. All the hours of writing, the days spent in fervent prayer. How he had suffered in life for the words on these pages, even unto the throes of death. The prophet's final anguished words as he slipped, trembling from the earthly realm were, "The book. The book. The book!"

Oh, how Phoebe now prayed as the pages curled and turned to ash and the smoke rose to Heaven, that her lord and master, the great prophet of the Almighty, had at last found an end to his suffering.

Gentleman

Of

Misfortune

A Novel

The companion to

Smoke Rose to Heaven

Available to order
wherever books are sold

1

A single small stone dropped onto the six of spades on the Faro table, drawing the attention of the only two men in the noisy smoke-filled gambling hall shrewd enough to notice. The dealer frowned at the development. All night he'd proven as quick as he was crooked, compensating for his small stature with his cold stare and quick hands, winning the house far more than strict probability allowed.

Equally interested in the stone was the player who sat to the dealer's right with an unimpeded view of each man around the table. Lyman Moreau, more observer than gambler, had played poorly enough all evening to attract little notice from his companions. Now he leaned forward in his chair, his eyes on the unusual token as the dealer indicated the offending object.

"What the hell is that?" Betting and conversation halted around the table at the dealer's words. Startled men followed his gaze to the tiny blue green stone etched with the outline of a beetle. His impatient fingers tapped the top of the box containing the remaining cards. "Get that thing off my table."

But Lyman watched the man who'd caused the commotion, a well-dressed, self-described merchant who'd been bragging and gambling and drinking all night.

"That, sir," the merchant slurred, "is an Egyptian scarab unearthed in the Valley of the Kings."

The dealer sucked in a breath and puffed out his chest. "I don't care what you say it is. If it can't buy a man a drink, it doesn't belong on my table."

"It hardly seems worth slowing the game." Lyman had said little throughout the night, preferring instead to listen. Gamblers of all classes came looking for trouble in this part of the city. Those who couldn't hold their liquor and their secrets usually found it.

And now the merchant had presented an opportunity. "I say let it play."

The dealer scowled at Lyman, but gestured toward the table and said, "Any more bets?"

Several men slid coins from one card to another, some placing copper tokens on top to wager on a loss. Lyman placed his bet on the jack to win. Satisfied, the dealer pulled an ace, followed by a four, an empty space on the table, and another victory for the house. The dealer slid his winnings into the bank and play returned to a furious pace.

Lyman suspected the box, or shoe as it was known, contained a mirror that allowed the man to see what cards to expect and how to most advantageously manipulate them. But the cheating didn't concern him, as he had seen the prize he most wanted and felt sure the dealer's indifference would work in his favor.

Three pulls later, the dealer placed the six of hearts beside the shoe and the merchant's shoulders slumped. When the second card, the jack of clubs, hit the table, Lyman fought hard not to smile. The dealer had no such concerns.

Grinning broadly, he slid the scarab toward Lyman. "I think this'll be your winnings then."

Lyman shrugged and scooped up the stone, dropping it into his coat pocket as he pushed back from the table in a single fluid motion.

*****

Like great brick tomes wedged together along a shelf, the line of houses rose around Lyman. No other city he knew swallowed a man as completely as New York.

The sun had just risen over the cobblestone streets and the city began to wake around him as he ascended the steps of number thirty-four. He rapped on the painted door for a full minute before detecting motion inside.

"Who the hell makes that kind of racket on a man's doorstep at this hour?" Lyman would recognize the voice anywhere, gravelly with age and hard living. Horace Laurent ripped open the door and stood with bare feet, unbuttoned trousers held up by one suspender, and a shotgun aimed at Lyman's chest.

"Horace." Lyman removed his hat and bowed, never allowing his eyes to stray from the end of the gun which, after a moment, the man slowly lowered.

"Oh, hell. Come in then, you cussed devil."

Lyman swept through the doorway and settled himself on an ornate sofa. "Thank you for your kind hospitality, my old friend."

Horace leaned the shotgun against the doorframe. "I know I'm in for something when Lyman Moreau knocks on my door. What brings you here?"

Lyman glanced around the richly furnished room. Above the carved mantel hung the portrait of a lovely young woman with dark hair and eyes. He opened his mouth to reply, but stopped when a lilting feminine voice drifted from the top of the stairs.

"Who is it, Horace?"

"Business. Stay upstairs," came his brusque reply.

Lyman's brow creased and the trace of a grin tickled the corners of his mouth.

Horace met his eyes briefly and groused, "None of your blame business." He sat in a chair across the room from Lyman. "Now, would you kindly tell me why you are knocking on my door at this ungodly hour?"

"I've come with an opportunity."

He looked long at Lyman, his eyes bright and piercing. "Just what kind of opportunity?"

In his younger days, before life had brought him to a lower place, Horace had been an adventurer and a scholar. Later, his black market dealings brought him to the shores of America and swept him into a mutually beneficial partnership with Lyman, a young swindler then down on his luck, but rich in knowledge of New York's seedy underbelly.

Lyman reached into his pocket and opened his fist to reveal the small stone.

"What is it?"

"A scarab. Turquoise. Have a look."

Horace stood and took the carved stone, rolling it between his fingers and examining the plain beetle-like etching. "Looks like it's from a setting—a ring or some other piece of jewelry. It's seen better days anyway, that's for sure."

The old man's tone was nonchalant, but Lyman understood that though surely Horace had seen many finer pieces of antiquity in his day, his interest had been piqued.

"And how did you come to possess it?"

"I won it." Lyman reached for the scarab. He let his arm drop again when Horace made no move to return it.

"Well, is it genuine?" Lyman prompted.

Horace nodded. "It's real enough. What do you mean you won it?"

"Won it off a well-to-do merchant in a game of chance at the port."

Horace smiled now, his fingers trembling. He tossed the scarab back and asked, "Is there more?"

Lyman placed the prize in his coat pocket and grinned. "Five crates, I hear. And mummies, too."

"I've no use for mummies." Horace's flushed face glistened with a fine sheen of perspiration, peculiar for the cool of the house on a spring morning. "What is it you hear, exactly?"

The old man's appearance gave Lyman a moment's pause, but Horace's stiff manner at mention of the mummies did not invite polite inquiry about his health.

"There's a ship out of Trieste carrying cargo from an Antonio Lebolo." Lyman slowed at the name, reproducing it as best he could from his recollection of the gambling merchant's drunken babble. "You know him?"

Horace rubbed his whiskered chin. "I know of him. A Frenchman. He worked for Drovetti in the Valley of the Kings."

"Well," Lyman continued, relieved his recently acquired information had so far proven reliable, "evidently he shipped his plunder to America to be sold by Gillespie & McLeod. Then he up and died. All I need is documentation to support my claim as his nephew and heir. Am I right to assume you have connections who are able supply that?"

Horace sagged against the back of the chair and waited a silent beat before responding. "I might know a man. Not a reliable sort, but could make you the heir of the Viceroy of Egypt. If he had a mind to." The old man's cracked lips spread into a smirk that soon faded.

"Now that would be fun, but hardly necessary."

"What would be fun?" The female voice came from a figure of loveliness descending the stairs in a voluminous skirt and puffed sleeves. Lyman watched as the woman from the portrait emerged.

Her fingers tucked a wayward strand of dark hair into a knot at the back of her head, which sat atop a long, elegant neck. Her eyes met Lyman's and she offered the hint of a curtsy before entering the sitting room.

"Mariana, may I present Mr. Lyman…" Horace stood, pushing off the arms of his chair with a low grunt. "I forgot to ask. What name is it you use now?"

Lyman stood as well, bowing to the olive-skinned angel. "Johnson will do."

"Well then, Mr. Lyman Johnson, allow me to introduce my wife Mariana."

"An absolute pleasure." Lyman bowed again and was pleased to see a faint blush rise on Mrs. Laurent's cheeks.

Horace lowered himself once again into the chair, seeming to deflate with the effort.

"And what was you two gentlemen discussing?" She stepped around Horace's chair and settled onto the end of the sofa. Lyman remained standing and thought to answer her, but noticed Horace give a subtle shake of his head.

"Nothing to fret about, darling. Mr. Johnson was presenting a business proposition, but I'm afraid it won't work out."

"Why not?" Mariana patted the sofa, inviting Lyman to sit by her side. "He seems like a good sort of fellow. Did I hear you say mummies? How intriguing."

Lyman sat stiffly on the edge of the sofa, close enough to his friend's wife to detect the faintest scent of lavender.

Horace narrowed his eyes. "Eavesdropping is a nasty habit, my dear."

"Nonsense. It isn't eavesdropping if it's in my own house. And it is a wife's duty to aid her husband when she can. Don't you think so, Mr. Johnson?" She swiveled to face Lyman and to both his delight and discomfort, she placed a hand on his shoulder.

"I have to agree." It was his turn to blush.

"Smart man." She turned to her husband with such a flash of anger Lyman could feel the heat of it, even if he did not fully understand it. He watched Horace wither in her gaze.

"If it's papers you need, Quinn will get them for you."

"Trouble is I don't trust Quinn," Horace grumbled.

Mariana swept away his protestation with a wave of her hand. "You don't like Quinn, Horace. That's not the same as mistrusting. I'm going out this morning. I'll fetch him. You'll send a note with what you need."

Horace said nothing, but he soon rose from his chair and shuffled to a writing table in the corner of the room where he closed and nudged aside a slim book, pushing it against a glass sphere on a wooden frame. Withdrawing a sheet of paper from the drawer, he scrawled a brief note, folded it, and held it out for Mariana.

"There's no reasoning with you," he said with a sigh that implied reserved pride.

"You're a wise man, Horace. Occasionally." She slipped the folded note into the bodice of her dress and leaned toward her husband, kissing him lightly on the nose. The gesture struck Lyman at once both condescending and intimate, and a wave of embarrassment rushed over him.

Mariana straightened, smoothing her dress. "Mr. Johnson, it was a pleasure to meet you. Will you be here when I return?"

"You may depend on it."

Her eyes sparkled as she reached for a wide-brimmed hat hanging by the door. She donned it and re-tucked her disobedient curl before disappearing through the front door.

Lyman watched her exit. "You've done well for yourself, my friend."

"I'm in a lucrative field," answered Horace, settling once again into his chair.

"Lovely girl." Lyman indicated the portrait, which, though stunning, had failed to capture the beauty of its subject. "A bit young for you, perhaps?"

Horace waved a spotted hand in front of his face. "It's not age that matters so much as the experience. She keeps me young."

Lyman settled once again onto the sofa, sizing up his friend. He could still see, in many ways, the vibrant, barrel-chested man he'd once admired almost like a father, but he could not deny that Horace's fire had cooled with age, and perhaps more. Some unnamed illness plagued the man before him, revealed by the careful way he held himself, like every movement demanded a moment of recovery.

"Not sure that's working, Horace. Are you well?"

"I'm well enough. And what about you? Thought you married a zealot and became a farmer or something."

Horace was business first, but with that out of the way, it pleased Lyman to know his former partner had kept tabs on him. Their relationship was a tenuous one, often coated with deception with perhaps genuine concern at the center.

"Were you afraid I'd gone off the crook? Made myself respectable?"

"I wouldn't presume to hope as much as that, but I thought a change in situation might settle you."

Lyman was fourteen when he'd met Horace—the younger man grasping to rise out of the mire of his childhood and build a life for himself, the elder a gentleman turned burgeoning criminal. Lyman ran hustles for Horace, helped him navigate the coarser parts of the city, as he stole and cheated his way into the black markets of New York. In the process, the two men developed if not trust, at least fondness for one another.

"I chose a different path." In truth, Lyman had been in love with a religious woman, but she had turned out not to be as forgiving as her faith might suggest. "Found myself a wealthy widow instead, became a landed gentleman."

"This wife of yours doesn't mind if you hop up to the city to dip your toes in the black market?"

"I doubt she's terribly concerned. She's dead." Lyman had become practiced at feigning grief, but he would make no attempt to deceive Horace.

"I'm sorry to hear that. Was she good for you?"

"Yes. Much too good." Katherine had been his wife for only six months. She was a few years older than he, a widow alone and unwell. She'd put her faith in an untrustworthy trickster who offered her hope, giving him her heart in exchange. If only he'd been more deserving of it.

"And why, if I may ask, does a comfortable widower decide to come back to the city and commandeer a shipment of antiquities?"

Lyman shrugged. "I missed the life, the action of it all. I can't see myself retired to the countryside. It's not in my nature." He changed the subject before Horace could dig deeper. "Who is this Quinn fellow?"

"Martin Quinn, a clerk in the Office of the Collector of Customs. He's an ambitious, conniving cutthroat, but he can be useful when he stands to profit enough."

"How much is enough?"

"Elegant crime takes commitment and capital. I believe I taught you that."

"Will he help us?"

"If you want that shipment, he's the best man in the city to get it for you. Maybe the only one." Horace frowned. "And I doubt he'll say no to Mariana."

"So you don't trust him."

Horace leaned forward, fixing him with a hard glare. "I trust him as much as I trust you."

Acknowledgements

The journey of a novel is long and winding, but it is certainly not lonely, and I am very grateful for the people who walked beside me through the process. Many thanks go to early readers Velma Finnern, Ruth McClintock, Susan McClintock, David Michaels, Amica Grimberg, and Margo Dill. Also thank you to my Willammette Writers friends at Tuesday Night Critique whose insights helped to shape this project in its earliest stages, and especially to Sandra Shaw-McDow for reading a late draft and for offering constant encouragement.

Thank you to Bruce Irwin who introduced me to the world of dowsing and took the time to share his wonderful stories. I also owe many thanks to the librarians at the Salem Public Library in Salem, Oregon who worked hard to fulfil my strange requests for sources. To my fellow Missouri writers in Coffee & Critique, you came into this project near its end, but in so many ways helped me to put on the final polish. I am so thankful for all of you. A million thanks also go to my husband for his unwavering support and to our boys, the greatest cheerleaders a mom could hope for.

A novel's journey is never completed unless there are those who believe in it enough to guide it across the finish line, a line which for this novel moved several times in unanticipated ways. Thank you to Steven Varble for a stunning cover design and to Megan Harris, the best editor ever. And I am especially grateful to the many readers who have encouraged me and so patiently waited to hold this book in their hands.

Author's Note

Smoke Rose to Heaven is the first novel of two that include the characters of Ada Powell and Lyman Moreau, though due to the sometimes complicated business of publishing, its companion *Gentleman of Misfortune*, derived from the strange history surrounding the *Book of Abraham*, beat it to the bookshelf by more than a year. Both novels emerged from a quest to better understand the faith of many of my neighbors when my family and I briefly lived in a tight-knit subdivision in Oregon on the corner of which sat a Latter-day Saints church.

Initially my research had nothing to do with writing a book, but when I stumbled on a nineteenth-century conspiracy theory referred to as the Spalding Enigma, I was intrigued. First suggested by excommunicated church member D. P. Hurlbut and put before the public by newspaper editor Eber D. Howe's 1834 anti-Mormon book, *Mormonism Unveiled*, the theory claims that the *Book of Mormon* was largely plagiarized from an earlier, unpublished manuscript by Revolutionary War veteran Solomon Spalding.

Hurlbut, who surely had an ax to grind, gathered numerous affidavits from neighbors, friends, and family members of the then deceased Spalding testifying to having read or heard read-aloud portions of a story called *Manuscript Found*. The witnesses claimed this work was nearly identical in plot, characters, and style to the *Book of Mormon*, a scriptural work said to have been translated, through divine revelation, from ancient golden plates discovered by Latter-day Saints founder Joseph Smith.

The alleged connection between Smith and Spalding was Sidney Rigdon, a Calvinist preacher turned Mormon convert who served as Joseph Smith's right-hand man during many of the early years of the Latter-day Saints movement. A direct connection between the two men is difficult to prove, but much circumstantial evidence exists to place them in close proximity to one another and to give Rigdon both motive and opportunity to obtain a copy of the manuscript.

The one piece of evidence that eluded Hurlbut and Howe and many conspiracy theorists since is the original Spalding manuscript itself. Two copies are believed to have existed—one in the possession of Solomon Spalding's widow, Mrs. Matilda Davis, and the other in the hands of Sidney Rigdon.

If Reverend Rigdon had the manuscript, it seems he didn't tell anyone and, at his insistence, his wife burned all of his papers upon his death.

Mrs. Davis claimed she placed her deceased husband's writings in a trunk at the home of her niece Mrs. Zeviah Clark of Hartwick, New York. Though Hurlbut did find some bits of writing in the trunk, *Manuscript Found* was not among them.

It was the pursuit of this historical "smoking gun" that inspired *Smoke Rose to Heaven*. The character of Ada Powell is fictional, as are Aunt Harriet, Papa, and Lyman Moreau. The apostate Silas Allen is invented as well, though the ritual by which he was murdered is inspired by the theological concept of blood atonement and a troubling period of Latter-day Saints history.

The characterization of the elderly Sidney Rigdon is based largely upon Richard S. Van Wagoner's biography, *Sidney Rigdon: A Portrait of Religious Excess*. The couple allegedly in possession of the trunk containing the lost copy of *Manuscript Found* were named Jerome and Zeviah Clark, but though their names appear in this book, the characters are wholly imagined and should be read as entirely fictional.

William Miller was also a historical Baptist preacher who predicted the end of the world would arrive on October 22, 1844. Some of his followers were so distressed when his prediction failed that they committed murder-suicide. Miller's words at the camp meeting in this book are taken directly from his sermons. His Millerism became the roots for the Seventh Day Adventist movement.

Smoke Rose to Heaven is a story that I hope paints a portrait of a time and place in America's past. Historians refer to the sweeping religious movements and revivals of early nineteenth century New York State as the Burned Over District. Joseph Smith's church and its controversial new book were important pieces of that history.

As a work of fiction, *Smoke Rose to Heaven* offers no further illumination of the persistent questions surrounding the origin of the *Book of Mormon*. It is an exercise in imagination only and is not intended to convince or convert. If you would like to know more about the Spalding Enigma, I recommend the very thorough works of Wayne L. Cowdry, Howard A. Davis, and Arthur Vanick as a good place to start.

Questions for Discussion

1. What character(s) do you sympathize with the most in this story? What made you connect?

2. At a young age Ada witnesses the death of her mother in the birthing room. In what ways does this impact the person she becomes?

3. There are many villains in Ada's life. Do any of them appear, at least at times, redeemable? If so, which ones and when? In what ways do they each affect Ada, both positively and negatively?

4. Much of Ada's life involves a search for family, a sense of belonging, and a moral compass. Where does she seek these things? Does she ever find them?

5. Smoke and fire appear throughout the novel. What do you think these elements symbolize? Does their meaning change?

6. Papa and Harriet both speak to Ada of faith, but in very different ways. In what ways do their lessons shape how she views and interacts with faith as an adult?

7. At one point, Ada defines love as seeing the worst in someone and still being able to glimpse the good. What do you think of that definition?

8. Ada's feelings for Aunt Harriet are complicated. Even with many legitimate reasons to hate her, there are times when Ada reveals glimpses of grace. Why do you think that is? Do you believe there were times when Ada and Harriet came close to having the mother-daughter relationship they both craved?

9. Ada's final words in anticipation of her death are those of Psalm 130:3. Why do you think she turns to scripture in this moment, something that she often identifies as a source of terror in her life?

SARAH ANGLETON is the author of the essay collection *Launching Sheep & Other Stories* and *Gentleman of Misfortune*, a companion to *Smoke Rose to Heaven*. She lives near St. Louis, Missouri with her husband, two sons, and one very loyal dog. Visit her at www.Sarah-Angleton.com.

Thank you for reading!

If you have enjoyed this book, please take a few minutes to help others find it by leaving an honest review.